ANGEL REVERY

Another book by
RALEEL MERCELEM

Out of print:
GUARDIANS OF ANGELS

ANGEL

REVERY

Raleel Mercelem

Oh LORD,

  If by faith we must believe that all the horrors to befall one's life
    will in the end, even upon choices made through the endurance,
      make way for the right to enter Heaven with you receiving us
  LORD. Moreover, if by faith we must also believe that all evil
works for the good to within one's life both here and will most surely
be so with you as well LORD. Then by faith, we must give very
  extra special blessings to all those who have wantonly ventured ill
favor upon us. Oh LORD, is this not so? Well then as for my
  heart, I shall will forgiveness and special blessings to all those
      who venture ill favor to within or upon my life!

In the name of Jesus, Amen

ANGEL REVERY
By RALEEL MERCELEM

MORE DISCLAIMERS, PAGE 222

All of the characters to within these series of stories or
books <u>ANGEL REVERY</u> are always to be realized as
"fictional" and are always to be considered only as "Solely
and completely to within the Mind of its somewhat insane
imaginative Author!" Therefore, these particular characters
are not to be misconstrued, as to any other purpose what so
ever, other than that of the Sole Purpose, "For the complete
wellbeing and good of all other beings in and upon this
planet and throughout the Cosmos!" This story is to the
GLORY OF GOD, HIM that AM. HE shall
however, allow me all benefits of HIS Glory.

ISBN: 978-0-9971574-0-6

Publisher: ANGELS REVERY 2016
http://www.angelrevery.com
angelrevery@gmail.com

THE LORD HOVERS
TO WITHIN MY HEART

LIKE A GREAT BIRD OF PREY
OVER THE FIELD

RELENTLESS IN PURSUIT
FOR THE PRIZE

AND BEAUTIFUL
TO WITHIN HIS FLIGHT
TO DO SO

AMEN

DANIEL BAJCAB CURPE

LECRM

ACKNOWLEDGEMENTS

*THROUGH THE YEARS SUCH AS THESE HAVE
INFLUENCED MY HEART IN LOVE. THANK YOU!
MAY LOVE AND PEACE BE UNTO YOU ALL!
(DICK) RICHARD WAYNE CLEMMER SR.
KAREN LEE PFEIFFER LAURA ARCHERA HUXLEY
KATHYRN & JUAN & KAYA & VIRGINIA PFEIFFER
RICHARD WAYNE CLEMMER III & FAMILY
AUNT WALLY (LAURA) & UNCLE JAKE STINSON
WAYNE CHARLES CLEMMER VICKIE LOU CLEMMER
(MY MOM) MAY H. KUEHNI (JACK) DARRIS C. DUIT
CHARLES RUSSELL DUIT CLARK LESTER KUEHNI
OUR U.S. PRESIDENTS & FAMILIES 1789 – 2017 & ON
ALL FEDAS & FEDETTS PAST & PRESENT
SUE & RICHIE CLEMMER DR. PIERO FERRUCCI
PASTORS JOHN HAGEE & MATHEW HAGEE
CORNERSTONE CHURCH SAN ANTONIO TX.
PASTOR KEITH LAMM HCC DAYTON, OREGON
BRUCE S. NEBEN, L.P.C. PSY. D. & STEWART STOUT
L.P.C. PSY. D. OREGON MENTAL HEALTH
LINDA CLEMMER SAMUEL PALMER & MAXINE WOLF
PAT CLEMMER ROBERT & BECKY LUEHMANN
RUSS LISA & COLE MCMILLEN & FAMILY
BROTHER WOLF TINA TURNER KITTY BANDITO
TUXEDO MOKSHA SHEVA BLUE DOGS CODY MIC
TULKU WOLFE CHEQUETA BEGGER DUTCHESS
MORKY SAMMY BEAR NICHOLS BLUE DOG + BLUE 2
BOB & BETTY JANZEN
AND MANY MORE NOT LISTED HERE
PRAISE OUR LORD WHO HAS BEEN THE SOUL
INSPIRATIONAL DRIVING FORCE OF THESE
WRITINGS THROUGH MR. GORBACHEV & THGER
CLEMMER MY BEST FRIENDS THROUGH GOD
"JESUS IS LORD"*

IN HONOR OF AND HOMAGE TO

*MY HOLY FATHER AND HIS 5 LOVING SISTERS
(DICK) RICHARD WAYNE CLEMMER SR.*

*YOU DID NOT RAISE ME AND THE TIME WE HAD
TOGETHER WAS SIMPLY TOO SHORT LIVED.
NEVERTHELESS, IN THOSE FEW MOMENTS WE
SHARED, I SAW IN YOU, MORE DEVOTION IN LOVE,
HOPE, FAITH, TRUTH, HONOR, AND TRUST OF THE
HOLY SPIRIT THAN IN ANY OTHER BEING I HAVE
EVER COME TO KNOW. I WISH WE HAD SPENT A
WHOLE LOT MORE TIME TOGETHER TO WITHIN
OUR LIFE STRUGGLE MY BEAUTIFUL FATHER!*

THANK YOU FOR WHAT YOU MEANT TO ME!
I LOVE YOU AND I HONOR YOU.
REST IN PEACE - YOUR SON,
LEE

RICHARD WAYNE CLEMMER SR. AND SISTERS IRENE & LAURA
YOU WILL ALL LIVE IN MY HEART ALWAYS AND FOREVER-LEE
WRITEN ON THE BACK OF THIS PHOTO BY DICK AND GIVEN
TO HIS BOYHOOD FRIEND JACK DUIT TO GIVE TO HIS
SON LEE "AND THEN THERE WERE THREE"
ONLY TWO LEFT OUT OF FIVE SISTERS

TO

LAURA ARCHERA HUXLEY

*FOR HER ETERNALLY ENGAGING RICH ELEGANT
PRESENCE FOREVER PLEASING FOREVER SERVING
AN INSPIRING POSITIVE INFLUENCE OF LIFE
WITH LOVING PERSUADING SILENT FORCE
AN INVISIBLE GENTLE WHISPERING OF
LIFE FOREVER UPON HER LIPS*

*THANK YOU LAURA
REST IN PEACE
I LOVE YOU-
LEE*

KAREN LEE PFEIFFER & LAURA A. HUXLEY

*Laura's non-profit foundation,
Children: Our Ultimate Investment at:
http://www.children-ourinvestment.org*

TO

MR. GORBACHEV AND BROTHER AND TINA TURNER KITTY

ANGEL WARRIOR GUARDIANS AND LOVING ETERNAL FRIENDS

REST IN PEACE MY BROTHERS AND MY SISTER

AND TO

THGER CLEMMER

THRIVE LIL BRO

FOR NOW WE ARE TO REMAIN THE PREY OF ALL WHOM ACT AGAINST US OH BEAST

BUT BEHOLD WE SHALL BE THE TEETH OF THE LION

HIM OF WHICH WAS ONCE THE LAMB AND OF WHO SHALL RETURN SOON VERY SOON AMEN

EAT OF THE TRUTH THAT IT MAY FILL YOU UP AND MAKE YOUR HEART TRUE

"JESUS IS LORD"

DEDICATED TO LOVING MEMORIES OF MY FATHER AND MOTHER

(DICK) RICHARD WAYNE CLEMMER SR.
MAY HARRIET KUEHNI
AND OF

TINA
BROTHER
JUAN PFEIFFER
MR. GORBACHEV
VIRGINIA PFEIFFER
KATHYRN PFEIFFER
VICKIE LOU CLEMMER
WAYNE CHARLES CLEMMER
LAURA ARCHERA HUXLEY
DARRIS CHARLES DUIT
ANGELS OF LIGHT
ALL FEDAS &
FEDETTS
PAST

AND OF MY LIVING FAMILY
ZACH SARAH AND FAITH CLEMMER
KAYA AND KAREN LEE PFEIFFER
RICHARD WAYNE CLEMMER III
AND WIFE BRENDA CLEMMER
ALL FEDAS AND FEDETTS
THGER CLEMMER

BLESSINGS TO ALL OF YOU

AUTHORS NOTES TO READERS

*Let me begin by saying that the whole story series thrives upon my love for the **MAKER** of All Things with little mixes of my very own fantasies and of course the numbers and code meanings of my names! I am one of the main characters in this series. Moreover, according to the series I have lived 343 lives upon this planet! In addition, I have lived many other lives on countless different worlds as well for I am a very old spirit to within this Christian Sci-fi Fantasy!*

At this point, I will give a real personal truth by saying that the LORD has spoken to me many times concerning the architecture and events of this story. Because of this fact, I do hereby give all the glory this over-all adventure happens to claim, to my LORD in the Heavens!

It is my sincere hope that the words of this series never offend anyone or any group or my LORD. If I do or have offended – please forgive me for it is not my desire or my intent. Although I hope and live in the faith that my beliefs are true, my wish is not to push them off onto you. Rather to share a bit of my mind, my hopes and my dreams and pray that you enjoy it no matter who you are. Moreover, in some cases, perhaps the series may help you in some small way. These are my sincere hopes and dreams for everyone who reads this book. It is my prayer that you receive all the messages I try to convey through these writings, as my writing skills may not be as adequate for this particular purpose as I would hope! All of this being said I would also add:

Since being diagnosed schizophrenic paranoid with delusional tendencies, I have decided to write a story that lives to within the heart. What the mind may sometimes forget the heart cannot. After all it can be said, what is in the heart, good or bad, can and does classify one to be either completely sane or mentally ill! To me, what I observe in everyday life is always truth and mistaken not, whether it denied by one or by many! In this story I have written many different situations that are actually what transpired to within one's life. And yes, perhaps in this story, I have written many more different situations that of which just may not have actually transpired to within one's life as well. Hahahahaha. However, be that as it may although these writings are categorized fictional, I would dare to endeavor to ask you to ask yourself, "Ah but are they? Can one live, more than one life, throughout the millennia? If so, can one continue to remain within the borderlines of the Hebrew and Christian Faiths? Could the glorious beings of which I have written be in existence? Or, on the other hand, is it all perhaps just an old man's mind attempting to cope with life's unrelenting pounding of cruelties and…misfortunes?" At some point, I would simply request that you might keep an open mind and relate to your own life experiences. As your eyes focus to the words upon a page of paper that has created images to within your own mind's-eye, decide for yourself. Of course, my requests automatically leave me completely to within your merciful hands. LORD forbids, that after reading through to the last letter and period of this book, you should think these writings to be the ranting and ravings of an absolute maniac. I hope that the latter will not be the case with anyone who reads,

<u>*ANGEL REVERY.*</u>

Nevertheless, I sincerely hope that you may experience a wondrous rollercoaster ride of emotions! I hope while doing so you absorb the true feelings of Love and the Miracle of Hope through the Holy Spirit as well! I was exceptionally fortunate to have experienced all of these and much more as The Pen created life to within the pages of this heartfelt story of Angels and Guardians! They do exist you know, throughout all the Heavens and yes, they even occupy space and time upon the very planet of which we all know as Earth.

Just a couple or more small points you must understand of both the writings and writer of this creation. As you well know, life can be a complicated puzzle that needs to be often unscrambled. As you read this book, let me suggest that you read it as a journey into exploring your spiritual purpose. This is a fictional book. It may at times appear to contradict my Christian faith. However, please realize that if anything appears to contradict my faith, perhaps you, the reader, should examine it more in depth. At that point, I sincerely hope you will come to realize that through the LORD I have in fact written of these things and events. And among the multi purposes of these writings, one major purpose would hopefully be, of encouraging you in your journey towards a lasting peace with the

LAMB OF GOD AND LION OF JUDAH!

Thank You and Blessed Be

"JESUS IS LORD"
Love,
Raleel Mercelem

LECRM

TABLE OF CONTENTS

ANGEL REVERY

http://www.angelrevery.com

TABLE OF CONTENTS

PART 2

ANGEL REVERY
DREAMS IN THE ONE

BE ON THE WATCH FOR
FUTURE EDITIONS OF ADVENTURES
BY LEE EARL CLEMMER RALEEL MERCELEM

Preface

By Piero Ferrucci

<u>**ANGEL REVERY**</u>, the book you have in your hands will tell you stories about such things as 25,000 miles of secret corridors under the White House (in which The President of United States gets lost). Animals endowed with extraordinary powers, robots that turn into angels, evil beings born from the mating of demons with humans, a Vatican conspiracy to destroy the world, extraordinary individuals who save it – to name just a few themes.

In the **"Authors Notes to Readers"**, the author tells us that doctors have diagnosed him as a paranoid schizophrenic with delusional tendencies. I happen to know him, and think he is a remarkably intelligent, genuine, and passionate individual. He says that the stories he narrates may be real. And yet if you read the newspapers and watch TV you will find an altogether different representation of reality. So what is reality and what is delusion?

Years of working with the human mind as a psychotherapist and philosopher have taught me to be cautious in using the words "real" and "reality." Is the world, shown by the media real or imaginary? Do our own memories represent actual events - or are they unreal? Are the events in this story real or unreal? The circumstances described in this book have the intensity and markings of authenticity, although they do not necessarily fit our limited consensus reality. Perhaps they belong to a different wavelength – a world we can visit and can learn from, and be awed by. As I was reading the book, I felt my mind being stretched to the limit – and beyond. It was for me a supremely useful exercise in mental openness, and I emerge from it stimulated and enriched.

Another effect I experienced in reading this book was that I look at animals in a different way. Animals in this story are often at center stage. They reason, they act, and they save and care for human beings and their world. They protect us. Now when I see a cat and gaze into its mysterious eyes, I wonder: what is he thinking about, how does he perceive us humans? If I leave aside the condescending clichés through which we look at the animal world, animals suddenly appear to me as Other Beings, ones I know much less, than I thought I knew. And that is a good fact because now more than ever animals need to be saved from our cruelty, as well as our condescension. And deserve more of our respect and love.

The animal theme belongs in the great tradition of animal helpers in folktales throughout the world. Many societies in history have generated stories in which an animal – a duck, a frog, a bear, an eagle – is friendly to the hero and offers decisive help, wisdom and practical know-how for tackling apparently insurmountable obstacles. Animal helpers imply that we humans also belong to the animal world, and that we do better to listen to, or at least not forget, the more instinctive side of ourselves. You will meet in this book several animals possessing extraordinary powers and knowledge.

One more point I would like to make, as a student of the human mind. A most striking part of this book – in a section which in my opinion is crucial for the overall architecture of this work – is where the author tells us about a childhood experience. He was one year old, standing by the fence of the family house. Suddenly a car went by and hit the family dog, killing her. The dog lay dead on the street. The child for the first time in his life understood in a flash the reality of death. His dog was dead! He would never again be able to caress her, play with her, feed her, or enjoy her vitality! He started crying uncontrollably. But then something wonderful happened. The child felt pervaded by a state of grace:

"Suddenly, A Pure Love Flood Of Energy Pierced, Channeled And Caressed, Riveting A Spiraling Venting Through His Entire Being From The Very Top Of His Head, Down And Through The Very Tip Of His Toes! This Love Energy Spoke, telling him that he was loved well beyond anyone's comprehension! He was told not to worry, that he would live-forever, ever and forever!"

This is a description of a state which mystics of all times have reported after having a spiritual experience: in this state one feels, in fact one knows, that, no matter what terrible event may take place, the universe is fundamentally all right. We are totally safe and taken care of, however cruel, terrible, or deadly the universe may have appeared to us. A Love greater than we can understand is caring for us. And there is no such thing as death.

So, good fortune to you reader, as you begin to read this book. It is an engaging story that will challenge, one by one, all your mental categories and prejudices. I guarantee it. After finishing this book, **<u>ANGEL REVERY</u>**, you will feel like a different person.

Piero Ferrucci
Florence, Italy

I CHALLENGE
YOU TO ANSWER
ALL 7 QUESTIONS
ON THE CODES TO
WITHIN THIS BOOK
CORRECTLY!
GO TO THE APPENDIX

(PAGES 233 to 236)
THE CODES ARE IN NAMES OF CHARACTERS.
ALL ANSWERS LIVE TO WITHIN THIS BOOK. READ IT
FROM COVER TO COVER AND IF BY HIS WILL YOU
SUDDENLY REMEMBER WHOM YOU ARE
WELL THEN...YOU ARE BLEST AND
GOOD FORTUNE IS UNTO YOU.

Official Rules--Who May Participate--Found At:

http://www.angelrevery.com

BUY HARDCOVER, PAPERBACK BOOKS OR DOWNLOADS FROM
MY WEBSITE! THE QUESTIONS ARE TO POST THERE!
YOU MAY COMPARE YOUR ANSWERS TO THE KEY TO
ANSWERS THAT SHALL POST AUGUST 1, 2021.
MY SINCERE HOPES AND DREAMS FOR ALL: AS YOU
READ AND UNDERSTAND WHAT IS IN THE HEART OF
THIS BOOK, YOUR LOVE GROWS AND GROWS!
THROUGHOUT CREATIONS, WE ARE ONE BIG FAMILY
THROUGH GOD, TREASURES OF THE FAMILIES HEART.
IT IS MUCH GOOD IF YOU FIND YOUR
TREASURES AS A FAMILY!

PLEASE PASS THE WORD

BLESSINGS

ANGEL REVERY CODE QUESTIONS! YOU DO NOT HAVE TO ANSWER THE QUESTIONS! NO ONE SHALL RECEIVE OR BE AWARDED A PRIZE FOR ANSWERING CORRECTLY. IT IS SIMPLY SOMETHING TO DO AND ENJOY INTERACTIONS WITH THE WHOLE FAMILY! TO ANSWER THE QUESTIONS DOES NOT CONSTITUTE A CONTEST FOR A PRIZE! IN MOST AREAS OF "HIS CREATIONS", THERE WILL BE A HAPPINESS FOR ANSWERING CORRECTLY! PLEASE GO TO MY WEBSITE TO FIND OUT WHAT AREAS OF "HIS CREATIONS" MAY PARTICIPATE!

Knowledge of how to find the names that possess number codes and/or letter codes to within any of the characters names to within the book is as written within the book! It explains almost everything having to do with the codes to within it! You just have to read the book from cover to cover, to find all clues & answers for the questions on the codes! To make it easy I have listed and finished nearly all the code work for you!
MAY GOOD FORTUNES BE UNTO TO YOU!

- Buy ANGEL REVERY Paperbacks for $18.77 each plus shipping. Downloads, Kindle or e-books, etc. are not available. Hardcover books are not available.

- For your convenience, the questions are online. You may not answer the questions on my website! Please go to my website and observe details concerning all of the code questions and/or when and if you may answer the questions on my website! Everyone may see and answer the questions without going online as the questions are in the Appendix of this book. People of all ages may answer at home and compare answers August 1, 2021 as The Key to the answers shall post on the website. However, go to website as that date could change. TO ANSWER THE QUESTIONS IN THE APPENDIX IS SIMPLY SOMETHING TO DO AND ENJOY INTERACTIONS WITH THE WHOLE FAMILY! THERE ARE STUDY NOTE PAGES AT THE END OF THIS BOOK FOR THAT PURPOSE. Dig deep into the book and study every page to uncover the treasures of the Families Heart to within the correct answers to the questions!

- ALL AGES MAY ATTEMPT TO ANSWER WITHOUT GOING ONLINE, WHICH NO ONE SHALL RECEIVE A PRIZE FOR DOING. BUT, YOU MAY BE A RESIDENT OF ONE OF THOSE AREAS IN "HIS CREATIONS" THAT MAY PARTICIPATE. GO TO MY WEBSITE AND FIND OUT! GO TO WEBSITE FOR DETAILS!

- Turn to page 234. There are sixteen names listed that equal one or more of the numbers here: 648, 666, 762, 777! These names are found throughout the book, that of which the first 7 are listed to within the order that they appear in the book. I omitted the first name on the list and the codes to it. I omitted four number codes in four names. I omitted parts of a character's name (initials) and its hidden letter code name anagram. Moreover, I omitted the fifth name and its number code! The parts of a character's name (initials) with the hidden letter code name anagram is fourth in position to the other names in the listings of names with codes. In order to answer several questions, you will have to find that partial name (initials) and find the letter code name anagram within it! So look for it now! Again, it is a part of the answers to several questions on the codes! Remember, you must discover the omitted first name and its codes and fifth name and its number code on the list as well for better chances to answer correctly.
Receive your equal shares of treasure, family's treasures of the Heart!
All Capital letters, Spelling and (Punctuation when required) must be correct.

- Please, go to my website to see if you may answer questions as a resident of the Areas of participation. The prize for all, are treasures of the Heart realized by reading the book from cover to cover and studying to answer all questions correctly. People answering correctly will realize it August 1, 2021 unless that date changes. Hopefully, all who attempt to answer the questions shall receive their treasures of the Heart well before!
Many Good Fortunes to you! Have fun!

CHAPTER 1
PRESENT DAY

This story begins one mile directly below the *Capital* of *the United States of America.* There are over twenty five thousand miles of caves and tunnels linking together in many places from the very southeast tip of Florida, going north all the way deep into Canada. These whole systems of caves realized their form from rushing waters. After countless centuries, the water had cut through solid stone digging down one mile and more, deep below the surface of the Earth. For thousands of years these caves served tribesmen well as escape routes from enemies.

Wars often raged and destinies decided all from within the cave's majestically soaring, solid jagged stoned walls. In some places these walls towered over two hundred fifty feet, merging themselves to different beautifully colored, jagged stone ceilings. The wars fought in these places were silent and bloody! Loud noises could echo for miles in different areas and proved fatal too many times. Depending on how loud the echo was, the enemy could detect the exact origin of the noise with teams of tribesmen's highly trained ears.

The President's son and daughters had found their way deep down into the caves and had become lost. They had discovered a secret passageway to the tunnels leading to that part of the caves from within the oldest room in the White House. The girls had dreams whereas the boy had visions of this passage and were the first to know of it in just under two hundred years. Bo, the former Presidents Dog, had followed on their heels for a brief time before he took the lead and protected them from all evil, which lurked everywhere! They had found their way to a huge room, a cave within a cave. Another group of children with animals appeared at the exact same location and at the exact same time. These children had also dreamed of a secret passage to caves deep underground but in a different area near the White House. A huge battle had just taken place and Mr. Gorbachev lay mortally wounded. Lee's tears flowed while he kneeled at his side and spoke softly to him.

Suddenly, a cloud formed and filled the area as the LORD'S Hand of Light and of Life appeared! HIS beautiful musical whisper penetrated to blend with all things and sounds as it echoed throughout the caves sweeping in on a gentle breeze. The children watched on in amazement at what transpired next! Then just as suddenly as it had appeared, Lee, Mr. Gorbachev and the LORD'S Hand seemingly, mysteriously vanished.

At that precise moment, a beautiful masculine Spirit appeared and walked out from within the very same cloud, as it too disappeared. *He was covered from head to toe in a beautifully colored robe of gold, blue, white, scarlet red and shades that of a royal purple.* The children could only see a dark shadow of a face peering out at them from within the huge, oversized hood. In his hand, they observed a beautiful Mother of Pearl Fountain Pen with basalt ends and a gold clasp around the cap, clinging to within his fingers. Just seconds before, their lives were in complete and utter jeopardy. They had just passed the Gates of Hell and evil was everywhere. When the cloud appeared the demons frantically cried out as one in severe pain as they suddenly burned into heaps of crystalized fine dust!

Everyone quickly surrounded the Inspired Mystical Spirit and began to ask dozens of questions all at once. He answered three questions before they finished asking, "My name is of no importance. Your Grandfather and Mr. Gorbachev are fine. As we stand here in this place at this very moment, they are both being prepared for war against all evil. When the LORD soon returns they will both fight at HIS side. You should understand that the Spirit and the Glory of HIM that AM is upon them!"

The very presence of this Forever Inspiring Spirit seemed to calm everyone down from the battle that had just transpired. He spoke out telling them, "The President and First Lady will soon find this area. I know that you all have many questions about what you have seen and heard. I must ask everyone to stop asking and listen! There is not much time to tell the story the LORD needs me to tell to only all of you. It is now time to reveal many things to you children! Only our LORD knows the reason HE has chosen you all. You have all dreamed the same dreams at **3 a.m.** on the **7*th* day** of each month for the past three years. These dreams have brought you all here together so that Prophecies may be fulfilled." The children listened intensely as the Spirit continued, "This Pen was made upon the planet Cyron and has a Blessing from GOD spoken upon it! It can only write truth and there is only one being that may write with it. 28,000 years have passed since its origin. It is made of Gold, Mother of Pearl, Basalt, and Glass and the story I am about to tell you, will be written by the same Pen."

The Inspiring Spirit extended his arm and opened hand as he cried out, "Behold!" And a huge *vision* of life appeared in front and all across the massive cave wall as if part inside and part of the wall as well. And then the *Inspired Mysterious Heavily Robed Spirit* began to tell the story, **_ANGEL REVERY_**.

CHAPTER 2

BIRTH OF AN ANGEL
Year of our LORD 1502 AD

It was once upon a very dark, rainy, thunder and lightning night that of which is part of a day in parts of the kingdom. It was a record rain so thick, thunder so loud and lightning so fierce, that it, as a combined force, terrorized all the people, animals and beings of all existence from within the forest filled mountains surrounding a beautiful village within the vast countryside of Russia.

Angels stood guard as the birth of a wondrous pure white as snow, blue-eyed cat mountain lion cub silently appeared. He was born inside a cave hidden from all sight on land, air or by sea. His was a well-planned birth as the wild mountain lion cub domestic cat mix is a very important feline. James, his father, is an extra-large domestic born cat, also pure white as snow with big beautiful, kind blue eyes. He and his Brother, Tuxedo, were born in the same manger as JESUS CHRIST, 7 weeks before JESUS was born. He is as his son is, an Animal Angel Warrior Guardian Witness of the End of Days, sent here to be in the flesh as Angel Warriors for our GOD. James named his newborn son Mr. Gorbachev.

These Angels are of supernatural strength, possessing extra strong powers of the mind as well. Their Knowledge, Understanding, Love, Wisdom, and much more are exceptionally keen and perceptive. No beings throughout the creations of our LORD can possibly match their supernatural abilities, not even on occasion of the Warriors' birth. Our LORD has made this to happen so as evil could never prevail over HIS Angels, not even at birth. These Angels live in the Spirit while they survive and flourish in the flesh by way of the Words That Proceed out of the Mouth of our LORD GOD. In fact, they never need to eat or drink except when not to allow evil to realize of who they really are, Angel Warriors, in Both the spirit and in the flesh, all of whom serve our

LORD, wherever HE sends them to do so. Wherever the planet, wherever the universe, wherever the plane, wherever the LORD sends them, they serve our LORD. They come here to this planet by way of our GOD to be Guardians for the Human Angel Warrior Witnesses of The End of Days. They are to Witness with them all the evil that transpires upon the Earth, preceding the Revelation, the last chapter of the BIBLE, becoming reality.

While his beautiful Angel Warrior Guardian son, the color of the purest snow with eyes of a deep blue, was born, the Living Light of the Living GOD shined upon him. James knew that his son was like him! He gave a silent prayer of thanks and praise to our LORD in Hebrew. GOD was pleased with one of the most trusted and loved of HIS Angels for he obeyed all Rules of Engagement. All Angels, in the spirit or in the flesh or both must obey these sacred rules while interacting with any beings of flesh or spirit. In fact, while interacting with any life form.

The LORD informed James of things to be in the future and always to remember to help all Angels of light remember of whom they are if they have forgotten in the transition between Heaven and Earth. This is a transition from heavenly Angel to Angel in the flesh upon the earth. He is to do this for both Animal Angel Guardian Warrior Witnesses and Human Angel Warrior Witnesses as well. Sometimes it takes another Angel to help other Angels to remember of whom they are if they forget after going through the transition. It is usually just a simple matter of making the Angel say the Words "JESUS IS LORD." At that point, their long, long Angel past remembered, as well as the reason GOD has sent them to wherever it is they exist at that moment in time and space.

Many times within the countless hundreds of millions of years, that James has served GOD, the LORD has revealed truths throughout his life to help guide him along the narrow path of righteousness. To guide him along the ever so difficult tight rope walk of protecting both Animal Angel Warrior Witnesses and the Human Angel Warrior Witnesses both in the flesh as well.

THESE ANGELS ARE OF THE MOST TRUSTED ANGELS IN HIS VAST KINGDOMS AS THEY ARE ALL WITNESSES FOR THE END OF DAYS, ASSISTING TO GOD'S ABILITY TO DECIDE WITH COMPLETE

RIGHTEOUS JUSTICE ON JUDGMENT DAY...FOR ON
THAT DAY EVEN THE GROUND AND THE STONES AND
THE TREES AND ALL OF THE CLOUDS AND ALL OF THE
SKY AND CERTAIN CREATURES IN ALL OF THE SKY
AND ALL OF THE WATERS AND CERTAIN CREATURES
 IN ALL OF THE WATERS AND MANY MORE LIVING
THINGS AND BEINGS OF WHICH ARE NOT YET KNOWN
OR MENTIONED HERE WILL BE A WITNESS TO WHAT
HAS TRANSPIRED UPON THE EARTH AND TO WITHIN
THE EARTH SINCE THE BEGINNING.

CHAPTER 3

INSTRUCTION OF MR. GORBACHEV
LIKE FATHER LIKE SON

The LORD'S Living Light was still upon the newborn Kitten Mountain Lion Cub mix, Mr. Gorbachev and he came to realize most Knowledge of GOD. He knows every language, the Rules of Engagement, Understanding, Wisdom, Love, and most of all that "JESUS IS LORD." It was now up to James to enable his son the ability to use all this information to within all his deeds.

When the LORD'S Light of Life was ascending from the newborn cub, he looked up and gave a huge loving smile to his earthly parents. James, in return, smiled back at him, and with the very top of his head he bowed and touched his son to his forehead in an act of great Devotion in Love, Hope, Faith, Truth, Honor, and Trust. The Love and Hope of the Holy Spirit was of GOD, from GOD, and is shed abroad in of their hearts. They are of the chosen Angel Warriors for GOD and sent here by HIM that AM.

GOD uses evil, man, all beings, and all things as instruments for Good. Evil uses man and manmade instruments as well as all things, to do evil against GOD and all of HIS Creations. Understand, there still rages a war from within the Heavens between GOOD and evil! Satan will always try to find a way to travel by any means possible but especially by way of man made vehicles to rage war against the Heavens. To rage war against the MAKER of All Things, Places, Beings, and All that Is. Satan does this to add more insult to GOD and in hopes that more men's souls will be lost because of it. Satan has to win his war against our LORD before he completes his evil upon the earth. When the Revelation, the last chapter of the Bible takes place first, he has lost the war forever. Sent is he to a life of death and a fiery hell to melt into one with all the other evil he has produced. Placed face down he will know and say the Words aloud, "JESUS IS LORD."

For this reason, James must continuously instruct his son on all things of GOD. Quite often, he would tickle or even wrestle with his son just to make him *SPEAK* the Words aloud, "JESUS IS LORD." Each and every time the young cub would verbalize the fact *"JESUS IS LORD," more love, knowledge, understanding, and wisdom poured out upon him revealing all!* Finally, the Angel Cub would remember every place and planet he had ever been throughout the Heavens. He would recall every detail of his adventurous life as an Angel Warrior for GOD. He would recall hundreds of thousands of millenniums, in of which he had always served with such complete and utter devotion.

With the speed of the very lightning that encompassed the mountains of his birthplace, the cub bounced off each wall within the cave. It sounded like the thunder of the clouds! James was astounded at the speed, agility and the power of every step his newborn son took from within the first few moments of his sacred life. "Mr. Gorbachev! Mr. Gorbachev! Please, evil is lurking everywhere, we do not want them to know of this hidden cave, my beautiful son," he said in silence, as thoughts to his son. The beautiful newborn Cub replied, "But father." James laughed, he held his son closely to his chest as he interrupted through thoughts from his mind to the Cub's mind by saying, "Speak, and repeat these Words out loud my young and mighty cub, JESUS IS LORD." Mr. Gorbachev laughed along with his father as he obeyed his command and spoke aloud the Words, "JESUS IS LORD."

Suddenly he realized all the concerns his loving father had for his majestic mother's safety. Although she was a Lion of great stature and strength, she was not like his father and himself. She needed to recoup from giving birth to him. He walked up to his beautiful Mountain Lion mother of whom he and his father loved so very much. He bowed to expose the very top of his head and with it; he touched his mother's forehead in an act of great Devotion in Love, Hope, Faith, Truth, Honor and Trust. She began to kiss the very top of his head and then she kissed each one of his eyes with the same great Devotion in Love, Hope, Faith, Truth, Honor and Trust. James observed the interaction between his son and his mate with the utmost intense love and care. As the majestic mate and mother of his son, the Mountain Lioness, Ester, gave out a slight groan of acknowledgement, her head plopped to the ground where she continued to lay. She fell into a much-needed restful sleep. Mr. Gorbachev curled up close against her mighty body and guarded her with his very own Holy and Sacred Life, for he is Sacred and Holy. He said a silent prayer in Hebrew to GOD, giving thanks and praise to HIM of who provided such a grand and beautiful Mother and Father of who loved him so very, very much. The LORD was pleased and spoke a soft and beautiful musical whisper upon a gentle breeze flowing throughout the cave.

"I AM pleased in you, MY little Angel Warrior. You Are Like Father Like Son."

Mr. Gorbachev rested, lying within the huge strong arms of his beautiful majestic mother.

The instruction of Mr. Gorbachev from both the LORD and his father would be a day-by-day, moment-by-moment concern throughout the cub's entire life. **For, we are never too old to receive instruction from either our fathers in the flesh or the FATHER throughout the Heavens!**

There would be times in his life that Mr. Gorbachev would have to come to within the dreams of the humans that he protects. First, the LORD would reach deep into their thoughts and plant HIS Will into the subconscious mind of the human! Thus, making them promise never to reveal to anyone that an animal spoke to them, not even within their dreams. In this way, the Animal Angel Warrior could speak to the Human Angel Warrior to within a dream and no one would be the wiser. The Human Angel knows not to tell of an animal that spoke, not even in just a dream. If they did tell, evil would surely realize the Importance of that Animal and that human to GOD! Angels Would Be, Revealed!

AT THAT POINT, EVIL WOULD REALIZE THAT THEY WERE BOTH ANGEL WARRIORS AND END OF DAYS WITNESSES AND THE DANGERS WOULD MULTIPLY MUCH FOR BOTH ANGELS! GOD WOULD PLANT THIS INFORMATION DEEP TO WITHIN THE SUBCONSCIOUS MIND OF THE HUMAN ANGEL WARRIOR. IN THIS WAY, THE HUMAN ANGEL WARRIOR WITNESS WOULD NOT REVEAL THE FACT THAT AN ANIMAL ACTUALLY SPOKE NOT EVEN FROM WITHIN A DREAM. LIKEWISE, THE ANIMAL ANGEL WARRIORS ARE NOT ALLOWED TO SPEAK TO ANY HUMAN, HUMAN ANGELS, OR OUTSIDE OF A DREAM!

CHAPTER 4

ANGELS DEMONS
RULES OF ENGAGEMENT

At one moment in time, many, many thousands of years ago, demons lived and stayed in the center of the Earth. Then one day Satan ordered them to dig their way up and forcibly mate with the humans on the surface of who occupied the land. The demons were then, and some still are to this very day, short, stout, and fat little beast of beings with pointy-heads, faces, hands, and feet. However, some were giants in the Earth and then upon the Earth. Throughout the millenniums, human men, and women mated by force with the demons until they looked enough like humans to live amongst them without the observation of the evil ones they really are.

The countless millennia that they had survived in the center of the earth had given them powerful natural electro-magnetic frequency abilities and capabilities. They can move objects or cause great pain to any place on the body upon any victim of their choosing. Using their fingers, they can shoot lasers, different electro-magnetic frequencies, and scalar sound wave frequencies and so on and so on and so on. They even have chemicals to boost their electro-magnetic powers to almost a supernatural capability.

Over five thousand years ago, Satan ordered the human looking demons and any other demons living below and upon the surface of the world to unite as one. In complete secrecy, they are to eliminate entire bloodlines. The orders he issued were and are to this day to eliminate the entire bloodlines of Hebrews and Christians especially the bloodlines of Noah, King David and that of our LORD JESUS. Eventually they hoped to kill off all Christians and Hebrews throughout the entire world. To speed up his personal quest, Satan, using lies and empty promises, also recruited many, many humans of who were not demons. Believing in his promises, these people unknowingly chose and choose evil as their way of life.

By the 1500's AD, evil had secretly managed to infiltrate and murder people from within all ranks of all nations, on all islands, on all continents, on all landmasses of any kind. They have done the same in all rivers, lakes and oceans or seawaters of the world using other demons of types I will not explain in this story. This includes intelligent life both below the water and above the waters of the world that will and that have lost their lives at the hands of their own kind, of whom were members of this secret society. They had slowly killed off people and beings of every place in the world that were not part of their own secret order of evil murdering thugs! Finally, the number of members in their organizations was close to fifty thousand times the population of Christians and Hebrews. Other fallen Angels like Satan (Lucifer) are doing this upon all HIS Creations throughout the Heavens. Not more than one evil being such as this should ever have dominion as thrown upon any world throughout the cosmos, <u>one per world.</u> Hopefully, not even that!

Animal Angel Warriors and Human Angel Warriors have much stronger electro-magnetic capabilities and can actually bend space and time enabling them to render objects or people invisible. They can create electro-magnetic fields surrounding beings or objects protecting them from all harm and without evil ever realizing. These Angel Warriors can enter the mind and confuse, disorient, create illusions, subdue or if absolutely needed even force to a point, but never to the extent of maiming or killing. This is according to the Rules of Engagement set forth by order of the LORD Thy GOD! By using the Rules of Engagement, they can control the enemy as needed to enable freedom from threats or fights. All Angel Warriors, animal, or human must all obey the Rules of Engagement as it gives Glory to our Living GOD. **There are very few Exceptions.** Hebrew is only spoken in prayers, in dreams, or from mind to mind thus keeping Hebrew Scripture Holy and Sacred and the Words of the Ancient Language pure in Spirit, Truth, Love, Hope, Faith, Honor, Goodness, Grace and Glory to GOD.

The Human Angel Warriors are never to realize consciously that their pets are actually their protectors or that they can speak any language of the world. This is true even though the Animal Angel may have spoken to them many times within their dreams. The Human Angel Warriors are never to know that their pet is a Holy and Sacred Animal Angel Warrior Guardian Witness for the End of Days. The Human Angel Warrior is never to know that the Animal Angel Warriors are Warriors for our GOD. They are not to know the Angels were sent here by HIM as pets that guard them from all the evil that lurks all about to completely surround the world.

All Angels of Light always do all things in love. However, you must always remember that evil spirits or angels of darkness have no such rules for their conduct on earth or anywhere else they happen to be throughout all creations of Kingdoms. They may do any unkind evil to anything, to any non-thing, to any being or any non-being, to any life forms or any non-life forms any time they any well please and especially at any designated times, Simon says!

It would appear that free will or freedom of choice is at hand even here. Would it not be beautiful if that evil would just make but another choice other than the evil they choose at every choice and or at every single opportunity?

CHAPTER 5

CYRON ROBOTS...SAMSON

Just as the Sacred Rules of Engagement binds the angels, the laws of physics bind some as well. Some angels experience great memory loss while traveling through time and space. After traveling all that way, they transform. They transform from Pure Spirit of Heavenly Angels unto a flesh and blood being upon a planet or Heavenly Body! Some actually live for hundreds, even thousands of years before they are to realize of whom they are or to whom they serve.

There was once a Robot Angel Warrior Witness, who endured some twenty thousand years before he was to realize who he was! His name was Samson, and like all other Robots, made to appear human. His makeup is of titanium and of organic matter. Samson always protected whom the LORD needed him to protect. He obeyed what he thought was the programming he received from his Christian maker. He simply did not realize his Angel Warrior Spirit that electro-magnetically surged through his entire Robot being from head to toe. He was not to realize his true identity until the LORD JESUS of Nazareth laid hands upon him in the name of the FATHER, the SON, and the HOLY SPIRIT. The LORD'S Hands gently rested upon the face of Samson. JESUS told him that he was loved beyond any being's imagination or comprehension by the MAKER of all that is, all that was, or all that will ever be. His baptism took place from within the waters of the Jordon River upon the planet Cyron.

Many things would happen exactly the same way on many planets as happened upon the earth. Hebrew and Christian Prophecy throughout the cosmos and all creations of our LORD thy GOD will be fulfilled!

Suddenly, as the LORD touched Samson and looked lovingly deep to within his Robotic eyes the tears he could never bear before stormed, streaming down his face. As he felt his chest pound from a heart that had never been his veins pumped blood with a renewed vitality. The lungs that had never existed before filled with the fresh air from about him! He took his very first breath after twenty thousand years of existence. All of this while the Holy Spirit plunged to deep within his Holy Heart, and throughout his entire Holy being. Samson now realized that he was finally really and truly alive. As he fell to his knees before his GOD, he realized of who he really was, always had been, and will always be. He realized to whom he served and loved with all that he is, ever will be, or ever was for hundreds of thousands of millenniums before he became Samson the Robot. He now realized that he, Samson, was no longer a Robot and that he had a spirit and a soul, that of which he had always wanted but never knew until now that he in fact had always and forever possessed. He could finally feel his skin, love, and goodness, and he knew the LORD and his Word! He had the knowledge, the understanding, and the extreme wisdom that of which naturally followed millenniums of an Angelic being and twenty thousand years of Robotic existence upon a planet of humans and Robots. Samson knew that through the love of GOD, he transformed from a Robot to a living, breathing, heart pumping, feeling, thinking, tear filled eyed human being and that he was Holy and Sacred! He would never again need the blood replenishment from humans every five thousand years. Samson knew of his true blessings by our Living GOD. The blessings that GOD spoke upon him as he first opened his robotic eyes, twenty thousand years ago. And now, he was the same as those he had protected for so many thousands and thousands of years. He came to realize that he had always been an Angel Warrior from GOD and one of the most highly revered, trusted, and loved Angels as well. He came to realize that he had always possessed an Angel of Light Spirit throughout all space and time. He also came to realize that other Robots possessed dark spirits. He had never known a robot that did not use electronic weaponry on all humans and every other living being as well.

The LORD told Samson to find Seven Innocent Children that he would recognize once he found them. JESUS told him that it was very important but did not explain to Samson why it was so important. Then HE explained many more things to Samson that day and gave to him many more different names, one for each and every life that he would have to live, suffer, die, and witness too as well. And Samson remembered the names for each life, all but one. This was to ready him for the long journey ahead, trekking billions of light years through space and time, electro-magnetically hurdling to a very small planet. The LORD needed him to witness while living upon that Sphere within the Heavens. From within a flash of light, the LORD of Host sent Samson on his way to Earth.

Samson's conscious mind sang a prayer over, and over again while hurdling through the space-time continuum. It was a prayer of the human who built him. He would later call it, "A Prayer of Cyron." Samson, no longer a robot, loved this prayer. He had heard Hebrew Christians sing this prayer aloud for 20,000 years, since the day this man built him as a robot. The humans passed it down from generation to generation, all his robotic life.

"THE LORD HOVERS TO WITHIN MY HEART LIKE A GREAT BIRD OF PREY OVER THE FIELD RELENTLESS IN PURSUIT FOR THE PRIZE AND BEAUTIFUL TO WITHIN HIS FLIGHT TO DO SO   AMEN"

In every life Samson would have upon the Earth, he was to look for the seven children of innocents. The LORD told him that he would easily recognize them. HE explained,

"The children will appear in the last place you will expect to find them! With two women Prophets from Cyron revealed, the children will be near! THAT LIFE WILL BE THE VERY LAST LIFE OF SUFFERING YOU WILL EVER HAVE TO ENDURE FOR THE LORD, YOUR GOD, AGAIN!"

Samson had no knowledge of how, or when, or even what he was supposed to do once he found the children. He knew only to obey his GOD, and look for them in every Life until they appeared before him. Then HE gave to Samson the Holy Prophet's Pen, Lineage Book, and Compass, and said to him, "Remember the Prophesies." The frame in time HE sent him to on the planet Earth was 3000 years before Moses. From then until this present day, **June 04, 2017**, he has lived **343** consecutive lives! **7x7x7 = 343.** In every Life evil stalks and harms him, using every possible method, in attempts to kill and, or to veer him away from GOD'S Master Plan!

IT IS ALMOST TIME TO WITNESS FOR OUR LORD
THE CHRIST IS RETURNING SOON VERY SOON

CHAPTER 6

FREEDOM OF CHOICE
(FREE WILL)

This finely honed tool, "Freedom of Choice," upon the moment of Judgment by our Living GOD on all planets of human, robot, living beings, plants and, or inhabitants of any kind, would in fact separate the men, or any beings from the Angels to be, or of whom would have been. Freedom of Choice enables the transformation from man or any being to pure spirit of the Heavenly Angels to unfold miraculously. Or, on the other hand, would just as miraculously transform them to a fiery pain filled life of death.

Because evil beings had all acted as one in their plight to harm other beings so shall it be on the Judgment Day. They shall all melt and bond into one with no identity, creating for them a life of death and fiery hell and searing unrelenting pain forever and ever and ever.

You see, GOD has to know of what your heart truly feels toward HIM. All the people, beings, robots and things of all the worlds, about all the vastness of all the Heavens are filled with Heavenly Angels in the spirit only, as well as in the spirit and in the flesh. Almost all beings in the flesh are not aware of whom they were before their birth in the flesh upon whatever planet they were sent to. If their Hearts were true to GOD when they were Angels flying throughout the Heavens, they somehow, no matter what the circumstances, find a way to obey the Rules of Engagement and remember of whom they have forever served.

Even while war still rages about the planets and throughout all the Heavens between Angels of Light (Warriors For GOD) and Angels of darkness (warriors against GOD), this tool, "Freedom of Choice," is in fact the most powerful and valuable tool that GOD has to realize the purity, love and truth from within ones Heart.

This tool allows GOD to know exactly who truly loves HIM and is devoted to HIM!

This same most valuable and powerful tool of which brings such glorious and great victories from within all HIS Creations also begets great unrelenting pain and sorrow from within our Heavenly FATHER'S infinite Spiritual Heart. Remember HE is after all, a FATHER first and foremost. Truly, each and every soul of which is lost to this Most Holy and Sacred powerful tool, "Freedom of Choice," is an Angel, that of whom HE shall never see again from within HIS so very vast Kingdoms of Creations! HIS Love for even those of who rage war upon HIM, their MAKER, is truly a great love. As much love as HE has ever had for any and all upon any and all planets, places to within all-star systems, shadows, black holes or any other place that exists through HIS loving grace. When even one should perish by way of this most powerful tool, I say to you all from within all parts of HIS vast, so very extremely vast Kingdom of Creations that you all shall hear HIS Sorrowful wailing Cries from having to send a loved one to a life of death, erasing them from the Book of Life forever! All will know of the FATHER'S Love, HIM that AM!

CHAPTER 7

HEART OF AN ANGEL

As he stood in silence listening to his forest filled mountain birthplace, Mr. Gorbachev observed, heard, and felt all the things and beings around him. Blades of grass moving gently in the breeze, tiny ants walking up the trees, caterpillars transforming into beautiful butterflies, the Falcon diving upon its prey.

Suddenly he realized that four humans were methodically stalking his mother. As he entered their thoughts, he knew to act swiftly whereas in just a few more moments one of them would kill her for merely a trophy to hang on a wall from within the den of a Russian home! His heart filled with both fear for his mother and pure rage against these trespassing, would be murderers! In less than a millisecond, he flashed through the forest a quarter of a mile. He was to waste no time as he pounced upon two of the want-to-be assassins with shear brute force and speed. As their weapons flew, the men bounced off the trees as well. As he turned to combat the other two, one man fired a blast from his rifle that struck his mother. In complete desperation, with a single thought, he disoriented all the men while he pounded upon the shooter! He held him with a death grip of teeth wrapped around his throat. This was the same man's throat, who would murder his beautiful mother!

The other three men, still disoriented, saw five other mountain lions circling that were simply not there. Their hearts filled with fear of the cat-mountain lion cub of who had attacked them but had not yet attempted to kill. They had never seen such speed and accuracy in any animal on any hunt they had ever been. All three fled in all different directions to escape what they thought was in fact certain death.

As Mr. Gorbachev's teeth tightly gripped around the man's throat, the same man of whom thought of his mother's head hanging in his den, the heart remembered what his mind cared not too. The Lion's big beautiful blue eyes gazed deep to within the Muslim's terrified brown eyes and his heart filled with the complete Love and Forgiveness of that of our LORD. He could see, feel, and smell the fear of death from within this man's heart as he trembled, trapped in an inescapable death grasp! As he released his hold of the Muslim's throat, a small trickle of blood splattered to the ground, all while the man still trembled and began to cry as like a small child. With love and understanding in his Heart, the Mountain Lion Cat-Cub gave the man a very slow but meaningful bow of his head, while cocked to one side. As he searched deep to within the eyes of this man, the cub furiously blurted out a roar, his face twisting into a snarl. Then, completely relaxing his face, he slowly shut his eyes and even more slowly opened his eyes again as if to say, "It is alright, I forgive you." With his head still cocked to one side, he ever so slowly bowed it once again, and in a flash of light, the cub completely vanished into thin air!

The want-to-be assassin, in complete awe, thought, "His eyes spoke to me!" Then, he said aloud to himself, "I saw and I felt love, kindness, goodness, knowledge, understanding, and wisdom all from within his eyes." He felt a great sense of guilt, not only for firing on the majestic mountain lioness, but also for his thoughts as he pulled the trigger; thoughts of her head hanging upon the wall in his den. He desperately hoped she would survive and that somehow he might see her and her heroic young majestic cub once again. He would like to see the same cub to which he owed his very life. The cub of who was blue eyed and of who was pure and white as a fresh snow. The cub of who had a penetrating stare that could somehow explain of whom he was, his gentleness, and good intent. He sensed that this young beautiful cub truly had The Heart of an Angel!

Throughout his life, he had heard tales of certain Animals that were Angels in the flesh with great supernatural powers. These Angels protected other Angels in the flesh. It was said that they would not kill for any reason and although could speak any language, would never utter so much as a word to any human. They say it to be "The Rules of Engagement" of which were set forth by the GOD of Abraham for all Angels in the flesh of who walk the earth. He had thought that it was all just legend, that is, until now!

The battle of life and death between man and animal was taking place as James looked on with great concern. If the young cub violates the LORD'S Rules of Engagement and kills, even by accident, there could be very, very serious consequences indeed. James had sensed awesome danger for his mate and arrived at her side just as she cried out in severe pain from the lead ball that penetrated her shoulder. He stood close to her and at the ready. Moreover, he had engaged an electro-magnetic force field all around her as well. At the same moment, he rendered the lioness invisible to any one's eyes. Just as his thoughts were going out from mind to mind to his son, telling him to remember our LORD'S Rules of Engagement, Mr. Gorbachev had let his death grip go from the invading assassin. With a forgiving gentle look and a slow meaningful nod, the cub was gone in a flash of light! He quickly reappeared by the side of his wounded mother and concerned father. James was already in the process of healing her as both escorted her back to the safety of their secret cave within the forest-filled mountains.

"I AM truly pleased in you, MY merciful, loving, Angel Cub, yours is surely The Heart of an Angel of the most trusted kind, anywhere throughout the entire Heavens."

Once again, the Voice of GOD rang out as the most beautiful of all music. The Most HOLY of HOLIES softly whispered as one with the wind, all that is, was or ever shall be! HE softly musically whispered as HIS Life Giving Light remained upon the family three.

"Your Heart shines as a beacon, brightly of all goodness. Soon you must become the guardian of a Muslim man called, Daniel Adjac Pruce. This man has forgotten who he truly is and who he truly serves, the very man that hunted and shot your Lioness Mother."

Mr. Gorbachev nodded in obedience and gently smiled as he answered, "YOUR will is my will, LORD."

The four hunters that had stalked the cub's mother were all devout Muslims! Each one had a different story to tell about what had happened that day but all agreed on one simple fact, the Cat Mountain Lion Cub that so heroically saved his Lioness Mother's life that day, spared each and every one of their lives as well.

CHAPTER 8

LAURIE

She was born in Italy in the year of our LORD, 1901. As a small child, her parents, of whom were exceptionally well educated, made her to study with great discipline, violin, the sciences and among many other subjects, Catholicism. She attended a very old, respected and Grand Catholic School connected to the Vatican itself.

A super loving child, she was abundantly loved as well. Every day, while on her way to the Catholic School, that of which she so faithfully attended, she walked straight through the central part of the Vatican until it turned into a long winding hallway. It had many separate rooms adjoined to it and somehow the hallway eventually connected to the school itself. She often times would stop and innocently, secretly observe and listen to Cardinals and sometimes even the Pope praying or discussing Worldly affairs.

At seven years of age, she had already become a child prodigy as an accomplished Solo Violinist and performed concerts throughout the entire known World at that moment in time. She would feel the music completely throughout her entire body and soul, and the LORD loved her very, very much.

One day, while on her way to Catholic School, she once again hid in the hall. She secretly observed and listened to a Cardinal speaking to a man all alone from all the other Cardinals or other Church Officials. This time it was very different from any other moment in time that she had ever observed or listened in secret before. There was a stench of the most foul of odors and as she entered the long, wide hall, she could not see anything but darkness! It was absolutely the blackest, of any darkness, that she had ever experienced! Satan naturally employs certain darkness so black and thick, it is impossible to describe. This time, as she listened, she heard a very different sounding voice that was completely unfamiliar to her. She heard him saying exceptionally dreadful and unbelievable things to the Cardinal of who called him by name, "Lucifer!" "In just a short few years I will create a World War that will take the children away from GOD and GODLY things." He then added, "Less than twenty five years later I will create an even more devastating war that shall involve even more of the world. This will cause even more of the children and adults to leave the LORD *this* CHRIST!" She overheard this and much more as the Cardinal agreed to help accomplish Satan's agenda, by way of giving as much money and recruits to his evil cause, as necessary to succeed!

As Laurie overheard the Cardinal saying this to Lucifer she started to gasp for air from the stench that still poured into the hallway from the room they had been secretly plotting in. As innocent as Laurie was at the young and tender age of seven, she could have died merely from being to within the same general vicinity of Lucifer's overwhelming stench of evil! **While she fought, gasping for air to breathe, Lucifer heard her and smelled her!** He leaped into the hallway right beside, almost touching her, as he would have devoured anyone that happened to be there. **He could smell a strong scent of something or someone, someone young, something sweet! "It has to be a child," he roared!** "Where? Where?" She could feel and hear his footsteps all around as if almost on top of her.

Suddenly a bright light appeared that seemed to be coming from a rather large feline. He looked like a small tuxedo with eyes and ears. He was sitting very calmly and very quietly, right at Laurie's side. This feline, whom Laurie later named, "Tuxedo," was an Angel Warrior Guardian Witness of the End of Days. He had rendered Laurie invisible to all other beings around her. The foul odors and the darkness were no longer about Laurie! Although Lucifer himself was screaming, ripping and tearing at the darkness staring right through her and Tuxedo, all Lucifer could see was his own terrible darkness. All of this even as Tuxedo's light had completely lit up the hall with the energy of ten burning Suns all at once!

The truly innocent and the Chosen are privileged. Thus enabled to see Angels as this in all of their Glorious GOD'S Life Giving Light. Thus, Children thrive in the Light and the Angel serves them as well. And so it was, likewise, when Lucifer kept screaming, ripping, and tearing at the darkness, almost on top of Laurie and

Tuxedo, he simply could not see them side by side nor could he see Tuxedo's Life Giving Light of our LORD.

You see, if an Angel shines his Holy Sacred and Pure Spirit of Love, Goodness, and Grace Magnified by the LORD'S Living Light, the devil's eyes are not capable of observing. It is fortunate for him, for if his eyes were able to observe they would burn from the inside out! Although Lucifer could not see the Light, Laurie, or the beautiful cat Tuxedo, he remained very suspicious and knew that something was not right. Lucifer decided to walk with the Cardinal down the hall another 200 feet and entered another conference room to finish planning another one of his evil plots.

Now that Lucifer and the Cardinal were a safe distance down the hall in another room, Tuxedo led Laurie away from danger and to within her classroom in the Catholic School. Laurie was aware that this beautiful feline had saved her very own life, and tried desperately to coach him into her home as he had followed her after school. The beautiful Tuxedo was content to follow Laurie wherever she went but always kept a large amount of distance in the background, the same applied to Laurie's home.

Although it is usually the LORD that would come to within the humans mind before the Angel Guardian comes to within a dream, GOD instructed Tuxedo to do this task. To plant thoughts into Laurie's mind of not telling a soul about any of her experiences with evil or even with him as her life would be in grave danger! The LORD decided this for HIS own purpose concerning the faith of HIS beautiful Laurie. Tuxedo also made her to realize that these experiences would serve her and the LORD later on in her long, long, life. In fact, her experiences at seven years of age, concerning evil would much, much later in her life, not only serve our LORD and Master, but would serve all life in the world as well.

CHAPTER 9

WARS AND A LOST HERO

When World War I broke out into tragic, furious, and unmerciful killing, Tuxedo saved Laurie and others just like her, many times over. Even through all of this, Tuxedo kept a great distance between Laurie and himself. This was exceptionally difficult for him as he loved her with much of his strength and had to feel her from afar. Tuxedo knew too well the danger it would impose if Lucifer observed in any way, shape, or form, his being too close for too long or too many times to Laurie. In addition, Tuxedo did not want Lucifer to sense or remember anything of that day in the Vatican, the day that Laurie overheard evil plots masterminded by Lucifer! It was the same day his foul orders overwhelmed everything in the hallway as he explained to the Cardinal more of his evil schemes! If Lucifer thought for even one minute that they were the ones in the hall that day in the Vatican, he would follow them to the ends of the planet. He would never stop plotting their deaths until the very End of Days when the LORD would prevail over him in Judgment!

In Laurie becoming a young woman she continued to perform concerts throughout the world and came to be married to a young man close to her own age and vocation. The years passed and her faith in the LORD slowly grew weaker with the tragedy of her husband's death after only five years of marriage. In addition, her faith grew even weaker with the tragedy of observing another world conflict, as war and killing became a way of life for many once again to within her very own lifetime. She no longer had Tuxedo to rely on to strengthen her faith in GOD as it seemed that even he had abandoned her in these, her greatest hours of need. She longed just to look upon the gentle face of the special feline of who, throughout her youth, had always been there to save her and her loved ones from sure destruction. Europe had endured much unwanted evil and many had come to perish.

Toward the middle of World War II Laurie had traveled to America where she had met a British Scientist. They fell deeply in love and were married. His name was Alden Blade and he was a well-known writer throughout the world as well as being a top-notch scientist. They came to have many scientist and writer friends. Most of them lived close by in the Hollywood Hills of California where they had built one of their homes.

They were, for a time, very happy. But as both had witnessed two global conflicts, countless and senseless smaller wars, not to mention police actions on whole countries as well, their faith in GOD and JESUS and the Holy Spirit, for a moment, was no more! She was now on the other side of the world and had all but forgotten Tuxedo and that day his light shined upon her as he led her to safety from Lucifer. After all, that was way back in 1908. Throughout the years, she had often wondered and had many questions about that surely miraculous day at the Vatican and the years that had followed. The years that Tuxedo had seemingly performed miraculous deeds for her and others like her, before her very own eyes!

#1---Who exactly was he?
#2---What was he even doing in the Vatican?
#3---When did he come to the Vatican?
#4---Where did he live and where did he come from?
#5---Why was that wondrous cat in the hall that day?
#6---How did he perform those miraculous deeds over the years?
#7---Was he perhaps an Angel Warrior of Legends past? It was said for centuries now that angels in the flesh, both animal and human, guarded certain people and beings in and at the Vatican!

Laurie had often thought about all of these questions and many, many more with no answers throughout all the years that had streamed by as like the clouds in the sky. Laurie did not realize that Tuxedo was in fact an Animal Angel Warrior Guardian Witness for the End of Days on the planet Earth and sent here by GOD. There was absolutely no way that she could have possibly realized that Tuxedo was on a Holy and Sacred mission for GOD.

He was to protect the Pope from all evil, evil thoughts and the foul odors that Lucifer would project upon him to hinder his

Judgment on all matters twenty four hours a day, seven days a week. When Laurie was a child, Tuxedo was to protect her as well. When she became an adult Tuxedo continued to secretly follow and protect her all the rest of her days by order of our LORD. He left the Vatican when Laurie left the Vatican and he followed her. But up until that moment, Lucifer was always bewildered at how the Pope could still function properly while being constantly bombarded and under attack. No one protected the Pope as well as Tuxedo and Moksha, his father. Together, they were unbeatable! It is duly noted that both Laurie and Lucifer simply did not yet realize of who Tuxedo truly was in the Eyes and Heart of our LORD.

CHAPTER 10

DREAMS OF TRUTH

In the home of Daniel, while sitting comfortably to within his den, he could not stop thinking of the magnificent Mountain Lioness and her most merciful and wondrous cub. He now felt an overwhelming bond that somehow miraculously bridged him to the white as the purest snow, blue-eyed wonder. The blue-eyed Lion who refused to kill and had come to within his dreams as of late. The cub would soothe and care for him in two separate on-going nightmares as he pervaded them with Love and good news of his being chosen by the LORD GOD!

The cub gently infused to within the first nightmare and told Daniel his name, Mr. Gorbachev. He reminded Daniel of the Prophesy of the Pen, Compass, and Lineage Book concerning his stepfather and his brother, James Adja Pruce. He also informed Daniel that his brothers were not of his blood. They had plans of murdering him while in the forest, supposedly observing and hunting for food as to enjoy a large feast with the whole village. The LORD had already entered into the subconscious mind of Daniel and filled it with thoughts of silence. Silence as to talking to anyone of an animal speaking to him to within his dreams. This protected his and Mr. Gorbachev's identity, and importance to GOD, from evil. However, Daniel dismissed this dream as something that happened to ease his conscience of the guilt. The guilt he had so deeply felt ever since his eyes had seen to within the eyes of the majestic and merciful Mr. Gorbachev. The cub of who had released his death grasp from Daniel's throat even though he had tried to murder his Lioness Mother.

Just as he had finally dismissed his dream as an easement for his own conscience, he yet still had another dream of Mr. Gorbachev and his warning. Once again, the picturesque majestic blue-eyed cub pervaded Daniel's nightmares with Love and good news and made of them a beautiful and wondrous dream. In this dream, he gently asked Daniel to say the Words

"JESUS IS LORD." As Daniel Adjac Pruce obeyed and said those Words aloud to within his own dream, "JESUS IS LORD," he realized who he really was and had been throughout eternity! He knew of whom he had served all that time. He remembered JESUS, while upon the planet Cyron, where he had been Samson, the Robot. He remembered the LORD JESUS laying hands upon his face baptizing him in the Name of the FATHER, the SON, and the HOLY SPIRIT transforming him into a human being! He remembered the flash of light that had sent him hurdling through space and time, billions of light years to Earth, to witness the End of Days upon this planet for the LORD. He remembered that he was an Angel Warrior for the MAKER of all that is, was or that will ever be! He remembered all the other lives he had witnessed too, while upon this Planet! He remembered his need to find the 7 innocent children for our LORD.

As he awoke from his dreams, he thought that his own conscience was once again playing tricks on him! Besides, everyone knows that animals cannot talk, and who ever heard of being from another planet let alone knowing the LORD CHRIST!

Nevertheless, the lifelong nightmares, always a man in a heavy fog, bloodied and dragging a cross, and the dreams of Mr. Gorbachev just lately breaking into the nightmares, seemed so real, and the memories so vivid, that he felt he should perhaps consider what the young cub had said to within them. It was like an Angel's Revery covering the nightmares!

Over the years, before Mr. Gorbachev came into his life and within every nightmare, he would always praise the LORD and ask, "Forgive me, LORD?" And he would cry out and ask, "Am I the One?" All through these years, even as ugly and horrifying as they always were, his nightmares did seem to be less frightening as of late. However, in the end, Daniel decided to dismiss dreams pervading the nightmares as the easement of his own conscience once again.

CHAPTER 11

DREAMS PROVEN

More than a month had passed since he had the dreams of Mr. Gorbachev's warnings and the knowledge of whom he really was and to whom he serves. Mot Pruce asked Daniel to accompany him along with their other brothers, Tom and James, to the forest to observe and hunt for game. After the hunt, they would enjoy a large feast with the entire village for a certain religious holiday. At first, he was more than happy to hunt with his brothers and be with them in the forest.

Then, suddenly, he remembered the warnings of Mr. Gorbachev in two different dreams, and realized the truth of the unexpected invitation from his brother. Even as Daniel realized the truth, he went into the forest with his brothers anyway. He hoped that somehow the Mountain Lion Cub, warning him in his dreams, was simply a coincidence, and the desires for his brothers to murder him were not true. "After all, my brothers and I are all of the same blood. If the dreams are wrong about that then they have to be wrong about murder as well, and thus, simply an easement of my conscience for shooting the cub's mother," he insistently thought to himself.

It was a bright day with just a few clouds in the sky as Daniel and his brothers set out for the hunt deep into the forest. Walking along the edge of a steep canyon cliff during the third day of the hunt, Daniel saw a shadow moving at a very high speed from within the corner of his left eye. Just then, he stumbled and fell! Mot's sword flashed by his head missing him by less than a fraction of an inch. He jumped to his feet as Tom drew his dagger from its sheath and plunged at him. Daniel moved quickly to one side, but the dagger found its mark and pierced through his side. He clenched his brother's arm, and as he was falling backward, pulled Tom, forcing him back past himself and into James of who was rushing up from behind. By then Mot had regained his footing and once again reeled his sword with both hands raised high from above his head, straight down aiming for the very top of Daniel's head! With the reflexes and agility of an Angel Warrior, he tumbled to the ground sideways and right back up to his feet again, facing all three of his brothers. As tears streamed, flowing down his face, he gazed upon all three with the forlorn hope of their love and sobbingly asked, "Why, why, whyyyyyyyyyyy do you act out this unholy deed to kill your very own brother?" Tom pointed his riffle at Daniel as he picked it up from the ground and answered, "Our father, rest his soul, killed your whole Hebrew family, every man woman and child of them, while on a raid with other Muslims. You were just a newborn baby! He would not allow innocent life to end. So he took you in to be our brother. Now we shall kill you and take all that you have, and be clean of your Hebrew filth once and for all!" Mot added, "We have never wanted a Hebrew as our brother. Now that our father has been deceased from this world a respectful amount of time, we shall delete you from our family tree." Mot and James picked up their riffles, and with Tom, leveled them onto Daniel. All three men were laughing at his grief and all were about to fire the lead balls of sure death into him!

CHAPTER 12

SACRED RULES BROKEN

Mr. Gorbachev, of who had been secretly stalking the four men, hoped that the three brothers would reveal the complete truth to Daniel before he had to act and save him from their evil plight. When he observed the brothers picking up their weapons and were about to fire on Daniel, as they had already planned to do, he knew it was time to act!

Suddenly, once again with the speed of light, the mighty cub pounced, in seemingly one motion, on all three. Daniel quickly took advantage of this and leaped, sliding all the way down the steep slope of the canyon wall, 1500 feet or more, to the canyon floor. The men of whom he had thought were his brothers, not having his abilities, could not follow. He knew this place well, as the man of who he thought was his father had brought him here to hunt many times in the past.

The young cub slammed the three brothers all at once again. James and Mot rendered unconscious, their weapons flew to the very bottom of the canyon floor from the blow. Tom, the first struck by the Holy force, flew through the air, bouncing off a nearby tree! He tumbled over, and over and yet still over again, and again, all the way down the sloped canyon wall, to the very bottom of the canyon floor! He landed within the thickest part of the forest about 100 yards away from Daniel. There was a space between the canopy of trees giving Mot and James a clear view of their brother from the top of the canyon wall. His body was twisted and broken as he laid there fighting to breathe, he was dying. The young Mr. Gorbachev, realizing what he had caused, gasped frantically for air as his heart completely filled with unrelenting sorrow. In a millisecond he pounded to the canyon floor at Tom's side touching him with great care as the tears flowed down the white fur on his face! Tom, looking at the cub in complete awe, felt all the sorrow and all the love from within the Lion Cub's Holy Heart as their eyes slowly met. Tom's arm ever so slowly rose as his hand gently touched the tears streaming down the beautiful face of the mighty cub warrior. Mr. Gorbachev bowed, exposing the top of his head to Tom, and with his forehead, he touched Tom's face with great Devotion in Truth, Love, Hope, Faith, Honor, and in Trust, as he cried uncontrollably. While gazing into Tom's eyes, the love, goodness, and sorrow in his Heart gave way as he broke the Holy Sacred Rules of Engagement. He gently sobbed and spoke, saying, "Please forgive me my brother, I did not mean." Tom, now realizing that Animal Angels were not only legend but also beings of our LORD GOD, the GOD of Abraham, Isaac, and Jacob, interrupted. And while gasping desperately for air said, "I do not mind as to die at the might of whom I now realize to be an honorable and Holy Warrior. You have honored me greatly by words spoken from your mouth, my Angel!" Struggling to use the hand that still rested upon the head of the mighty cub, he gently pulled him closer as he kissed Mr. Gorbachev with great love from within his heart!

In that instant the cub knew that this was a man of who had a chance, even still, for life everlasting with Angels of Light. At that moment the cub whispered, "Please say the Words, JESUS IS LORD." Tom replied, "But, I am not worthy." The Angel Warrior answered, "An Angel of darkness or men with dark hearts will not say those Words but an Angel of Light, or a man with a pure Heart can and will." Once again, the cub softly asked as he sobbed, "Please, Please say the Words, JESUS IS LORD." As Tom looked lovingly deep within the beautiful blue eyes of Mr. Gorbachev, he gasped for air to breathe once again. He slowly whispered with an overwhelming abundance of love from within his very own lonely heart, "JESUS IS LORD."

Before Tom could finish saying those mind-expanding Words of truth, the canopy cover of the trees opened, spreading widely apart to expose a large cloud that had appeared directly over them!

CHAPTER 13

ALL IS FORGIVEN

Suddenly, a brilliant light piercing through the cloud shined down upon Tom and the majestic cub! The Huge Hand of Life Giving Light reached out from within the cloud and touched them both, as it ever so gently and lovingly caressed them! Tom, struggling, looked up into the cloud; he slowly and painfully raised his other arm up to touch what he saw as unbelievable beauty and grace! He was looking directly into the Holy Face of our LORD, JESUS! He cried out, "You are so beautiful, my LORD! You are so beautiful! You are so beautiful! Please forgive me for I have sinned against you so terribly, so horribly all my life, I just did not believe! I did not know you then! I am so very truly sorry, my LORD, JESUS! I truly love you LORD. I truly, truly love you! I love you! Do with me as you wish, oh LORD do with me as I deserve. Just know that whatever you decide, whatever befalls me, I love you LORD! I love you, the Most Holy of Holies!"

As Tom said these words from his heart, the LORD'S voice, in a soft whispering musical tone, rang out from within the cloud! It was the most beautiful music in all of creations' singing whispers, as one with the wind and all that is, was or that will ever be!

"I now realize your love, as the words spoken from your mouth that come from deep within your heart are forever true! Therefore from this day, and throughout eternity, you shall be with ME always in paradise to within MY FATHER'S House, you are forgiven."

Tom's eyes blinded with loving tears and regret of his sins. He still gasped for air as he pulled the mighty Cub even closer with all the strength he had left in his dying body. He struggled to whisper, "Thank you, and thank you." With his last three laboring breaths from upon the planet Earth he ever so gently whispered, "Thank you, my young and beautiful Angel. You have made me find the absolute truth in our LORD. You have helped give to me what I never would have received without you in all of the days of which I have walked upon this Earth." Tom's soul and spirit received to within the Heavens and our LORD'S Life Giving Light remained rested upon them both.

Mr. Gorbachev felt a deep sense of guilt, shame and overwhelming grief for what he had caused to happen to the Human, Tom! With his tail tucked between his hind legs and his ears lying completely flat down upon his head he begged in Hebrew, praying silently to GOD for forgiveness as his mighty paws caressed the face of Tom. As the LORD'S Huge Hand of Life Giving Light was still upon them, HE began lovingly petting his wondrous Angel and Mr. Gorbachev felt GOD'S Love and HIS Wonderful Grace and Forgiveness. The LORD answered his prayers as once again HIS soft whispering voice rang out as soft, gentle music to within the Heavens,

"Today you have brought to ME, three souls, two of whom I could not have been certain of until today!"

The young cub replied, "But LORD, I broke the Sacred Rules, not once, but twice. I have killed and I have spoken out loud to a Human." The LORD, in HIS infinite wisdom, once again musically whispered to HIS devoted Angel,

"You were not aware of your own heavenly strength as you fought so courageously to save Daniel, for this reason Tom fell to his death. When you spoke to him, your tears and words were in love, kindness, and good wishes from within your very own loving heart. This caused a man's name, which once was erased, to be entered back into The Book of Life! For causing ME to come here, two others have also found their way into The Book of Life! Daniel now remembers and knows of whom he is and has been for all eternity. James Pruce now realizes that I AM and he will respond in a proper manner. I love you MY Angel Warrior, go forth and break The Holy Sacred Rules of Engagement no longer."

As suddenly as the canopy of the trees had spread open and the cloud had appeared and opened as well, both closed and the LORD'S Living Light vanished back into the Heavens.

CHAPTER 14

FRIEND FOR ETERNITY
HARDENED AND UNHARDENED
HEARTS

Daniel had observed from the distance what had transpired with Tom, the cub and the LORD as he was approaching their location. He was now aware that his dreams were of truth and that somehow Tom had also found truth and favor with our LORD! This made him very happy and very sad as well, for when he reached his brother, Tom, he saw that he had died. He had heard the LORD speak, and although he was not aware that the cub had spoken, he knew that somehow Mr. Gorbachev had everything to do with Tom gaining favor with the LORD. He looked down upon the great Lion and thanked him and then he looked up and prayed, thanking *GOD* as well. The cub purred loudly as he leaned in close and rubbed up against Daniel walking back and forth rubbing against his legs over, and over again.

Daniel somehow knew that this majestic young Lion would be with him always, and together they would walk the Earth. He reached down, laid his hands upon the head of his new loyal friend, and kneeled in front of him. Mr. Gorbachev knew that this friendship was Eternal. He bowed his massive head and touched the very top of it to Daniel's face in Love, Hope, Faith, Truth, Honor, and Devotion in Trust.

On top of the canyon wall, over 1500 feet up, Mot and James Pruce, had also witnessed the cloud and the Hand of Life Giving Light reaching out, caressing their brother. They heard the soft whisper of the Voice of music that spoke Words of forgiveness. They had heard nothing more than that, but it was enough to turn James toward the Living GOD, and the event had changed his life forever!

Although Mot had heard and seen these same things of Holiness as well, he could not and would not, accept what had happened to his brother. His heart remained hardened more so than ever before. The numbers of his name, Mot Pruce, added up to the number 666. Throughout his entire life, Mot would continue to do, as Lucifer wanted him to do, evil to others, including to his very own brothers, Daniel and James. His evil would ultimately be against himself as well.

Although the numbers of their names, Tom Pruce and James Pruce came to 666 as well, the LORD, with the assistance of the mighty cub's love and good will, had unhardened their hearts. In the end, the Holy Ghost ignited, dwelling to within both their hearts. The Truth, Love, Faith and Hope of GOD, through the Holy Ghost, had defeated all of the evil of which had resided within both men's hearts and from within both men's names. The Holy Ghost Resides where evil used to live! Therefore, the LORD had forgiven them!

Then the LORD added Adja to their names and Adjac to Daniel. The name Daniel Pruce equals 648+6+4+8=666. Daniel Adjac Pruce equals 762+7+6+2=777. The LORD added Adjac to his name for he was Holy and his Heart was Pure. This was the same for Tom and James as Adja became part of their names.

IT IS WHAT TRULY RESIDES TO WITHIN YOUR HEART THAT WILL IN THE END, TELL THE "TRUTH OF EVERLASTING LIFE!"

CHAPTER 15

THE WOLF AND THE MOUSE

The dew had gently settled upon the trees, plants, and ground and the morning air was amazingly fresh and crisp. Everything still sparkled to within the early morning rising sun. The Mouse awoke and raised his little head above his home from within the serene forestry of the Russian Mountain landscape. Looking up over his mound, his mouth opened wide as his voice rang out, "Yaaaaaaaaaaaaaaaaaaaaaaaaaaaaaaaaaaaaaaaaaaaaaaaaaaaaaaaaaaaaa aaaaaaaaaaaaaaaaaaaaaaaaaaaaaaaaaaaaaaaaaaaaaaaaaaaaaaaaaaaaaaa aaaaaaaaaaaaaaaaaaaaaaaaa...yaaaaaaaaaaaaaaaaaaaaaaaaaaaaaaaaaa," giving a great big, long, lazy yawn. His short little arms reached higher and higher and yet still even higher up over his head in a much-needed early morning stretch of his tiny little body.

Mot Pruce was out hunting with his large ungodly dog who was just like him, an angel of darkness. He was in an especially foul mood as he had lost two brothers to the Holy Ghost in of the LORD. Satan had shamed Mot by expressing to him his wishes of death to his brother James and the Hebrew, Daniel. James Adja Pruce and Daniel Adjac Pruce were not responding to Satan's will. The Holy Spirit had heroically rescued them! This angered Satan very, very much. Mot was shamed and hated anything and everything Holy. This included his blood brother, James.

James Witnessed the Holy event of his brother's death, and therefore received the Holy Spirit at that exact same moment. He knew of Mot's Hate for him or anyone else that is Holy. And so it was he also knew that Mot would now try to kill him. James fled from that part of the forest that same day, hid from his brother, and planned to flee Russia as well.

So as Mot Pruce headed out with his unholy companion to hunt wild game, his thoughts were to track his brothers down as well. He simply wanted to kill anything and everything living or that happened to cross their path! Suddenly, as Mot's dog had ventured far up ahead on the beaten trail, the ungodly hound saw the mouse who was right in the middle of his long, lazy morning yawn and stretch. The evil beast plunged himself at the tiny creature and snatched him up whole to within his very large and foul mouth. The mouse had the supernatural powers of a Holy Angel but did not realize who he really was as of yet. He bit the inside of the dog's mouth while at the same moment disorienting the huge beast. As the ungodly dog gave out a painful crying howl that could be heard, for miles, his jaw dropped all the way to the ground. The mouse was exceptionally upset as his stretch and his yawn had been completely disturbed. He quickly leaped out from within the hound's mouth, dripping wet with slobber. He looked directly into his eyes and said, "Man, your breath is foul, to say the least." Then the mouse, still being very upset, began to slap the beast repeatedly all the way back up the trail twenty yards or more.

Mr. Gorbachev had been observing all of these events in amusement. He realized that the mouse, speaking and doing mortal combat with a huge animal and winning, was truly very special. He had to be an Angel of who did not yet remember his long past with GOD! He also realized the tiny mouse was very old, as he knew of his own powerful abilities!

Finally, with one big swing, the mouse clubbed the poor dog into complete unconsciousness, laying him flat on his back within the middle of the trail. As the mouse turned, wiping his hands as a job well done, he saw the mighty cub calmly sitting with his head cocked to one side and looking directly at him. Observing this, the mouse stomped, then planted his feet firmly in the ground as he said, "What? "You want some of this too. Huh? Yeah, you! Want some of this? Come on. Come on you over grown kitty catty watty datty, huh? Come on then!" As the majestic white cub looked at the tiny being, he laughed and softly replied, "No, I do not think so my mighty little friend." The mouse was very surprised as he very gently and slowly said, "You are like me aren't you? I mean I have never ever heard another animal speak that is other than a human being." The great cub answered, "Yes, I Am as you are my little friend. Please say the Words, JESUS IS LORD." The mouse, feeling slightly threatened, said in a very sassy tone, "What do you mean say the Words, *JESUSSSISSSSSSSSSSSSSSSSSSSSSSSSSS LORRRDDDDDDDDDDDDDDDDDDDDDDDDDDDDDDDD?"*

As the mouse was still saying the Words, his memories had all come completely back to him after 800 years of life on this planet! He was so very happy to remember that he began running around and around in circles screaming, "I am an *Angel*, I am an *Angel*, I am an *Angel*, all of these years, I've always been an *Angel!*" As the mouse stopped running in circles but was still screaming, he ran from the very tip of the young cub's tail all the way up to the top of his head. While leaning over with his own head upside down he looked Mr. Gorbachev straight in the eyes and repeated over and over, "Thank you, thank you, thank you, thank you so very much!" Then, still looking deep into his eyes, he kissed the cub right between them on the very bridge of his nose.

Gorbachev could not help but break out into a hearty laugh and reached up with his mighty paw to allow the tiny, happy mouse, to jump on it as he gently set him onto the ground in front of him. Mr. Gorbachev, being in constant tune mentally with the mouse, realized that the mouse had no name, and asked through thoughts if he could name him Timothy or Tim for short? As the mouse was now in tune mentally with the cub as well he agreed, but only if he could call him Gorby.

Timothy began to tell the young and impressionable cub all about his *800* years of life upon this planet called Earth. He told Gorby all about the happiness he had once felt as he was growing up with his parents and how he raised his own families throughout his youth. Then all his loved ones, one by one, began to die as he remained in good health and seemingly indestructible! After a long while, he began to think of it as a curse and stopped making friends and trying to create other families, especially another wife. It had broken his heart over, and over again as the loved ones of his youth would die and die and die and die. Finally, he became a loner and walked this planet for over *700* years all alone. *700* years of no friends, no family and never knowing of whom he truly was as well. He only knew that he was different, much different, from any other being that he had ever encountered before, that is, until this day. He finally found someone like himself, and now to know of who he is, was, and will always be. To know of whom he had forever vowed his allegiance and to whom he served. This all had in fact, made him extremely happy! Now, after *700* years, he had not only found a friend but he had found his GOD as well, and would serve HIM from this day forth knowingly and willingly.

Tim began to explain many things about the forest and about other animals and creatures even more tiny than him or that of the ants. Tim talked on and on about the many exciting tales and adventures that he had experienced of life and death! He told Gorby about traveling the world by land and on the high seas and even by the air. Mr. Gorbachev listened with great interest and intense extrapolation! Then he told the bewildered cub that he had never felt such a wonderful feeling before as in the moment that he had actually come to fly. To fly by air in the skies above the mountains and the trees and all the other wildlife from upon the planet is truly a treat. Of course, the excited young cub had to ask, "But Tim, how did you come to be able to fly?" The mouse gave out a great laugh as he began to explain. "I had seen an Eagle flying majestically. He was flying high above even the mountains and clouds. As I observed I began to feel a deep desire to see for myself what wonders he surely saw from that viewpoint. I decided to invite danger by running in circles until he noticed me. In fact, it took so long for him to see me that just as I thought he would never do so, he suddenly snatched me up into his claws! It was all very funny because every time he tried to drop me, within his nest of young Eagles, I would hold on and enter his thoughts at that same moment to fly high and try to drop me. Finally, I would grow tired and bored and as he would fly close to the ground, I would allow him to let me go. I swear he truly seemed grateful each, and every time he was able to drop me from his or shall I say, from my grasp. Every time I would repeat these events with that *Great and beautiful Bird of Prey*, he seemed to enjoy the experiences as a challenge of will and of strength. We, together over many, many years, seemed to have built a sort of bridge or bond if you will, between us. Over these many past years, I have come to enjoy his company even though he is a great bird and I am his prey!"

As Tim talked and talked, Gorby came to realize that this little being was truly an exceptionally good soul. He found himself trusting, loving, respecting, and even looking up to, so to speak, this tiny wondrous creature called, Timothy. He began to think of him as an older, wiser, and stronger brother. Within the very short time they had been conversing with one another, the cub truly developed a deep and meaningful connection with this, his newfound friend.

The two Angel Warriors were enjoying each other's company very much, as the mouse felt the same love and admiration for the mighty cub as the cub had been feeling for him. In fact, they were so excited and so much involved into the conversation with each other that they had not realized the wolf who had been stalking the both of them. He had been doing so for the past three hours. He waited, watched, and listened for just the perfect moment in which to pounce upon the majestic cub, as the mouse was just too small to combat with any dignity.

The wolf was a massive 250 pounds of bone, pure muscle, and sheer size. He had tri colors on the very tips of his hairs, very light colors. A beautifully colored Star shaped image in his fur softly settled just between his beautiful deep blue eyes and reached straight up onto his forehead. He had a huge fluffy tail of which was long and curled all the way up around with the very tip touching to his back. This all set him apart from any other wolf in existence upon the entire world, as he was truly a stunning, beautiful, majestic, and noble looking being.

Tim and Gorby had stopped on the trail to sit as Tim had finished yet another story, and as both started to laugh and still talk, the wolf decided to act. Suddenly, without warning, the wolf leaped into the air with his sights and aim for Mr. Gorbachev of who had not even noticed. Tim, of whom had an over whelming feeling of the nearby danger, looked up in just the nick of time and saw the air borne wolf. Without hesitation, the tiny being disoriented the huge animal as he quickly pushed Gorby out from within his path of attack.

By this time both Gorby and Tim were already inside the thoughts of the wolf. They both realized at the same moment that this huge beautiful and majestic looking animal was in fact exactly like them. As they looked back and forth at one another, they began to laugh. They looked onto the wolf as both asked him at the same moment to speak aloud the Words, "JESUS IS LORD." The wolf, understanding what they had asked him to say aloud, replied, "No!" The wolf once again set himself firmly to leap at the cub. With their thoughts, both Tim and Gorby made the wolf crouch down low in pain as they asked him once again to say the Words,
"JESUS IS LORD." Once again, while in much pain the wolf replied, "No!" And still, yet one more time, they put him in just a little more pain. They made him crouch even lower with his chest and jaw touching the ground as they once again asked him to say the Words, "JESUS IS LORD." Once again as the wolf was very

head strong, answered, "No, I willllllllllll, willlll, nottttttttttttttttt!" As they both looked at each other in complete disbelief, they once again put the Wolf in even worse pain. They made his head to bow face down with his eyes and nose touching all the way to the ground with the rest of his body as they asked the wolf one last time to say the Words, "JESUS IS LORD." This time the wolf, in compliance with their wishes answered, "JESUS IS LORRRD!" As the magnificent animal said those mind expanding Words, they completely let him up and relieved all of his pain.

Still halfway disoriented the wolf asked them, "Why did you not kill me?" As the two Angels looked at one another and then upon whom they knew to be an Angel as well, asked, "You do not know?" As the great wolf began to recover and consciously think without pain, he answered, "Ve, ve, ve, ve, ve, ve, ven, vengeance is, vengeance is mine says the LORD….I remember!" As he remembered this, he remembered all things throughout his long, long existence as an Angel Warrior for the Living GOD. He finally realized the purpose of his long *500* years of life upon this planet. This allowed him the time of which he so desperately needed to gain the knowledge, understanding, and wisdom that of which he would need to guardian others like himself. He could now Guard the Angel Warrior Witnesses of the End of Days for our LORD GOD. He was now properly equipped.

The great creature was very grateful that the mouse and the cub had made him to say those beautiful Words that allowed him to regain his loving memories as an Angel of our LORD! The three of them together repeated many silent prayers in Hebrew to our LORD, giving thanks for making them all come together and become friends.

After thanking GOD in Hebrew, they all began to play uncontrollably. They ran up trees, then down trees, all about the forest until finally after a long time of playing they came to rest and calmly sat to talk. The wolf, realizing that they both had names and he did not, asked them to call him Brother for he felt that they should be his brothers. In this way, they could think of him as being their very own brother. Tim and Gorby both agreed with great joy and from that day forth all Angels would call him Brother.

As the three continued to talk, Brother told them of a man that he had seen in the forest of who had found a place to hide. He told them that entering the man's thoughts, revealed his plight to him.

Brother went on to explain that the man's name was James and that he was in fact running away from his very own brother, a man called Mot Pruce.

Suddenly Mr. Gorbachev thought, "If the Holy Spirit had entered to within the heart of Tom then perhaps at the same moment he entered into his brother, James." Tom had died to within his very own arms just days ago as the LORD had come down to receive his soul. Gorby knew HE would send the Mouse, Wolf and his father to where James Pruce hid from Mot. They would bring him back to his family's lair, hidden to within the mountains.

After Tom died, the cub had brought Daniel to the lair as well to hide him from Mot Pruce and his evil demons of which were everywhere. Now, Mr. Gorbachev would also have to take Timothy and Brother, the wolf, to the cave as well. He knew his father would understand and would in fact explain it all to his beautiful and mighty Mountain Lion Mother. As it was, when he had taken Daniel to within their cave his mother acted very uneasy at first. After his father explained in his or her own Mountain Lion language, she became unbelievably calm and serene as she completely accepted the human. She even touched up against him as she slept by his side to protect him from all danger. He was always amazed at how his father would gain absolute control and complete trust of his huge beautiful Mother with just a look or just a word.

Mot had found his ungodly dog on the trail sitting; he seemed very dumfounded and bewildered as well. Mot decided to go back to the village. He would round up as many evil beings as he could to swarm the forest until they found the cub, Daniel and his brother, James. When he would find them, he would kill all three. If he should come across the Cub's Mountain Lion Mother and Father in the process, he would murder them as well.

The mighty cub carefully took Timothy and Brother to within the secret cave. Daniel simply could not believe his eyes! First, he saw the cub walk in and right behind walked the wolf and just as he thought he had seen everything, in walked the mouse, just as happy as could be. The mouse was jumping onto the cub then onto the wolf then back to the ground and then around and around in circles. Daniel even thought that he had seen a smile on the face of this tiny little creature of GOD. Gorby greeted his mother and his father. The mouse jumped onto the back of Brother who walked right up to Daniel. He laid by his side touching him with the very top of his great majestic head in Truth, Love, Hope, Faith, Honor, Devotion and in Trust. Immediately after all of this, Gorby, his father, and his mother, Esther, walked over to Daniel and lay up against him as well. The five formed a circle completely around him. In all of his days upon all of the planets or Heavenly Bodies he had ever lived in the flesh or as a robot throughout the millenniums, he had never felt anywhere near this level of love or trust. He silently gave thanks in Hebrew to the LORD and without Daniel realizing the others bowed their heads with him as he prayed. Daniel began to think to himself, "These must be Angels like me; why else would they take me in and protect me as family?" All at once, as he felt all of them loving him, he knew that he, Daniel, loved each and every one of them as well. He truly loved beyond any comprehension, the Mountain Lioness, the cat, the cub, the Wolf, and the mouse. By now, Tim had climbed up onto Daniel's chest as he lay on his back in the very middle of everyone. He lifted his arm to pet the tiny head of the beautiful little creature as the mighty mouse slept upon him. He felt truly loved and extremely happy to be within this cave with his newfound family, even as he hid from Mot.

That night as all in the cave were fast asleep, GOD came to every one of them to within their dreams. There was much to explain and HE had to instruct each one on their part in order to do HIS Will. HE told James, Gorby's father, that he and Timothy would soon have to depart from Russia with James, the brother of Mot. They were to go to Italy and live for a long period until HE would once again instruct them to go to another place. As the LORD entered Timothy's dreams as well, HE instructed him on the very same matters, as they would have to protect and guard the human James.

GOD entered the dreams of Mr. Gorbachev and explained that he would team up with the Wolf, Brother, and that they would travel with Daniel to Italy to stay for a while. Then they would travel to another far away land and continue to be the Guardian to Daniel all the while. GOD explained the very same to Brother, as HE had entered to within his dreams as well.

The LORD interrupted Daniel's regular ongoing nightly nightmares and explained that he must travel to Italy with Mr.

70

Gorbachev and Brother, the wolf. HE further explained that Daniel must watch over them and protect them at all cost but HE did not explain why. The LORD further explained that, after a time had passed, he would travel with them to another far away land.

Finally, HE entered the dreams of the beautiful Mountain Lioness, Esther. HE tenderly told her that HE loved her more than she could ever understand. GOD explained that soon she would come to be with HIM in the Heavens. HE explained that someday, not too far into the future, she would once again be with her family to within the Heavens. The LORD told her that she would once again be an Angel Warrior for HIM within the Heavens. HE needed her with HIM for a short moment in space and time. HE touched and thanked her for all that she had accomplished for HIM on the Planet Earth. HE told her that once she was with HIM she would completely understand.

The LORD did not explain these things to Mr. Gorbachev or his Father nor did HE tell them of HIM entering to within Esther's dreams. HE did not want them to worry. You see our LORD has perfect plans for every one of us, and it is HIS will not for us to worry or be sad.

The next morning the Wolf explained to the mouse and James exactly where to find the brother of Mot, James Pruce, from within the forest where he was still hiding. They went directly to the hiding place where they easily found him. He had been waiting for them because GOD had come within his dreams and explained everything to him as well even though he is not like them. The LORD told him that he would travel to Italy with a mouse called Timothy and the Father of the Mountain Lion Cat Cub, James, of who was a cat. The LORD told James Pruce to protect them at all cost. Although the human named James was not exactly as the other Angels and did not possess their supernatural powers, he was still a Witness for The End of Days upon this planet. GOD now entrusted him with some of the same Knowledge as HE had entrusted with the Angels. After all, James would someday fly yet one more time to within the Heavens with all the other trusted spirits and souls. For he now possessed the Holy Ghost to within his own Heart within this lifetime.

All three quickly traveled through the forest and back to within the secret cave. Daniel was very happy to see his brother of who was not of his blood but possessed a change of heart just as he had towards our Living GOD. James was just as happy and they both exchanged truths of the dreams they had the night previous. They shared what the LORD explained to each of them. They both new that it was the Will of the MAKER of all that is, was or that will ever be and they were happy and content with this knowledge.

James observed all of whom dwelt to within the cave. They all seemed to have the same desire to touch him. He felt all the love that they projected upon him and knew that he now had an exceptionally loving family of which he had never before possessed.

Everyone realized that soon, so very soon, all would have to go forth and fulfill what the LORD had told each one of them to do. As for now, they would all enjoy each other's loving company, protect one another, and know that GOD intended this for all of them. They would all take advantage of the next week to rest for the long journey ahead. They would learn from one another of life from each of their own perspectives, according to each of their own life experiences. They would all become very, very close to each other and love one another as much as any family could possibly love their own. Each and every one of them felt so much love towards one another that they could not ever understand it, nor could they ever begin to come close to explaining it!! After all, they are Angel Warriors for the Living GOD, each one of them on a special mission for HIM that AM. Being together as they were now they were all happier than they had ever been. Well, at least in this lifetime.

CHAPTER 16

THE SEVENTH WARRIORS

**"THE LORD HOVERS TO WITHIN MY HEART
LIKE A GREAT BIRD OF PREY OVER THE FIELD
RELENTLESS IN PURSUIT FOR THE PRIZE AND
BEAUTIFUL TO WITHIN HIS FLIGHT
TO DO SO   AMEN"**

In the cave, Daniel could not help but to express his love in a Prayer of Cyron for all to feel. He spoke out in the Greek, singing aloud this prayer as all of the family listened in great awe for these words gave to describe exactly to what was truly within each of their own Hearts as well. This prayer brought to Daniel pleasant memories from Cyron and the people he loved and protected.

It was four days now gone by and within three more, they would all start their separate journeys on their quest for GOD. They spent most of their time now praying for guidance as well as a safe venture for each one of them. All were about to go out into the unknown! Each one prayed for the others, as family would all do for each other.

The Lioness paced back and forth, back and forth, back and forth, over and over, over and over, and yet still over and over again, as she was already well aware of the dangers that would unfold before them. She had not worried for herself but for all of her family for she was a true Warrior with the power and strength of at least 20 demons. Her husband, James, and her young Cub stayed right at her side pacing the cave with her to let her know they truly loved her and everything would be all right. Soon everyone was pacing the cave with her until she finally became amused and gave a long and loving look to all as she calmly sat down. She shook her head ever so slowly and looked at all of them one by one, for what seemed to be a long time. She cocked her head to one side and gave out a long and loving moan while still gazing upon all her newfound family in complete awe. The whole family broke out into a long and hearty laughter all at once, and all together. The whole while, it even seemed that she was laughing at herself as well! This definitely eased all the tension that had seemed to fill the air from all around them.

By now, Mot had gathered a huge army together of very large men and even larger animals, and every single one of them, evil demons working for Lucifer and taking orders from Mot. They were a murderous looking bunch and were over 20,000 in numbers. Mot was fully aware of what he had put himself up against, and he would not have a shortage of demon power. He knew that these could very well be Angels of GOD in the flesh, and if so, they were of more than supernatural strength and powers of the mind. He would not chance good beating down evil again as Satan would surely punish him severely.

Mot sent out yellow jackets, flying scouts, to spot his brother and the cub, the cub's father, the cub's mother and Daniel. As one of the yellow jackets came back to tell what he had seen in a report to Mot himself, it became evident that he had finally found his enemy. The scout had reported 1 cat, 1 Mountain Lioness, 1 cub, 1 mouse and only 1 human! James, the brother of Mot, stayed in the cave with Brother, the Wolf. Brother stayed at the side of James until their departure on their separate journeys. He had somehow managed to remain unobserved by any of Mot's scouts.

Mot's army would march for 3-days to reach the point in of which the Yellow Jacket scouts reported to have seen the Angels. Mot grew more and more impatient by the moment, as he could now taste a victory that was very close to within his grasp. He imagined all of their blood spilt upon the ground, as he would personally cut off each of their heads one by one allowing each of them to witness the one before them! He wanted to see, feel, and smell the fear that he could inflict to within their Hearts. Mot did not know that his brother, James, was among them nor did he realize that the Wolf would be in the battle as well.

As the demons marched on it became nightfall and the whole army made camp for the night. There was much tension scenting the air that completely surrounded and paralyzed the army. In addition, many stories circulated throughout the entire camp. They were stories of great peril and terrible defeat as the rumors spread that they were stalking Animal Angels. Until now, they had all thought that Angels in the flesh were just mythical legends. Men and demons told many stories throughout the centuries of how no army had ever come even close to defeating them. In fact, it was legend that the GOD of Abraham Isaac and Jacob assured every one of the Angel's battles to be victorious, thus wiping out whole armies of any nation that had the will to go into battle against them. No one knew for sure if the army was in fact going up against Angels, but just the thought of it struck fear into each demon's heart, as GOD had placed it there. The demons had begun to think, "Even if the Angels are not just legend, we have no idea of their numbers and strength." Fear surely spread throughout the entire army, even its Generals, for this was GOD'S Will. These Are HIS Angels and HE would not let anyone defeat them, especially Mot's army, of who all answered to Satan.

Fights began to break out all around the camp as the commanders tried to stop all the confusion and hostility among themselves. When they tried to tell the troops of demons that these beings had few in numbers, none of the demons believed it. They were already convinced that these were not just any beings but were in fact Angels of Light. Moreover, if they were so few in numbers, "Why then do we march with 20 thousand murderous demons?" As they kept demanding to know the answer to this simple question, the commanders kept repeating the same answer and the more they would answer, the more confusion and hostility prevailed throughout the encampment.

The next morning Mot's army resumed marching while violent fights continuously broke out to within the ranks that of which slowed the army down tremendously. Many men and animal demons died in these vicious brawls as the march slowly moved on. The closer they came to the Angels, the more fights broke out and the more vicious killing came of it. The LORD had hardened each one of their Hearts. As the army was only 10 hours away from the Angels, the numbers of the demons had diminished by over 7000 men and animal demons because of the vicious warring to within their very own ranks. The 10 hours of marching they had left to do was all along the long canyon wall, over 1500 feet above the canyon floor, not far from where Mot and his brothers had attacked Daniel.

When it became nightfall, it was once again time to camp, as Mot's army needed rest from all the hostility and confusion that had seemed to take over the entire force. Mot held a special meeting with his commanders, as now he had become very, very concerned of the battle yet to be. You see, the LORD had also entered to within the heart of Mot and fear truly lived within him. Although he tried to hide the fear from his commanders they could clearly see the sweat of which poured from his brow even to within the coldest mountain air in Russia.

Back in the cave, they had no idea that Mot had such a huge army out looking for them. They did not realize that in fact the whole army was on the march toward their approximate location and would be there in hours.

Mot's army of demons would have to travel down from the very top of the canyon wall into terrain extremely saturated with huge boulders. They lay sporadically in the path from the top of the wall all the way down about 1500 feet or more to the very bottom of the canyon floor, and were not very stable. They would have to be somewhat careful as they traveled that distance downward to the floor of the canyon. They were all very experienced soldiers. They would handle the situation easily. This was the only place the army could march down to get to the Angels last observed position. Mot would send out yellow jackets to scout the floor of the canyon. They would hopefully spot the Angels as he approached that part at the top of the canyon wall where the army would travel downward. They would camp there, at the top of the canyon wall, for a much-needed rest. Once the scouts would report to him on their whereabouts, he would send out 300 men to engage the Angels and act as decoys. This would allow the army time to march down the slope and reinforce their position. Mot knew he could possibly catch the Angels off guard and that would be his very best possible weapon, surprise!

Mot's army approached the position at the top of the canyon wall to march down the slope to the canyon floor over 1500 feet away. It was then that he began to have second thoughts. He sent 400 men and animal demons as the decoys rather than the 300 that he had first decided on. The 400 would silently travel down to the canyon floor and hide until the scouts would report to them on the exact position of the Angels at daybreak.

In the Angel's cave that very night, all were about ready for their journeys, and were both happy to serve their GOD and sad to have to split up what they now had considered to be their very own loving family. They were all content to spend their last night together touching each other as they slept. As they were lying there together, Esther, stood up, plopped right down in the middle of all the bodies, and rolled over onto her back with all of her paws up. She simply wanted to be the center of the attention and as everyone laughed and laughed, one by one they all cuddled right up against her. She purred and purred and purred all night long. The mouse quietly walked up her body and lovingly curled right up nice and cozy to upon her mighty chest. Timothy loved this family with more than all his heart for you see; he had no family or friends for *700* out of *800* years of life upon this very lonely, lonely, lonely, planet. He truly loved every single one of these beings who were a part of him. Observing these beautiful Godly creatures, you simply would just not ever know that they were in fact Mighty Angel Warriors! They truly were loving and very peaceful.

As the morning came, everyone awoke and began to yawn and stretch in a lazy sort of spirit. As Timothy thought of the Eagle of whom he might never see again, he gently put the thoughts of singing the prayer about GOD and the bird of prey into the mind of Daniel. For some reason, perhaps unknown to him, Daniel began to sing that particular prayer, as all the others seemed to bow their heads in prayer with him as well. He always enjoyed singing this prayer aloud while thinking of Cyron. All the people of Cyron from within his heart and all the family sang aloud with them in the Greek, a Prayer of Cyron.

"THE LORD HOVERS TO WITHIN MY HEART LIKE A GREAT BIRD OF PREY OVER THE FIELD RELENTLESS IN PURSUIT FOR THE PRIZE AND BEAUTIFUL TO WITHIN HIS FLIGHT TO DO SO   AMEN"

The mouse listened and could not hold back the tears that flowed from his eyes, streaming down his little face. The others could clearly see that Timothy was very sad. They all gathered around him as they fumbled to hug his tiny little body.

When an Angel feels sadness, everyone with a spirit and or soul of light feels it as well. His newfound Angel family told him through their thoughts that they loved him very much and everyone cried together. Daniel and even James, the brother of Mot, felt these things as well, but did not understand why as they cried too.

As the LORD was secretly watching HIS family of Angels and even as HE knew that Timothy would see his friend the Eagle yet again, HIS tears flowed down as domes as well. HE felt the loneliness to within the tiny heart of HIS little Mouse Angel.

The small group of Angels, along with James Pruce, went out into the early morning sun as the dew sparkled under its fresh rays of a hazy light. In just a few more hours, they would have to say their goodbyes to one another. Then they would depart on their separate journeys to the Vatican in Italy. All seemed to drag their feet in sadness and gloom as the anticipation of leaving Russia, their home, began to take on reality. The Angels all formed a circle as each held the other's hand and paw and began to pray together once again. Daniel and James hugged and as they looked deeply into one another's eyes, they realized the true love of brother-to-brother. Both knew that in this way they are of the same blood!

The yellow jacket scouts had found tracks leading up to the secret cave and birthplace of Mr. Gorbachev. An hour earlier, they had reported to the commander in charge of the 400 demons hiding nearby. This allowed the demons to take ambush positions against the Angels, as they would come out of the secret cave. The four hundred hid behind trees, up in the trees, behind large boulders and even behind large mounds of dirt and awaited the word from their commanders to attack. The yellow jackets rushed up to the top of the canyon wall and reported to Mot as he waited for a signal to march down to the canyon floor. As the first arrow would fly through the air Mot's Army would begin to march.

Suddenly, the Lioness could smell the foul scent of demons and gave out a low troubling roar to warn her entire family. Just at that moment, an arrow sliced through the crisp morning air, finding its mark, piercing through Esther's leg as she moved around to observe the danger. From within the trees above her, 30 demons using their electro-magnetic fingers to shoot waves of bad energy in an attempt to weaken the Lioness, jumped down upon her, swinging their swords. Again, Esther wounded, leaped up to within the tree biting, ripping, and tearing as she so gracefully moved. She jumped back down to pounce upon seven more demons as they were attacking her mate. James could not believe his eyes to how fast and sure she moved, even with her terrible wounds. Tears welled up and began to drip down his white fury face. As much as he wanted to shield her by fighting by her side, he knew that he had to protect James, the brother of Mot, for our living GOD. He thought, "She is truly a warrior of who is more deadly than that of any demons he had ever fought, more deadly than *25* demons combined." His mind went out to Timothy telling him of her danger. The mouse, hearing the thoughts of James, looked and saw 30 more demons pounding upon Esther. In a frantic fit, he disoriented all of them and dashed to her side, as she lay almost completely helpless and dying.

Demons were everywhere and upon every Angel and James, the brother of Mot as well. James was not subject to the Sacred Rules of Engagement and as he did battle, his sword and dagger swung true in great strides to within true warrior fashion. The Wolf proved himself in battle as well laying out at least 60 demons to unconsciousness. Daniel did the same as did the great cub as well protecting Daniel's back. As Timothy fought off all the demons from Esther, a demon rushed up from behind and stomped upon the mouse. The demons sword was swinging downward and less than a foot away from cutting Tim in half. Suddenly, a flash from above struck the demon with a force that hurled him to bouncing off trees. Tim felt something familiar and looking up, he thought, "No, no, could it be, no it just could not be." His eyes searched the sky and then, "Yes! Yes! It is! It is! The Eagle has not forgotten me!" It was the Eagle of who had watched his back and saved his Angel life. The Eagle was not to stop at saving his life for he was attacking the demons as if with the very Wrath of GOD.

As this battle had come under control in favor of the Angels, Brother noticed Mot's army on the march down the rocky mountainside. The first row of demons was almost to the canyon floor where the battle was taking place. His mind went out to all of his family and as they saw the army coming down the mountain, they all realized that they were doomed. 13 thousand demons were marching down the mountainside. They were all between the top of the steep, wide path and the very bottom of the canyon floor.

Suddenly, out of nowhere, the Eagle of who had been soaring high above the canyon wall, stopped in midflight. He hovered for just a brief moment. Then in a 200-mile an hour dive, straight downward, he slammed the very top of the very biggest and most unstable Boulder that he could see! The boulder began to roll and roll and roll, rolling as it struck several boulders in its path. The other boulders did the same. More boulders struck other boulders, in turn striking other boulders, and in turn, those boulders hitting other boulders, and yet still more boulders pounding upon other boulders. Before Mot's army could respond, there were a thousand boulders rolling down the mountain, crushing everything and everyone to within their deadly path! As the Eagle soared high above, you could hear his battle cry going out across the canyon for miles and miles. Mot screamed aloud "no, no, noooooooooooo, no nooooooooooooooooooOoooooo, no, no, nooooooooooooooooooo, nooooooooooooooooooooooooooooooooooooooooooooooooooo, noooooooooooono, noooooooooo no, no, no, nooooooooooooono, no, nooooooooooooooooooooooooooooooooo!

When the boulders finally stopped rolling and tumbling and the dust had all cleared, you could see that there was not even one demon left standing. The other demons, of who had been in battle with the Angels, fled in all different directions as the fear of GOD pierced through their very hearts and minds! The Eagle had saved the Angels and James Pruce, as well.

All were still standing at the ready, all but one. While the beautiful Lioness lay helpless, the whole family, her family, gathered all around her. Each and every one of them were weeping and touching her in love and sorrow. A most deep and empty sorrow for they could not heal her. The wounds she endured were just too great. Weak from her wounds, she looked all around at them and spoke in her own Mountain Lion language. Whispering, she began to speak, "Do not be sad for you have all changed my life. Because you speak to your GOD so often in prayer to give thanks for everything in your lives, thanking GOD for having me as your wife, thanking him for having me as your Mother, and yes even thanking GOD for having me as your trusted and loved friend, I have now found that your GOD was always My GOD. For now, I do remember because of all of you. I love you all well beyond my own understanding." The Lioness looked deeply to within each of their kind blue eyes, her large strong paw slowly raised to pad their beautiful white fur faces of the tears that flooded down and around her. As the strength of the mighty and majestic Mountain Lioness slowly drained from her body she lovingly whispered, "Know that I love you forever my Husband and know that I love you of who is part of me forever my Son." With each one of their heads on either side of her face, James and Mr. Gorbachev each bowed to touch their foreheads to her lips one last time in great Devotion of Truth,

Love, Hope, Faith, Trust, and Honor in of the Holy Spirit. Straining to look at all her family surrounding her with tears rolling down their faces, her last whispering words echoed forever to within all of their Hearts, minds, Souls and Spirits; **"ALL CREATIONS RESPOND TO OUR LIVING GOD, SPEAK OF HIM OFTEN THAT THEYYYYY MAY HEARRRR."**

Suddenly a huge cloud formed over them and GOD'S Hand of Beautiful Brilliant Life Giving Light reached out and caressed Esther and her whole family. As GOD slowly lifted HIS Hand, they could all see the beautiful, the ever so majestically beautiful Spirit of Esther in all of her Angel Glory kneeling to within HIS palm, with wings spread wide, and gently smiling at them. She ever so lovingly looked upon her family one last time. The Eagle flew in circles around Esther to within the LORD'S Palm and began crying out as if in battle. While the Hand of Forever Life Giving Light suddenly disappeared to within the cloud over their heads, The Voice of GOD rang out as music. The most Heartfelt of the very loudest of all roars was echoing and echoing and echoing throughout the entire canyon from Esther's final and truly loving goodbye to her whole family. Her last loving roar and GOD'S soft musical whisper became one with the Eagle's Battle Cry, the wind and all that is, was, or ever shall be;

"DO NOT WORRY OF HER....SHE IS NOW AN ANGEL OF LIGHT...A WARRIOR....OF WHOM SHALL WAIT HERE WITH ME AND OF WHOM SHALL SEE YOU ALL AGAIN FOR SHE HAS DONE WELL FOR ME UPON THE PLANET...EARTH."

...... Then there was............SILENCE.........

....

*****

In this, the Angels all rejoiced even to within their own loving tears. Daniel, thinking of the Lioness, his newfound family, Cyron and the people he loved when he had been Samson, began to sing in the Greek the Prayer of Cyron once again. Nothing but love lives to within the heart of Daniel.

**"THE LORD HOVERS TO WITHIN MY HEART
LIKE A GREAT BIRD OF PREY OVER THE FIELD
RELENTLESS IN PURSUIT FOR THE PRIZE AND
BEAUTIFUL TO WITHIN HIS FLIGHT
TO DO SO   AMEN"**

CHAPTER 17

THE SUPREME INVESTMENT

As the years went by, Laurie and Alden became the godmother and godfather, of Kathy and Juan Tyner. Virginia Tyner came from a very fine and wealthy family and was the mother of Juan and Kathy. She worked hard through the mid and latter part of her life as a broker of realty. She sold Laurie and Alden Blade a very beautiful piece of property of which they built their home and a pool. It was set on a mountainside to within the Hollywood Hills of California. Virginia's sister had been married to Ernest Newfangled, a famous American Novelist and Prize Winning Global reporter on wars throughout the entire world for an American Newspaper. Ernest and Alden had known each other since early childhood and were close friends. Alden's family would frequently travel to the United States on business ventures. Often they would alternate between families, living with each other between travels. Ernest would sometimes even travel to Europe with the Blade family while school was out for the summer.

The Police Action in Korea once again proved as evil and bloody as any other Global war or conflict that had ever been. It brutally reminded Laurie and Alden Blade of all the unspeakable foul deeds men would do to each other for Religion, money and power. The two had belonged to a secret society for many years, even long before; they had become married to one another. They secretly used supposedly non-lethal electronic-weapons and chemicals on people not in the society. This seemed to make the world a safer place to live in and somehow meshed into the society's overall train of thought. This would make a better world, a brave new world free of Jews and Christians! These two groups seemed to be at the very root of both modern and ancient wars all throughout the world's recorded history. They felt that any group or religion that could do these kinds of gross afflictions to one another should not exist! Electro-magnetic frequencies and chemicals seemed to be the most merciful way to accomplish the secret society's agenda. All the people in this society feel as though they are doing the right thing. These people do not feel as though they are really harming anyone. They are simply slowing the people down so they have no strength to cause war or disturbances with others.

Once again, Satan deceived all who received these weapons. Satan gave the beings of this planet simple but stupid ways that would easily justify the killing of others. It was indeed a perfect way to keep their underhanded, cowardly, secret mass murders all one big secret as well. Electronic weapons are virtually undetectable and have the ability to kill gradually. These weapons also possess the capability to kill all at once. Using this method, people would not realize that the pain they felt was coming from beings all around them! Instead, the people would think that the pain they felt was in fact from old age.

Of course, this is the exact same method used by the Robots of Cyron to enable the over-throw, take-over, and the secret killing of all the people and people's governments of that planet. However, that in itself is another completely separate but extremely paralleled exciting tale of unbounded greatness, fortitude and Glory to GOD. I can only hope to tell you this magnificent story at yet still another moment in time and surely to all of our own mutual choosing, my fellow Angels of Light. Well, anyway back to the story at hand eh!

The secret society Laurie and Alden were prominent members of, recruited billions of people from around the world! Inserting billions of Trojan Horses within! Their recruiting methods enabled people to feel and believe as though it was the right thing to do for world peace. Every one of them, in the secret society, had computer chips inserted in various parts of the body. This enabled them to project lasers, electrodes, electrons and or all different kinds of frequencies. In turn, these frequencies would produce various violent radio type waves of energy. This was, and is still, used to accomplish the most desired level of sickness or pain to within any victims of their own choosing. The waves of energy pass through anything to get to their intended victim, even through walls of homes. As the waves pass through the walls they take with them any power in the wiring whatsoever, and deliver it to the victim along with the original radio type wave. Over a gradual period, in most cases, the victims would think that their body was actually failing them and simply responding to old age or perhaps even genetics.

The use of these types of electronic-weapons has enabled the takeover of any company, any nation, or any group of people anywhere and everywhere. This also includes any religious groups of people throughout the entire world. As they control the people, they control the land that the people possess.

These billions of people that are doing this throughout the entire planet have totally justified what they do. Just as they have on other planets as well. Satan is responsible for all and any weapons that can, or do kill. He knows that human nature will justify anything or any action. The stronger the electronic power they possess the more they will kill and justify killing whom they think deserves killing.

Laurie and Alden simply did not think about the fact that they, and all the billions of others in the secret society, had all fallen into the hands of Satan. Satan had completely candy coated the acts of his secret society. This society had completely taken over the peoples' civil and government infrastructures of all nations throughout the world. This Evil had traveled to America, with these types of weapons, many years prior. Along with unsuspecting people like Laurie and Alden, they were unknowingly, systematically taking over all jobs and killing everyone not in their own secret society. Of course, it is killing the ones using the weapons as well, as it is the nature of the use of these weapons. Satan leaves no stone unturned! The use of these weapons eventually kills the perpetrator. Or can kill right away, if one is not very careful. They end up eating their own. And the web continues to be spun!

Laurie, Alden, and all others in the society contributed money to do these things in America. This was for doctors to insert computer chips into people and their children, and paid for training as well.

When Alden died in the 1960's, once again Laurie was broken hearted. She moved to the large house that Virginia owned, and lived with Virginia, Kathy, and Juan Tyner. When Virginia died in the 1970's she once again was broken hearted! Virginia was not part of the secret society! There remained a great amount of guilt to within her heart knowing that she had even a microscopic part of her death on her hands. She could not wash her hands of this guilt for she truly loved this woman of who had been a true friend since the 1920's.

Kathy Tyner had met a young man named Lee Earl Clemmer in 1970. She introduced him to her family of which Juan, Virginia and Laurie were a part. Lee was not a member, nor was Kathy or Juan, of the secret society. Lee was a Christian, but never talked about it, nor did he fully practice it either. He was by far not a perfect man but a good and decent man. However, he did not yet fully realize his calling for the LORD.

When Lee met Virginia she absolutely loved him, and they felt a bond between each other as Virginia knew that Kathy loved him very much. One evening at the dinner table, Virginia told him an amusing story about Ernest Newfangled and a little white lie. He had told the world about a war wound he had received, a head wound, and the story was simply not true. The unveiling of that story shall not happen here but it made Lee feel very special because he had read about that particular war wound in school. He now was one of the very few who knew the truth because Virginia had told him at the dinner table. Everyone laughed and laughed along with this beautiful woman, Virginia Tyner.

Virginia had died just a year later and it truly had a profound effect upon all four, Laurie, Kathy, Juan, and Lee. They all felt overwhelming love for Virginia and in their grief stricken minds; the other three somehow felt that Laurie had something to do with it. All poor Laurie could do was weep for her friend.

In 1974, Kathy became pregnant and had a daughter. At the hospital, Laurie took complete control! She would not allow Lee to observe his own daughter being born. Laurie demanded he wait in the hospital waiting room. He obeyed Laurie's commands for she was to be his daughters godmother that day. Although he had observed in a previous marriage when his son Richard Wayne Clemmer had been born in Fallbrook, California, he was a Christian and he would always obey and respect his elders.

Lee moved to Las Vegas, Nevada in the mid-1970s and his relationship with Kathy and Juan became strained as he began to womanize and do drugs to a certain degree. Kathy followed him to Vegas and began to drink more and more. Lee, realizing that his daughter, as a small child, was more important than the two of them, made it obvious to Kathy that he wanted Laurie to raise their child. She would give her all the best in life, an education, travel, and meeting with important people throughout the entire world. He of course did not realize at that moment in time that Laurie in fact belonged to the electronic secret society. To her, none of it was evil, it was necessary in society.

In the later part of the 1970's Laurie began and launched an organization called The Supreme Investment, of which was for the children of the world. This organization was and is for the nurturing of the "possible human," beginning before conception. However, children in the womb, after birth, and through puberty were and still are just as great of a concern as well. Karen, her goddaughter, was a major part of this program. Lee was 100% behind her plight to keep Karen at this point, as he realized the importance of an organization of this type. Lee had complete trust in Laurie to raise his daughter in an unbelievable, excellent environment since that "one day" in an Oak Grove with **Krishna Murti**.

Lee had been under the impression that his daughter, Karen Lee Tyner, would go to Catholic school and become a Christian. Karen did at first go to Catholic school but it was not for a very long period, of time. He did not realize this as he tried to stay out of Laurie's way, that she might have complete control of all problems with the discipline that raising a child would take. He did not want the child constantly questioning authority coming from Laurie. Then, as he constantly fought verbal battles with Kathy about Karen legally staying with Laurie, Kathy became very distant to Lee. This hurt him deeply as he knew the love that Kathy had for Karen and he still loved Kathy very, very, much. Kathy had always been there for Lee whenever he needed help or anything, she was always there. She was the kindest, most giving and loving human being that he had ever met in his entire life. When she died in the mid-1980's it broke his heart and he would never recover. She had not talked to him for over six months before her death. He knew without doubt that he would truly love her forever.

Juan died just a few years after Kathy. Laurie began to wonder if she had performed as noble of a deed as she had first thought when she finally became a member of the secret society of electronic warfare. Her guilt became overwhelming for she knew that once again, she had been a microscopic part of some one's death, and this time it was Kathy and Juan's deaths. She never guessed that people would die at such a young age from the use of these non-lethal weapons. She once again could not wash her hands clean of those two deaths. Two more people of who were close to her since their births. It was at this timeless moment she realized that Lucifer's plans she had overheard way back, in 1908 at the Vatican had in fact gone the exact way he proposed. She had fallen into his hands just as billions of others had. At this timeless moment, she knew these silent weapons were by, and of, Lucifer! She vowed, never again to use her weapon. She solemnly vowed not to pass the electronic pain on ever again. She made a vow from that moment on to always endure the pain intended for others. In addition, she would teach the children to do the same.

Lucifer had woven his web too well around this poor woman! She still thought of that day, especially now, in the Vatican when Tuxedo saved her life from the evil one. She now longed for Tuxedo to save her once again. Just One more, one more, Just one more time, again.

CHAPTER 18

THE LORD SPOKE

Lee had known of peoples hate and contempt for him for a long time. In his youth he observed people using their hands and clothing to spread chemicals, disorient, and cause pain. He observed in the opposite way the first time at 3 years of age when he could feel his stepfather's fingers tickling him from three feet away before he even touched him to make him laugh. He loved his stepfather very much. He observed it in school as well many, many times.

When he was not even 1 ½ years old the LORD spoke to him. The LORD was within his heart. The LORD told him that the love HE possessed for him was well beyond all comprehension and that he would live forever and ever and ever. All of his life he thought that this kind of thing happened to everyone, for he was only a baby in diapers less than a 1 ½ old. Because of his youth, when it happened he did not think to tell anyone about it. It was not until much later in his life that he realized that this did not happen to everyone. The LORD did not speak to everyone. He realized more so than ever before of who his evil enemies were. The LORD came to him many times all through his life, both in his dreams and while he was awake! By the latter part of 2005, he began to write more poetry and different writings of which he began to save, per instruction by our LORD! In the past, he had destroyed or lost all other writings, from the times of his birth through to 2005.

While watching TV one day in the beginning of 2007, Pastor Hagee on the TBN channel explained how the word computer came to the numbers, 666! The LORD spoke to Lee as he heard the Pastor say it! The LORD told him, "If the word computer comes to 666, your name comes to 777." Right away, he added up the numbers of his name. Ten times in a row, it always came to 762. That same night as the LORD talked to him in a dream, once again he was told that the numbers of his name were 777. He told the LORD that the number 6 would not equate into 777 in any way! Then that night in another dream, the LORD told him once again, that the numbers of his name came to 777. He added the numbers of his name repeatedly and refused to accept the truth for the numbers came to only 762. Over the next weeks, the LORD finally explained much more in yet other dreams and how it came to **777**.

Simply add the ***762 + 7 + 6 + 2,*** which **equals _777._** Then, in another dream, the LORD said to look at all the letters of his name to realize a special letter code:

Lee Earl Clemmer = eeL CEll r a memre - Both the numbers and the letters of his name are that of completion. GOD has chosen him. But then, just as Lee started to think that GOD was not going to come to him again, HE did come to him again, and while he was awake! The LORD flooded his mind with telling him to look up his complete name within the dictionary, so he did; the meanings are everything Satan hates.

Lee---- A masculine name

Lee---- Shelter, protection, a sheltered place, especially one on that side of anything away from the wind, ship, farthest from the side from which the wind blows, of or in the direction toward which the wind is blowing, opposed to weather. Levites- Charged with care of the tabernacle, temple

Earl---- Noblemen, count, renown warrior, brave man, leader, ruler, noble, great bird, eagle, royalty

Clem---- To die of hunger or to starve To cause to starve The LORD went into the wilderness of the world without food or water for 40 days and nights and yet did not perish

Mer----- pertaining to meridian or meridional, of are at noon or especially, of the position or power of the sun at noon, of or passing through the highest point in the daily course of any heavenly body, highest point of prosperity, splendor, power, etc. Rare, southern, highest point of health, zenith, apex, culmination, prime vigor, imaginary great circle of the celestial sphere passing through the poles of the Heavens in the zenith, cutting the equator at right angles. A place or situation with its own distinctive character inhabitant of the

south of Europe, especially France, north and south - in the direction of the poles of a magnet, etc. etc. There is a lot more that I did not write here.

The name represents the title and dignity of the LORD for all that a name implies of authority, character, rank, majesty, power, excellence, etc. Name of GOD expressing HIS attributes.

In the late 1990's Karen had a beautiful baby girl she named Kaya. Laurie was there for her just as she had been for Karen as by now The Supreme Investment was a large part of all of their lives. Karen, Kaya, and all the children of whom this organization could help, might show GOD how she truly had felt all of her life, and she thought, "Who knows, it might perhaps redeem the things in my life that have in whatever way, interfered with life."

Lee Earl Clemmer had grown to love Laurie as much as he had loved Kathy, Juan, his daughter, his grandchildren, his own son, or his own parents. He knew her heart even as she desperately tried to hide it from everyone, and especially from him, for a reason perhaps not known to him. He realized his love for her since that day in 1977 when Laurie had taken him to listen to **Krishna Murti**. He spoke in the oak groves of Ojai, California, at the Oak Grove School. Lee overwhelmingly felt the LORD'S presence in those groves that day and knew the reason; The LORD was in this man, Laurie, and himself as well! Lee knew from that moment on, and into eternity, he would love her with all of his heart. From that moment on, Lee would entrust his daughter's life with Laurie Blade. She was truly a Godly being with a loving Heart.

The love had continued to grow and grow even after he began to realize her being a part of the secret organization. He knew that Laurie had always been entirely for his people, his blood; therefore, she was his blood as well! He had thought and felt for a long time that someday Tuxedo would return and make her say the Words, "JESUS IS LORD." Little did he know that later on in life, it would be him, 3,000 miles away, and nine years after her death, in this dream with all of you, the Eagle, Mr. Gorbachev, Tuxedo, Brother Wolf Dog, all the other Animal Angels, Laurie and the LORD that would in fact jolt the memory of her long Angelic Life behind! He would be the one to make her say the Words, "JESUS IS LORD!" Before you leave this place this day you shall see that wondrous dream as it took place over an hour ago and then the part that is now ongoing and continuing. Moreover, your faith shall grow a never-ending strength, for Lee is home in his bed dreaming, almost 3,000 miles away, yet he is here. All of this and all of you here and now and all that has transpired and all that will transpire are all to within his dream and yours. For all of you here and all who appear to within this dream are dreaming the same dream as well. To help reinforce Lee's faith these kinds of dreams are what Brother, the Wolf, and Mr. Gorbachev had done for him, first one, and then the other, years later.

Laurie was not quite ready to within her life experience to say those Holy Words as of yet. The Great Cat had explained to Lee what exactly had taken place that day many years ago in the Vatican as his brother, Tuxedo, intervened on Laurie's behalf the encounter with Lucifer! He had also revealed to Lee the importance of Laurie. He told Lee who she really was in the loving Eyes of our Living GOD.

The Inspiring Mystical Spirit began to recite poetry by Lee and gave insight to the rest of the story he was conveying to all within this dream. This would also charter a better foundation as to the understanding of the heart to within the character of this Guardian. The poetry hints as to who he really is throughout the cosmos and to within this adventure, with our LORD. For this book and the poetry within it are of the Pen of truth with Blessings of our LORD spoken upon it. Moreover, there is only one man that may write with that Pen.

CHAPTER 19
POEMS BY LEE EARL CLEMMER

FORGIVENESS IS STRENGTH

FROM THE WAVE OF A FINGER
SET TO KILL YET STILL LINGER
AS IN THE CASE OF MODERN MAN
ELECTRODES IN HIS HANDS
IN THE HEAVENS AIR LAND AND SEA
HERE IS WHAT IS TO BE
STRIPING TEMPLES WHEREVER BARE
UNTIL NOTHING IS LEFT NOT EVEN HAIR
WHILE HOLY SPIRITS WATCH ON
WEAVING IN AND OUT MOVING AND MELTING
BRAIN BONE MUSCLE AND SKIN
NOT GIVING EVEN A SECOND OF THOUGHT TO
WHAT NATURALLY SHOULD LIVE WITHIN
GIVEN THIS POWER BY OTHER MEN TO DO WHAT
SEEMS TO BE MIRACULOUS DEEDS BUT INSTEAD
UNMERCIFULLY BEATING TEARING AND BURNING
TEMPLES DOWN UNTILL ALL THE TEMPLES ARE
DEAD
WHILE HOLY SPIRITS WATCH ON AND ON
REMEMBER THE TEMPLE OF THE SON OF MAN
OF WHOM CHRISTIANITY WAS TRULY SPORA
THE SAME BEFALLEN HIM ALL
WHILE HOLY SPIRITS WATCHED ON ON AND ON

AS HE FORGIVES IF FROM YOUR HEART IS ASKED
SURELY I TOO AS WE ALL MUST FORGIVE
FOR SOONER THAN YOU THINK
THIS WILL ALL BE IN THE PAST
BE STRONG...FORGIVE

LEE E. CLEMMER

GOD FAVORED MOM

OH MOM MY LOVELY MOM I STILL LOVE YOU MORE AND MORE WITH EACH AND EVERY PASSING DAY

WHEN I'M SAD NO MATTER WHAT I'M SIMPLY FORCED TO SMILE WHILE THINKING OF ALL YOUR QUIET PLEASANT AND SUBTLY GENTLE WAYS

I CAN STILL FEEL MY EYES LOVINGLY KISSED AS YOU WHISPER SOFTLY I LOVE YOU LEE

MOM OH MOM I DO REMEMBER I WOULD LAUGH AND I'D GIGGLE AND ALL WHILE YOU HELD ME OH EVER SO TENDERLY

YOU MY DEAREST MOTHER TAUGHT US HOW TO PRAY NOW I LAY ME DOWN TO SLEEP MY HEART TO HOLD MY SOUL TO KEEP AND TO GOD BLESS ALL SOULS ESPECIALLY DURING THE VERY BLACKEST OF ANY DARK AND LONELY NIGHT

AND WHEN I WAS FRIGHTENED AS ALL THE LIGHTS WENT OUT...YOU MY GOD FAVORED MOTHER WOULD JAR THE DOOR SLIGHTLY OPEN YOU'D STAY TILL MORNING AND ALL WELL WITHIN MY SIGHT

YOU HAVE STRUGGLED ALL THRU YOUR GRACIOUS LIFE ALL FOR US YOU WORKED DEGRADING JOBS COOKED BREAKFAST FIXED LUNCHES AND ALL OF OUR DINNERS AND THIS I DO TELL

IN 1957 YOU EVEN BOUGHT FOR US OUR LORD'S SACRED BIBLE STORIES...CHILDREN'S BOOKS AND FOR OUR HIGHER LEARNING A COMPLETE SET OF THE ENCYCLOPAEDIA BRITANNICA AS WELL

YOU TOOK US TO CHURCH....AND ON ONE SUNDAY
JANUARY 13, 1963
YOU HAD THE PASTOR WILLARD W. BARTLETT
BAPTIZE US ONE AND ALL

THIS MY THOUGHTFUL MOM YOU DID FOR THE CHILDREN YOU SO LOVED TO BE BORN AGAIN AND

*IN THE EYES OF OUR LORD THY GOD WE WOULD
STAND UPRIGHT AND WE WOULD STAND TALL*

*WHEN ABSOLUTELY NOTHING GOES RIGHT
EVERYTHING WRONG SO WRONG THAT MOST
MIGHT JUST SIMPLY PULL OUT THEIR HAIR*

*MY MOM NEVER ANGRY KEEPS HER KOOL
GRACE AND PERFECT GOODNESS ALL IN THE
EYES OF OUR LORD THY GOD IS HOW MY MOM
HAS AND WILL ALWAYS FARE*

*FOR ALL WHO HEAR I TELL YOU NOW...THERE IS
NO MAN WOMAN OR ANY BEING CAN DARE TO SAY
CLAIM FOUL OR UPON DO TROD*

*AS MY MOM FOR ALL HER UNSELFISH LIFELONG
DEEDS IS AND FOREVER WILL BE FAVORED ALL
FROM WITHIN THE EYES OF OUR LORD
          THE LIVING GOD*

LEE EARL CLEMMER

PREAMBLE TO: SWORD FOR THE LORD
FREEDOM OF CHOICE (FREE WILL)

MY FREEDOM OF CHOICE ONLY EXISTS TO WITHIN A VERY ABSTRACT DISTORTED AND PERVERTED DELUSIONAL MANNER WHERE AS IT HAS BEEN BY MEANS OF SECRET COVERT ACTIONS, MAROONED TO A SOMEWHAT DELUSIONAL DIMENSION THAT SEEMS TO HAVE TRAPPED ME TO WITHIN UNHOLY PERIMETERS THAT OF WHICH HAS BEEN VERY CAREFULLY, METHODICALLY AND SO VERY, VERY UNMERCIFULLY BATTERED, RIPPED, TORN, PRIED, AND THUS FORCED TO IMPLODE TO WITHIN ITS SICKLY WEARY SORRY, PITIFUL, STIFLING STATE OF EXISTENCE. PERHAPS A MORE ACCURATE DESCRIPTION MIGHT BE A STATE OF EXISTENCE CONCEIVED AND BORN OF, THROUGH, AND BY WAY OF UNRELENTING TORTURE, PERVERTED DEADLY HUMOR, VAST ELECTRO-MAGNETIC WEAPONS TECHNOLOGIES AS WELL AS OTHER EVEN MORE DEVASTATING TECHNOLOGIES AND THE MOST EXTREMELY DARK AND EVIL, COVERT SECRECY KEPT BY GOVERNMENTS AND PEOPLE THROUGHOUT THE WORLD. THESE WEAPONS TECHNOLOGIES HAVE GIVEN WAY TO TERRIBLE PREDATORS. THEY INVADE, PARALYZE, AND NEUTRALIZE ALL BEINGS THROUGHOUT THE HEAVENS, AIR, LAND, AND SEA. *THESE PREDATORS ARE OF ABSOLUTE UNRELENTING INTENT AND URGENCY TO INFLICT UPON ALL VICTIMS, SLOW PAINFUL DEATHS OF LIVES MINDS AND SOULS AND SPIRITS.*

SO GUARD I WILL MY FREEDOM OF CHOICE BUT NOT WITH LIFE'S BLOOD OR LIMB. BUT WITH THE HOLY GHOST OF WHO LIVES FOREVER WITHIN MY HEART AND THRIVES INTIMATELY MERGED DEEP WITHIN MY LIFE'S BLOOD AND MY VERY LIFE'S BODY SOUL AND SPIRIT. THEREFORE IT WILL COME TO PASS MY SOUL AND MY LOVED ONES SOULS WILL ENDURE TO FEAR NO EVIL

WHEREBY BE SAVED FROM ALL EVIL. ALL OF WHICH LIVES, LURKS, AND WAITS IN AND ABOUT ALL NARROW AND OR WIDENED, DARK AND LONELY ROADS AND PATHS INTERWEAVING, AND INERADICABLE, ALL OF WHICH DESCEND ON DOWN DEEP TO WITHIN *THE VERY HEART OF THE VALLEY OF THE SHADOW OF DEATH*

LEE EARL CLEMMER

SWORD FOR THE LORD

BROUGHT UP TO TRUST AND NEVER TO POINT
THAT WOULD BE QUITE RUDE AND WAY OUT OF JOINT

STARVING FOR LOVE AS EVERY YOUNG CHILD WILL
LOVING LAUGHING CRYING AND PLAYING FOREVER
LEARNING NEVER STILL

ALL HAVE AS THEY FOREVER WILL STAY AT THE VERY
LEAST AT ARMS LENGTH
A TARGET SINCE BIRTH FOR BEINGS OF THE BEAST
JUST TRYING TO KEEP UP MY STRENGTH

WOUNDED FEELING YOUR PROJECTILES ALL CHARGED
AND TRAVELING AT SPEEDS OF SOUND AND THAT OF
LIGHT

COVERT SECRET DENYING ELECTRO-MAGNETIC
FINGERS IN PLENTY FOREVER TWITCHING FOREVER
POINTING TO SEND SURGING BURNING ELECTRONIC
FURY ALL AS ONE WITH ALL OF THEIR MIGHT

OH LORD OH LORD...AT EVERY POINT ON THE COMPASS
AS I TURN I FEEL PAIN THEN I ALWAYS SEE
COVERT SECRET BEINGS STALKING AND POINTING AND
ALWAYS WHILE CIRCLING ME

LIKE THE WALLS OF JERICHO TRIUMPHED BY GODS
PEOPLE THE JEWS
AS THE BEAST CARES NOT TO PURSUE WALLS
FOR IT IS ALL MANNERS OF BEINGS AND PEOPLE TOO
THEY DO SLEW

STEADFAST POSITIVE AND FULL OF LOVE EVEN
WHILE ENDURING GOOD OLD FASHIONED MID-EVIL
GRUESOME FORCE

AS EYES OF THE BEAST WILL BURN IF THEY SEE
THE HOLY GHOST LIVING THRIVING AND GENTLY
SPEAKING THRU ME
ALWAYS VICTORIOUS WHILE NEVER OFF COURSE

AS THE BEAST OBSERVES A SMILE FADING ON MY FACE
ALL WHILE MAGNETIC SPEARS PIERCE MY BODY IN AND
ALL AROUND

THEY DO SHUDDER AND THEY DO TREMBLE AND ALL
AS THEY DO WONDER HOW I STILL LIVE OR CONTINUE

TO STAND SOUND OR MY GROUND

ALTHOUGH I FORGIVE ALL THOSE WHO STRIVED TO CRUSH MY SPIRIT BODY AND MY SOUL
THERE WILL COME THE TIMES IN OF WHICH YOU'LL HAVE ABSOLUTELY NO CONTROL

SO IT SHALL BE ON THAT PURIFIED DAY GOD HAS ASKED ME TO STAND BY HIS SIDE AS WELL AS TO LEAD THE WAY

FOR I HAVE FORGIVEN IN TURN I'VE BEEN FORGIVED
AS IT IS IN THE HEART OF OUR LIVING GOD I DO
AND HAVE FOREVER LIVED

YOUR MARKS ARE NOW REVEALED YOU TERRIBLE TERRIBLE BEAST...I TELL YOU NOW IN TRUTH AND IN LOVE...TURN ABOUT FOR IT WOULD BE WELL AND WISE FOR YOU TO BE FOUND BY OUR LIVING GOD

FOR IF YOU SADLY DECIDE NOT TO TURN
YOUR THOUGHTS MUST BE OF INVINCIBILITY AS YOU SIMPLY JUST CANNOT BURN

OR PERHAPS YOUR THOUGHTS AND DREAMS OF WHEN YOU DIE
HEAVEN BOUND YOUR SPIRITS AND SOULS WILL SOAR AND FLY
THUS SO VERY QUICKLY GO GO AND GO

ALL DREAMS FOR WHOM YOUR SPIRITS AND SOULS SHALL SEE BY MY GODS SIDE SACRED SWORD OF JUSTICE UNSHEATHED AND IN THE HAND OF ME
TO WAIT HIS HOLY COMMAND TO SOW SOW AND SOW

I'LL HAVE WINGS STRONG OF PURE AS SNOW
AND I'LL BE YOUNG AND BEAUTIFUL FOREVER ALL OF THIS AND MUCH MUCH MORE
MY GOD HAS MADE ME TO KNOW

FOR I HAVE CARRIED AND REELED THIS MAGNIFICENT HOLY SWORD THROUGH COUNTLESS SACRED LIVES BEHIND
AS MY GOD DID THIS FOR ME THAT I MAY TRUTHFULLY SEEK AND VERY HOPEFULLY FIND

THAT THERE REALLY ARE ONCE ETERNAL SOULS SO VERY TRULY EVIL THAT THERE IS NO HOPE AND MUST

JUST SIMPLY BE THROWN IN HELL TO BURN
FOR MY GOD HAS SEEN MY TEARS AS I'VE REELED MY
TRUTHFUL SWORD ON ALL WHOM SADLY REFUSE TO
TURN

AS THE END COMES NEAR I FEEL YET ANOTHER
LIFE WELL IN BEING IS CONSTANT AND ALMOST
ALREADY HERE
AND ALTHOUGH I'LL STILL BE SAD AND WILL SHED IN
PLENTY MANY A TEAR

MY SWORD SHALL STILL REAP ALL EVIL SOULS AND
THUS HAPPEN ALL OVER AND ONCE MORE AGAIN
THIS HOLY SWORD OF JUSTICE SHALL ALWAYS REEL
UPON ALL UNFORGIVING AND VENGEFUL HEARTS
DRENCHED OF UNRELENTING AND UGLY SIN

FOR I NEVER ASKED FOR THE DOUBLE EDGED HOLY
SACRED SWORD OF JUSTICE OR FOR MAGNIFICENT
WINGS OF STRENGTH OF PURE AS SNOW
WITH GOD ONE HAS NOT TO ASK FOR WHAT IS ALREADY
EARNED PROVEN WORTHY AND THIS WOULD BE WELL
FOR YOU TO KNOW

IT IS FOREVER MY HOLY AND SACRED RIGHT
TO BE AT MY GODS SIDE SWORD UNSHEATHED IN MY
HAND WHILE WALKING RUNNING OR FLYING ALL FROM
WITHIN HIS NEVERENDING GLORIOUS RADIANT
AND LIVING LIGHT

FOR I HAVE SUFFERED LIVED AND DIED
PERISHED COUNTLESS TIMES ON COUNTLESS WORLDS
AND ALL FOR HIS NAMES SAKE TO STAY
AND AS MY HEART IS PURE ALL TRUE ONLY LOVE CAN
LIVE WITHIN I FEEL NOW I SHOULD DECLARE AND
VERY SINCERELY SAY

THIS DOUBLE EDGED HOLY SACRED SWORD OF
JUSTICE I SHALL NEVER UNSHEATHE DRAW RAISE OR
REEL FOR ME OR FOR ANY HATEFUL VENGEFUL WAY
IT HAS BEEN SAID THE LORD WORKS IN MYSTERIOUS
WAYS

THE VERY SAME POWER GIVEN YOU OVER LIFE IF YOU
 CHOOSE AS TO HARM ANYONE OR THE LIKES OF ME
TO SEND LIFE-ENDING ELECTRO-MAGNETIC SPEARS
HURDLING STRAIGHT IN AND ALL THROUGH

OH DO YOU NOT SEE

HAS AND FOREVER WILL GIVE BIRTH TO ANGELS
WHOSE SWORDS MUST SURELY REEL ALL UPON THEE

TURN ABOUT OR MY TEARS WILL BE FOR YOU
WITH EYES BUT CANNOT SEE FREE OF DARKNESS OR
EVEN PAST THE BLUE

LEE E. CLEMMER

JOSHUA

I come to this world to send a message of love and of hope to
All human spirits and to all spirits of all the types of all the
Species of all the life in and upon the World
for he is returning soon!!!

LEE E. CLEMMER

A MAN CALLED JACK DUIT

*A MAN CALLED JACK DUIT WAS MY STEP FATHER
AND I LOVED HIM SO VERY MUCH*

*HE WOULD TELL ME NEVER TO QUESTION ...TO
ALWAYS AND FOREVER SIDE WITH MY MOTHER
IN TIMES OF WAR OR PEACE GOOD BAD TOIL AND
OR PROBLEMS WITH EITHER HIM OR ANY OTHER*

*THIS IS SO VERY TRULY HOLY AND SACRED AND
IS MOST SURELY THE ONLY POSIBLE WAY*

*TO ALWAYS PROTECT YOUR MOTHER NO MATTER
WHAT LEE...WITH LOVE TEARED EYES HE SPOKE
IN SERIOUS TONES AS FIGHTING FLOWING DOMES
IS WHAT MY DAD WOULD ALWAYS GENTLY SAY*

*AND THEN HE WOULD EXPLAIN AND VERY
SINCERELY ADD
ALTHOUGH HE MAY HAVE REALLY SEEMED TO BE
HE COULDN'T EVER BE UPSET OR ESPECIALLY MAD*

*ABOUT WHENEVER IT CAME THAT I'D STEP UP TO
STOP ALL THE FUSS AND ALL THE FIGHT*

*HE ALWAYS HAD A DEEP RESPECT FOR ME FOR
MANY UNTOLD REASONS BUT THE LOVE FOR MY
MOTHER NO MATTER WHAT WAS ALWAYS FIRST
AND WOULD ALWAYS BRING OUR GOD'S ETERNAL
LIFE GIVING LIGHT*

*YES I LOVE MY STEP FATHER JACK DUIT WHOM AT
TIMES SEEMED SO SAD AND VERY WEARY AS IF
PERHAPS LONGING FOR SOMETHING EVEN MORE
THAN IS ALREADY TRUE*

*REMEMBERING CHILDHOOD ALL THAT WAS SAID
AND ALL THAT WAS DONE I COME TO SUDDENLY
REALIZE THAT THIS MAN CALLED JACK DUIT
MY FATHER HAD ALWAYS PROFOUNDLY HUMBLY
AND TRULY LOVED ME TOO*

O2/08/06 LEE E. CLEMMER

FOR THE GLORY OF GOD
LAKE OF FIRE

STONES AND TATTOOS ALL SIZES WHILE ALL SHAPES
PASSING MILES TO RIGHT ANGLES FLASHING THROUGH
THESE DEADLY GATES

COVERING ANGELS OF DARKNESS ALL UP AND ALL
DOWN
TO BOLT TO STRIKE OUT UPON ANGELS OF LIGHT ALL
FOR LIFE ENDING GROUND

STONES PIERCING TATTOOS THAT OF UNHOLY
LINGERS
FROM BEASTS ACTING ALL AS ONE SENDING
ELECTRONIC FURY STORED IN HEADS ARMS HANDS
EARS AND HAIR THROUGH ELECTRO-MAGNETIC
FINGERS

PIERCED ALL THROUGH DEVILED BEASTS EARS
SENDING PAINS OF DEATH TO ANGELS OF LIGHT
WITNESSES OF LATER DAYS WHOM HAVE NO FEARS
WHOM NEVER HATE NOR GIVE IN TO FIGHT

TATTOOS OF FIBER-OPTIC INK THAT TAINTS AS IT
TRULY SCARS THE TEMPLES BODY
TO ENDORSE THIS PLIGHT THIS UNHOLY HOBBY

AS THESE THE BEASTS SENDING PAINS OF TORTURE
THAT OF DEATH THROUGH ALL ACTING ALL AS ONE
SO SHALL THEY BE MELTED PULP ALL INTO ONE
TO FEEL INFINITE SEARING PAIN FOREVER AS CAST
AND THROWN DEEP TO WITHIN THE LIFE GIVING SUN

FORCED FACE DOWN CONSTANTLY HAVING TO SAY AS
WELL AS TO SEE..........JESUS IS LORD
TO KNOW HOW THEY SERVE GOD NOW GIVING LIFE TO
ALL OF WHICH WILL ALWAYS BE

THE DRAGON GIVES THE BEAST ITS GREAT AUTHORITY
OH BUT EVIL ONE YOU HAVE NO PLACE WITH ME
FOR NOW I AM TO BE RIGHTEOUS THAT OF WHICH
THE LORD CAN TRULY SEE
THE HOLY SPIRIT FREELY SPEAKING THROUGH ME

LEE EARL CLEMMER

CHAPTER 20

THE DEPARTURE

Esther's family endured crushing weights of sadness as she lay mortally wounded, helpless, and dying. Within the twinkling of an eye after her death, they witnessed our LORD holding their Lioness in the Palm of HIS Hand of the Forever Life Giving Light! HIS musical whisper explained that someday soon they would all be together once again. Suddenly, the crushing weights of sadness disappeared and happiness filled its place to within every one of their hearts. They now came to realize that Esther was in fact just like them. She is a Warrior of whom they would see once again through the Grace, Love, and Glory of GOD!

The Angels had now finally completed all the preparations they needed before beginning their long journeys to a fresh new life in Europe. It would be another two days before leaving as to give love and respect to Esther in prayer and burial of her flesh. Once the journey started, they would travel together 200 miles before splitting up into two separate teams. In this way, it would be much more difficult for Mot to realize where they were going. He would be looking for six beings. Two humans, 1 cat, 1 mountain lion cub-cat mix, 1 wolf and 1 mouse.

The family had decided that one team would take a western trek through Russia, then down through the Ukraine into Hungary, then through Austria, and finally into Italy. The other team would travel north to the coast of Russia. Then travel by way of the Arctic Ocean into the Greenland Sea then down through the Norwegian Sea around Norway then farther down into the Atlantic Ocean past Ireland, England, France, and Spain. They would then round the coast of Spain, passing through The Straits of Gibraltar and into the Mediterranean Sea, and finally to the coast of Italy. Their final destination would be the Vatican whereas both teams would thus meet and begin fulfilling their duties to GOD. One team would consist of James, the Angel Warrior, Timothy, the Angel Warrior, and James, brother of Mot. The other team would be three Angel Warriors, Daniel, Mr. Gorbachev, and Brother the Wolf. Although the LORD had explained to James Pruce that he would live in and around the Vatican with James the cat and Timothy the mouse, HE did not tell Daniel where he would finally end up living and serving HIM, THAT AM.

James, the brother of Mot, and the Angels were leaving to begin their long journeys to Italy as they painfully heard the terrible screaming battle cry of the Eagle. Suddenly, he soared down to land majestically near them on a fallen tree. He gazed upon the Angels with his head cocked sideways, wings spread, his beak wide open, his tongue wildly, viciously vibrating at the air. His ear piercing battle cry streamed through their bodies and then echoed out across the woods. Then he stood tall and erect, head held high, and two huge jagged scars parading all across his chest came into clear view.

It was at this timeless moment that Daniel remembered those same two scars on the Legendary Great Sacred Bird of Cyron! He was the very same Eagle Daniel had known over 28 thousand years past on the planet Cyron, and billions of light years away from Earth. He was Samson the Robot then! This Eagle Angel protected the High Priest and High Priestess of Cyron, Daniel Bajcab Curpe and Laura Ja Curpe. Laura Prophesied many things to him, as Samson, over 28,000 years ago. She Prophesied the robot's euphoric blood replenishments and the LORD Baptizing him, changing him into a human. She also Prophesied many things concerning the seven innocent children. She Prophesied that he, Samson, would serve GOD in another world, and through the help of an Angel, would find out many things using a Code derived from the Bible later known as The Bible Code.

Both Daniel Curpe and Laura Curpe were the Greatest Scientists and The Greatest Prophets of Cyron as well. Daniel Bajcab Curpe was his maker as Samson, and along with Laura, they were his teachers for hundreds of years, until their deaths 27,000 years ago and billions of light years away. This man wrote The Prayer of Cyron! This man made sure that he had an Angel spirit to within, as Samson, the Robot. This man made the Pen of One and of Truth from the planet Cyron with a Blessing from GOD Spoken upon It. The Holy Bird of prey protected him and his wife on Cyron and saved all the family here and now on this planet. Yes, and it was the same Great Holy Bird who is here on this planet now just as he is here now.

Suddenly the Great Holy Sacred Winged Bird's head turned and he peered directly into the eyes of Daniel for a very long time. As they recognized one another, a Devotion of Truth, Love, Hope, Faith, Honor and Trust of the Holy Spirit lived to within both of their eyes and to within both of their hearts. The two had felt each other's thoughts, and their thoughts were full of Devotion, Truth, Love, Hope, Faith, Honor, and Trust of the Holy Spirit. Still staring to within the eyes of Daniel, he shut and then opened his eyes very slowly simultaneously with an even slower nod of his head, yes, 3 times!

Then the Holy Birds' eyes moved downward glaring deeply into the eyes of Timothy as he gently floated down to the ground next to him. Tears filled both of their eyes as the Great Bird of Prey ever so lovingly picked the tiny mouse up. The Mighty Bird gently embraced the bewildered Timothy to within his powerful and deadly claws. He boldly gave to his GODLY little warrior friend one last flight, soaring through the air, high above the planet earth, and even higher to above the clouds. As he began effortlessly gliding into the Heavens, you could hear his loud piercing battle cries for miles and miles. If you watched carefully as he majestically soared, easily slicing through the cold crisp Russian wind, you might catch a sudden silent view of him using it advantageously. He would use the winds to quickly turn, or savagely dive downward or simply to change directions! Timothy screamed aloud harmoniously with the battle cries of his faithful friend, the Great Bird of Prey. Down below, all watched and listened intensely. They lovingly smiled in amazement of the unrelenting beautiful grace to which the giant and courageous winged creature of GOD made to within his every move.

After a very long while, The Great Bird returned Timothy to his family. He gently set the Mighty Little Warrior back to the exact same place on the ground where he had first gently picked him up. The Eagle promptly turned and jumped back up onto the fallen tree and stood majestically as he looked upon all of them. The whole family walked up to the Great Bird of Prey and he allowed each and every one of them to touch him. He began to move his head, up and down, then back and forth pressing up against their hands and paws.

Suddenly, the Great Eagle stepped backwards, spread his wings out wide, and stared deeply into each of their eyes with his head once again cocked to one side. Then, in an extremely slow and meaningful loving nod of his head, he ever so gracefully floated up into the air and flew out ahead of them into the very same direction of their travels. As the beautiful Warrior flew away, he blurted out yet another battle cry echoing out for miles and miles and miles.

Down below, all were humbly grateful to this Great Bird of who loved Timothy and had saved each, and every one of their lives through the grace of GOD.

THE GREAT BIRD OF PREY ON THE HIGHEST TOP SECRET MISSION FOR OUR LORD

Illustration by Karen Lee Pfeiffer (1974-Present)

CHAPTER 21

ANGEL WARRIOR REALIZED

The Eagle flew and followed their trek for the whole 200 miles before they split up into two separate groups to help insure their safety from Mot. As he finally turned and soared high above the Earth towards home, his scream pierced through the cold crisp Russian wind yet one last time. This last cry boldly echoed out into every direction, as love and good wishes to Timothy and his newfound family. As he flew in the direction of home, Timothy's eyes stayed upon him until the Great Bird disappeared into the horizon.

Tim told his Animal Angel family that he would miss the Eagle very much for they had been friends for over 200 years. The Animal Angels looked at one another and began to laugh as they explained to Tim that Eagles do not live to reach anywhere near 200 years. Tim replied, "You mean," James interrupted and said, "Yes, I mean he is like us! He is an Angel Warrior for our GOD!" Then Tim asked in bewilderment, "Why did he not come to within our thoughts?" James slowly replied, "Our LORD does things in ways that are mostly a mystery to us as to why or how. Just know that it is always for a very wonderful and glorifying reason." The Angels replied all at once, "Amen." Mr. Gorbachev looked intensely at Timothy and then deeply into the sky. He thought, "I have a funny feeling that someday, somewhere, we will have the pleasure of being in the company of that Great, Brave and Majestic Bird of Prey yet still another moment in time. Perhaps hundreds or even thousands of years from now, he may just save us yet one more time." As he stood there feeling these thoughts he smiled when he heard Tim say, "I hope with all my heart I see him again."

You see, there were actually two Seventh Warriors in this story, with Esther being one and entering into Heaven with our LORD after the epic battle. The Eagle is the other Seventh Warrior of who remains in the flesh and has given an oath of silence to GOD. His top-secret mission is to watch and listen for Lucifer as he talks to Mot and the other demons, then report his findings to GOD. He was simply not in a position to enable the other Angel Warriors to realize of who he really is. He truly loves his GOD, and his Angel Warrior brothers and sisters as well.

James Adja Pruce and the Angels split up into two separate teams. Both teams assured each other that they would all meet safely, in Italy at the Vatican! Upon departing, Daniel Adjac Pruce silently sang The Prayer of Cyron in Hebrew once again. This was in honor to GOD, to their friend the Eagle, to his newfound family, to the People and to a man, his maker on Cyron as Samson the robot. He repeated the prayer once again in the Greek, singing aloud for the family to pray as well for he never spoke Hebrew aloud. This keeps Hebrew Scripture Holy, Sacred, and the Words of the Ancient Language pure in Spirit, Truth, Love, Hope, Faith, Goodness, Grace and Glory to GOD.

**"THE LORD HOVERS TO WITHIN MY HEART
LIKE A GREAT BIRD OF PREY OVER THE FIELD
RELENTLESS IN PURSUIT FOR THE PRIZE AND
BEAUTIFUL TO WITHIN HIS FLIGHT
TO DO SO   AMEN"**

The Angels departed, following their two separate paths to Italy!

Just speak the Words

Go To http://www.angelrevery.com

KEEP TURNING THE PAGES TO:

ANGEL REVERY
PART 2

DREAMS
IN
THE ONE

Just speak the Words if you dare
"JESUS IS LORD"

RALEEL MERCELEM

KEEP READING ANGEL REVERY FROM COVER TO COVER TO ENABLE ANSWERING THE 7 CODE QUESTIONS IN THE APPENDIX

(PAGE 233-236)
READ THE BOOK FROM COVER TO COVER
THEN ANSWER THE 7 QUESTIONS.
DIG DEEP AND FIND YOUR PORTIONS OF THE
TREASURES OF THE FAMILIES HEART!
Go to http://www.angelrevery.com

ANGEL REVERY

PART 2

DREAMS IN THE ONE

RALEEL MERCELEM

FOR NOW WE ARE TO REMAIN THE PREY OF ALL WHOM ACT AGAINST US OH BEAST

BUT BEHOLD WE SHALL BE THE TEETH OF THE LION HIM OF WHICH WAS ONCE THE LAMB

AND OF WHO SHALL RETURN SOON VERY SOON   AMEN

THE LORD HOVERS TO WITHIN MY HEART LIKE A GREAT BIRD OF PREY OVER THE FIELD

RELENTLESS IN PURSUIT FOR THE PRIZE AND BEAUTIFUL TO WITHIN HIS FLIGHT TO DO SO   AMEN

DANIEL BAJCAB CURPE

LECRM

AUTHOR'S NOTES TO READERS OF
ANGEL REVERY DREAMS IN THE ONE

*Well once again, I have to say since being diagnosed schizophrenic paranoid with delusional tendencies I am still writing a story that lives to within the heart. Remember, what the mind may sometimes forget, the heart cannot! What lives to within the heart will make one to be either completely sane or mentally ill. Well anyway this is a second part of the story in of the series **ANGEL REVERY** and I sincerely hope you have enjoyed what you participated to read so far.*

Do you do as I do when you meet someone? You know, thinking that you might see through them just as they might see through you and know your love, goodness, and the wellness in of which you wish everyone. For example speaking down to someone is simply not in me to do. Thinking in those terms is not possible for me as I have a very deep sense of love and respect for all life. For this is what truly lives to within my heart. Evil would say and think contrary to that however, it is absolutely true when it comes to all my thoughts and feelings in life towards all life. It has always been that way for me. And I believe that as others begin to know and understand me they see these as obvious traits living to within my heart as well. So naturally, when it comes to others in of which I meet to within this so very short breath of life I like to think they are the same way. I guess that is what this story of people, robots, demons, animals, angels, and guardians is really about. Perhaps it is about what I, as a man need to imagine and believe of people and what life's situations, should really come to be. Don't misunderstand there still walks but a few people in life that through divine intervention are allowed to live either super long lives or many lives or in some cases both. Of course in my way of thinking it would all depend on what the LORD needs to accomplish to within their spirits concerning all things in of which HE has created. I truly live in the CHRIST the LORD JESUS who lived, died, and resurrected all for my sins and yours and in some cases for the sins of the dammed in hell itself. I hope that no man comes to perish by way of hell but that he rebels and does not do the evil ones bidding. And with a pure heart, leads others in hell to do the same for GOD. Repent For Salvation. I sincerely hope that in doing this the individual or individuals will succeed in overcoming death by grace of our LORD JESUS in of HIS loving kindness and mercy. For in rebelling against the evil one, while in hell, the infliction of pain and suffering that one would endure is unbearable! And the LORD would surely notice what transpired for HIM that AM. I hope all Races, Creeds, and religions love this story! Please, won't you come and move just a little bit closer to the

LAMB OF GOD AND LION OF JUDAH?

"JESUS IS LORD"

Enjoy and blessed be. Thank you.

Love,

Raleel Mercelem

LECRM

TABLE OF CONTENTS

PART 2

ANGEL REVERY
DREAMS IN THE ONE

BE ON THE WATCH FOR
FUTURE EDITIONS OF ADVENTURES
BY LEE EARL CLEMMER RALEEL MERCELEM

CHAPTER 22

THE PEN LINEAGE BOOK AND COMPASS-VISIONS CONTINUING

The guilt James felt in his soul simply would not allow him to stand it any longer and he turned to yell out to his brother, "Daniel!" He was over a hundred yards away as they had already split up into 2 teams and it took 3 strong yells before Daniel turned and saw James running towards him. Daniel, thinking that something terrible had happened, began running towards his brother and they met half way. Breathing heavily and looking deep to within his brother's eyes, James began to speak slowly. As he spoke, he held out a beautiful gold and sterling Lineage Book with angels carved into the cover and tiny precious stones inserted for eyes as well. It also had hallmarks from another World on the cover. And the beautiful Book housed golden pages along with a gold and sterling Compass and a gold, mother of pearl, basalt and glass fountain Pen, both attached, fitting perfectly to within as well. Although they are three completely different Ancient Artifacts, they are all as one within the beautiful Lineage Book.

James Pruce began, "Daniel, please say nothing and just listen my brother. My father found these beautiful Artifacts of GOD clutched to within your father's hand and in his other hand, you lay calmly kissing it. And he extended his arms outward to my father handing your life's blood to him. My father told me, it was as if you knew what was actually happening all around you, yet you were as calm as a true Angelic Warrior. This was all in the battle that was just in the process of taking your father's life and sparing yours. With your father's last dying breath, he told my father, "Take my son for he is as you and your son are, chosen! Do not be hard on yourself. For these things must come to pass." And my father saw the LORD'S Hand of Light and of Life reach out from within a cloud to receive his spirit!

Your father knew what was in the Lineage Book long before my father had slain him. He died for his GOD and his faith gave great life to my father from that moment on. My father realized your bravery and the love that lived to within your heart even as a newborn babe! And he, a Muslim, knew from that moment on he would love you, a Hebrew, forever. He would take you in as his own loving son. As his own life's blood! Forgive me my brother; I had forgotten these things for a while, I was very young when they came about. I just simply did not understand. Now I remember and I am understanding more and more. All Glory be to our LORD!

Let me tell you, my father's name, my name, and yours are to within the Lineage Book. Mine for the Compass, my father's name for the Pen and Lineage Book, and your name was right beside mine for the Pen and Lineage Book. Then your name burns upon the page again to add the Compass. When my father saw this and the explanation that the three articles had a Blessing from GOD Spoken upon them, he knew he had killed a Holy Man and his entire family. He would never forgive himself. He became devastated as he realized these Ancient Articles and the Family that had been laid to waste were all of GOD and for GOD. For the Heavenly Book is very explicit and documents, all in Hebrew scripture, many different things over a period of 28,000 years. Beginning from upon a planet called Cyron and ending here upon this planet, billions of light years away, according to this mysterious book. It is many books in one. It explains a code that is to within the Bible and documents the lineage of all the successors in the protection of these Ancient Holy Artifacts since well before and well after the very first moment of their conception. It is simply unbelievable unless you see it with your own eyes. My father's name, my name, and your name burned to within the page as our father opened the book to what he thought was the only golden page. But then, at that same moment, another golden page appeared and was blank. Then writing in script appeared as it burned into the first page and less than half a millisecond later our names in scripts appeared before his very eyes. You see, as we turn a page another page appears before our eyes. Then Scriptures miraculously appear as they burn to within the golden pages. No one else sees this happen and everyone else but us sees only one blank paper Page, not gold, to within this book. At that point, our father never again led a raid pillaging and plundering upon villages, or any being. He prayed 7 times a day for the redemption of all of his families' Souls for that deed so long ago perpetrated against an entire Hebrew Village and ultimately against GOD. Oh, and look, the Pen is longer than the Book. Yet if you place it to within its slot, it fits perfectly within it. And the Compass rests comfortably right beside the Pen. But once again, no one can observe this except for you, my father, and myself.

All three Items, the Pen, Book, and the Compass were not to function for anyone and in fact, only my father and I realized that I was the only one that could actually make anything work. And that was quite by accident. One day, right after our father cleaned the ancient artifacts I bumped up against the table they were laying upon and the Compass fell to the ground. I scurried to pick it up and once to within my hand our father observed the needle begin to move from within the Compass. It would not move for anyone else but me, both before and ever since. Our father decided I would be the protector of all three until such time, of my choosing, I would decide to give these Holy Artifacts to you. That time has come my brother. Only my father and I knew of all these Holy Articles for he spoke of them to no one but me. And now, you know. No villager or anyone else sees these items as they really are. Instead, they see tattered Hebrew junk that someone should throw into a burn. Hurry please, take them from me now and I ask you to forgive us for all that my family have done to your family and to you, my brother, please forgive me? If something should happen, if, if, if."

As tears welled up to within the eyes of both men, Daniel spoke, "There is nothing to forgive for we are family and we are Holy to within the eyes of our LORD GOD. We are as one, you and I my brother. I love you James!" "And I love you Daniel Adjac Pruce my brother," James cried out! "Thank you James Adja Pruce for you have fulfilled Prophecies concerning these Blessed Ancient Artifacts dating back 28,000 years upon another Planet." At that same moment, Daniel made the decision to take the Pen and the Lineage Book. The Compass would remain with James. Although it functioned for him as well, James still appeared to within the Lineage Book assigning him to that very special Blessing of GOD. This was Prophecy. Thereafter, they once again departed in separate directions to within their common goal, the Vatican. The mouse, cat, and Compass would serve James well to within that goal.

CHAPTER 23

JOURNEYS TO ITALY

The children watched on in great amazement as the huge visions of life upon the massive cave walls told tales of the past, present and future. And the two separate teams of GODS chosen began their separate journeys to Italy. And the Inspiring Spirit continued explaining the different visions as they were appearing upon and in the wall to within the mystically wondrous dream.

Timothy had already traveled far up ahead to scout and report any danger if any would exist along their first day as a threesome, in route to the Vatican. Tim had traveled this route many hundreds of years ago. It was on this route he had met one of his wives. It was much farther west from here in the Ukraine, nevertheless, the same route. He started to remember how he had met her. He had saved her from a large bird and they had stayed together from that moment on. He was traveling from Greece after he had lost another wife to old age that of which he had never fallen too. He had many memories of that part of the world of which he ran from by going east until he ended up in the eastern part of Russia. He now was on a mission for our God and he would not let those memories stand in his way. But he still could not help but remember all the wives and families that he had come to bore and had come to lose to old age of which could not happen to him. He was 100 years of age when he had met his wife in the Ukraine. She had been the last he would marry for he just could not bear to lose another loved one to old age. She had been the reason he moved once again farther east. He did not want to think of her every time he saw one of their mounds of dirt. Or a tree they would chase each other up or a place where they would wrestle each other and play.

Suddenly, his better memories interrupted, he heard a very loud noise not too far away and realized that his thoughts must transform and focus to the here and now. He did not want anyone to observe his group traveling as it could possibly get back to Mot Pruce. There was not much of a chance of being recognized. Nevertheless, he planned to be extra careful throughout all of their rugged travels.

As Tim listened for people on the trail, he also looked for anyone off the trail of who had set up a camp. He had seen two dogs off the trail about one hundred yards away. Two men with weapons were firing at a small target that they had nailed to a tree. "Why make a tree suffer with shooting into it," he thought as he continued on to scout up further on the trail. He had not seen anything really life threatening or hostile so far. However, he planned to have James meow or growl to show James Pruce another route when they would finally reach this point. As James approached, Tim gave the thought wave to James, father of Gorbachev, to make him take another split in the trail. James Adja Pruce knew that these animals were of superior quality of mind and in strength. He paid much attention to their gestures and followed where they went especially since it related well with the Arrow on the Compass. He had never gone this far west in Russia before and he hoped that they would not run into any problems along their journey.

Just as he was thinking about his hopes of not having any problems on their journey, two dogs attacked James, the cat. James, not wanting to attract attention, ran to climb up a tree while James Adja Pruce tried to discourage the troublemakers. It was to no avail as the dogs continued to howl and bark at the cat that stayed up in the tree. Repeatedly they tried to jump up into that tree to get James. They never knew just how fortunate they had been that day not to catch the Angel Warrior. James Adja Pruce just sat down and waited until the dogs lost all interest and returned to their own masters.

It had become dusk outside and nightfall was only minutes away as Timothy made it back to where his friends were. He asked James, father of Mr. Gorbachev, why they had not made their way up the trail any further? He had been waiting and waiting and waiting. James explained what had happened and Tim laughed as he thought, "I would have slapped the ill-mannered beast all the way back down the trail." James, the cat laughed with Tim as they both knew the mighty mouse would never have taken the risk of being seen acting out of the ordinary. They all bedded down for the night.

As the wolf, the mountain lion cub and Daniel all traveled due north towards the Laptev Sea the weather became colder and colder and yet still colder. It was a very harsh land with not a great many people to have to deal with. Daniel wondered if everything was going well with Tim, James and his brother on their journey west to Europe. He hoped they would not have a run in with Mot and Satan. He did not feel as though they had much of a chance against Mot without his group of warriors. After all, he had the 250-pound wolf and the beautiful majestic lion cat cub of which he knew had unbelievable strength. Daniel had truly hoped that if by chance Mot was on one of their trails that it would be his trail. Now that he had the chance to really know James, his brother, he did not want to lose him to anything or anyone or anyhow. He knew that James was not like him. James is a warrior but not an Angel Warrior as he is. He knew that if any battle took place on his brother's journey that his brother might not make it to Italy. Then he would remember that although his brother was not an Angel Warrior, the LORD had still come to him within his dreams as well. This could only mean one thing. He would make it in one piece after all. He remembered the mouse and the cat in battle. They were fierce and unstoppable. As he thought of all these things, his mind started to relax on the subject of James not making it to Italy.

As nightfall came, the three warriors decided to rest and continue again on their long journey in the morning when they could see a little better. The dangers in this harsh land were many and great. Daniel began to sing a prayer silently in Hebrew and both Gorby and Brother bowed their heads with him. Then they thought of all the other family members as Daniel sang aloud the Prayer of Cyron in the Greek! Then he continued and sang another prayer of Cyron in the Greek as well. And he remembered, with tears in his eyes, all of his robotic life and the very special loving people upon that planet as he sang.

**"THE LORD HOVERS TO WITHIN MY HEART
LIKE A GREAT BIRD OF PREY OVER THE FIELD
RELENTLESS IN PURSUIT FOR THE PRIZE AND
BEAUTIFUL TO WITHIN HIS FLIGHT
TO DO SO   AMEN**

FOR NOW WE ARE TO REMAIN THE PREY OF ALL WHOM ACT AGAINST US OH BEAST BUT BEHOLD WE SHALL BE THE TEETH OF THE LION HIM OF WHICH WAS ONCE THE LAMB AND OF WHO SHALL RETURN SOON VERY SOON   AMEN"

This was a cold, cold night as all three dug a deep hole, covered it with branches and slept, cuddled up close against each other. The sounds of the night to within a strange place were very unsettling; especially that Mot was still around in life and had the power of Satan within his weapons. Nevertheless, for some unknown reason to Daniel, this night did not give way to his usual ongoing nightmares and his question to GOD, "Am I the one?"

Back in the other camp, they had also dug a deep hole in the ground. The morning air was refreshing cold and crisp to the 800-year-old Timothy of whom awoke from on top of James, the father of his great young friend, Gorby. He raised his little arms up high over his head in his usual stretch position and just as he had done every morning for the past 800 years gave out a long, long, and loud lazy yawn. He looked over at his human friend James. He was still asleep and had his mouth wide open as he was loudly snoring away.

Tim jumped up onto a ledge on the wall of the hole and climbed his way up to the top, through the branches and onto the ground above. Both teams had decided to sleep this way at night to keep warm and to stay out of view of any would be attackers. It was also a good way to go unobserved by any of Mot's spies of who would constantly report to him. Tim once again went up ahead on the trail as scout. While he was walking and observing he chuckled at the thought of an insect going into the mouth of James as he snored. For some reason not known to him, he just found that possibility to be very funny to imagine. Suddenly he heard a noise up in a tree and as he looked, an eagle flew off from a large branch. At first, he thought it was his friend and he was going to tell him that he realized of who he really was. He felt discouraged when he saw the manner in which his body moved as he flew. For this told him that it was not in fact his Great Bird of Prey.

James the cat awoke and noticed right away that Tim had already left camp to scout. He was the team scout because he was the perfect size. He was difficult to see or hear by any would be attackers or by Mot's spies. He looked over at James Pruce and laughed at the way he looked as he snored with his mouth wide open. A small gnat kept buzzing around his lips. Every time he would take a deep snoring breath, the gnat sucked into his mouth. Then when he would blow forcefully out the tiny gnat blew back out of his mouth. Just so the gnat would not be choked down his throat, he gave out a very loud meow and James Pruce woke up suddenly. The very first thing on his mind was to eat something. He pulled a dried piece of beef jerky out of his sack and ate. He looked over at the beautiful white cat with the sparkling blue eyes and said, "Good morning." He looked around the inside of their small dugout and realized that the tiny mouse had already left faithfully scouting the trail up ahead. As he stretched his huge body, he looked over at James the cat and said, "Well I guess I am ready to go now. I have had my breakfast, got a very good night's rest and I have had my mornings stretch." The Animal Angel Warrior Guardian looked back over at him and shook his beautiful white head in an up and down motion as if to say, "Okay." Then he jumped up through the leaves of the branches and to the ground above walking up the trail slowly, giving time for James to follow. James said aloud as he followed, jumping up to the ground above through the branches, "You never fail to amaze me as I believe that you and Tim are smarter than I am. If I did not know better I would wager that the both of you could, if you wanted to, talk."

James suddenly gave out a very loud meow as James Adja Pruce laughed aloud and shook his head once again in amazement. The LORD had added to his name, Adja, for his actions came to match the numbers of his brother's names. For when Tom Adja Pruce had entered into the Heavens, our LORD added to him the same middle name, Adja, as well. This enabled his name to equal in numbers the same as his brothers, 777. Mot's name stayed the same for his numbers are 666 and to that end, his heart remained forever true.

There was an early morning glimmer upon the heavy fog. It seemed to lie upon everything like one huge heavy blanket completely unfolded to about the whole land before them. As the days of their travels became weeks and the weeks became months the trio walked across the majestically beautiful and rugged landscape of their mother Russia. Although Timothy had been born in Greece, out of his 800 years of life upon the planet Earth, he had lived to within the boundaries of the greatness of the country called

Russia for 700 years. For this reason he also felt of her as his mother country and often had said to James, father of Gorby, that someday they all should come back to see what changes the years would bring to her, if any, after a long passage of time. James knew, what he really meant was, would Mot still be around with his evil of Satan trying to control and kill off beings of GOD. As it was though, they would all miss their beautiful Russia and knew that someday they would in fact return for at the very least, a visit.

As the trio approached the border of Italy, they had traveled for 228 days through some of the most treacherous terrain on the face of the earth. They had trekked by land through Russia, the Ukraine, into Hungary, then Austria and finally down into Italy and into the Vatican. They had thought that their family and friends might already be there and waiting for them. They knew that although the distance was very close to being the same, Daniel's crew, did not have to travel through as rugged of terrain as they had. After all, that team had to travel a great distance by sea, which was over half the distance they had to travel to meet them here. They started to worry after waiting for them at the Vatican for over a month. They began to realize that having the mouse as their scout; it was a lot easier to travel unobserved. No one ever saw the mouse but he could see anyone and everyone. He was constantly on the lookout for any possible problems and effectively steered the trio from those problems. Between this and having the Compass, it had all made for a very smooth trip without too many problems. In fact, they all realized that the biggest problem they really had was food, water, and sleep for James. They began to worry that something terrible had happened to their other family members, Daniel, Brother, and Mr. Gorbachev.

The Inspiring Spirit began to tell all those listening throughout the dream a little more about Lee Earl Clemmer and about the times in of which he has witnessed.

CHAPTER 24

LEE EARL CLEMMER

> *A name, carefully constructed by a General in the KGB, (the robot Mot Pruce) was carefully inserted upon his birth certificate. This name signifies the last of His Kind.*
> *THE LAST OF THE EEL CELLS. EEL CELL R A MEMRE.*
> *The first and middle names inserted were of friends of Lee's family who had secretly infiltrated his family. (KGB Agents) No one realized it was GOD who made the KGB General do this.* Lee was born in The City of Angels on January 15 1950 at 7 minutes 7 seconds past the 7th hour of the 7th day, 3 days times 7 days or 21 days after Christmas. At his birth, the Doctor observed a scar on his left wrist, inside and out all the way through and a scar on top of his right foot, inside and out all the way through. Two huge ugly scars. He weighed 14 pounds 7 ounces and had the weight of the whole world lain upon him for he was as our LORD Is, a lamb of GOD. He is not "The Lamb of GOD" but he is a lamb of GOD. His bloodline is within the same line as that of Noah and...King David which is the same as that of the Mother of our
> ### LORD JESUS THE CHRIST

There are those who believe that the LORD has not yet existed as a man upon the Earth. And some engaged to within an old practiced reality to give to the LORD a child and to keep that child out of the loop, so to speak. Knowledge will always hide from them and the lack of it is and always will be their ultimate demise! These children are to be in the dark, concerning any training with electronic weapons and many other things as well. Informed on nothing, as they are in fact a lamb therefore separated from the family and others concerning many matters. Anyone singled out to be a lamb is subject to everyone having a part in his or her slaughter. They believe that this enables atonement for sin for themselves and others as well as to within the perpetrators of this electronic warfare.

Of course, there will be many others having many other reasons for joining the secret society against the lambs. The lambs must suffer so that others will not. Satan is the Master Organizer against GOD. Once again, Satan has used the Old Testament and New Testament in explaining why and how to allow people in justifying their actions through using electronic weaponry on others. Satan is extremely resourceful when it comes to anything against GOD but especially resourceful when it comes to recruiting new members of his secret society. This, his secret society, brings all the souls to him through their negative actions. The actions of a being, if performed over and over willingly, will ultimately end up living to within their heart forever and forever and forever.

Most had a conscience when they first began in childhood to use their electronic weapons on others through the teaching of their parents. Repetition is the most harmful element in this equation and imports murderous imprints to within the hearts. For the more they do these acts, the easier, and the more urgent it becomes to justify them through the easement of their own conscience. Children realize the wrongness of these acts but accept it by way of the parent or parents teaching them how to use the chips inside their bodies.

There are however, other huge factors in the acceptance of these teachings. One factor is simply the constant interacting with so many others, circling and firing on their victims, covering them with different chemicals thus enabling more efficiency to within the use of these electromagnetic weapons. With so many others doing this, all as one, and all together, it makes it very easy to accept. Another factor is the training since before birth. At first, some young people might question these teachings. However, most of those some will ultimately justify their actions. They would possibly do so by simply thinking or saying aloud, "If my parents and my friend's parents taught us to do these things to others, it must be right." As they become older it becomes harder and harder for the Heart to remember what the mind had forever forgotten concerning these kinds of deeds to others.

Because of these interacting kinds of behavior, even since before birth and carrying on throughout childhood and into adulthood, these people have no clue that what they do is in fact Satan's plan for them. To ultimately, receive rejection by GOD by doing his will and not GODS WILL. Unfortunately, their actions remain camouflaged to them, through the misunderstanding of The Old and New Testament. To use the LORD'S Word against the LORD and recruit more souls through the causing of misunderstandings of HIS Bible and HIS Torah will forever be the evil ones greatest triumph.

Most of the people that use these weapons are not aware of the reason that they are firing on someone. They only know that they are not giving the proper signal thus not being a part of their society, tag teaming them with electronic weapons is appropriate. Or they fire on who they think is an infidel.

Some of these people are not religious but love the power and love to use the power men have given them. It is of course Human Nature to use power if one has it to use and most will end up using their power whether it be wrong or right. People use their power to win, to overpower others in any and every situation from within their own social environment! It is natural to use this power to within your own life however most of these people become like bullies who know karate and use it whether they need to or not! Again, even the latter is of the same natural order of things. If you have the knowledge of karate and if you have the ability to use electronics as a weapon, you will find a way and or a reason to use them even if it is just simply to practice. After a while, one might even venture to enjoy doing so, whether used in a proper fashion (right way) or in a wrong way (harmful fashion) to within any given situation. Especially that the electronic weapon is part of your body (computer chips in ones being) and as a result becomes part of the mind. Just as the knowledge of karate becomes part of the mind and as a result becomes part of the body as well. As one would use all senses, knowledge and physical strength, if needed, to deal with any situation in one's environment, so it is with these weapons, because their design is to be an intricate part of ones being. Therefore, the use of this weapon is in one way or another against their own living being as well. All of this said, I will get back to the story at hand and the chapter of Lee Earl Clemmer.

I have already told you that the LORD came to Lee and spoke to him many times throughout his entire life! In fact, the LORD is still communicating with him. I will now describe to you what happened and just how a few of those times came about! For whatever reason, only GOD knows, I cannot explain most of these happenings to within the life of Lee for that is not the will of our GOD. Most of the communications to Lee from GOD are private and or Top Secret! I will however tell you of a few things that do not interfere with such matters.

The very first time the LORD came to Lee was in East Los Angeles, California! He was only one year old and in his diapers. He was standing and clenching the chain link fence for balance just outside the front yard of the family home on the sidewalk. A cars loud screech from frantic breaking tires ripped his head around towards the noise. The car pulled over to the curb. The family dog, Chiquita, a Chihuahua, lay on the ground, not moving. For some reason unknown to him at the time, he realized that she had died and understood this fact. He began to cry uncontrollably and the sad thoughts in his mind were simply just too overwhelming for someone so young and so innocent!

Suddenly, A Pure Love Flood Of Energy Pierced, Channeled And Caressed, Riveting A Spiraling Venting Through His Entire Being From The Very Top Of His Head, Down And Through The Very Tip Of His Toes! This Love Energy Spoke, telling him that he was loved well beyond anyone's comprehension! He was told not to worry, that he wound live-forever, ever and forever!

Just as suddenly as the Love Flood of Energy caressed and came upon him, it was gone. The LORD came to Lee over, and over again. In 1952, at two years of age and in the middle of the night, the LORD told him to wake up the whole family. Somehow, a lit cigarette had lodged itself and started a fire in the couch. The whole house had filled with murderous gagging smoke from the very top of the ceiling all the way down to about 10 to 12 inches from the floor. Lee crawled over the floor, room by room, to wake everyone as instructed by GOD. Life, was as always, upon the Lips of our LORD. And so it came to pass everyone in the family lived another day.

One time the LORD came to Lee in the middle of the night, it was in 1954. The LORD informed him to go downstairs to tell his beautiful mother there was someone within the house, who did not belong. She was sitting in the living room writing a letter to Jack Duit who was Lee's stepfather and was overseas! Lee was 4 years old as his mother spoke softly to him saying, "Oh Lee you were just dreaming. You wait here while I get another cup of coffee." His mother stopped writing, got up and preceded down the hall to the kitchen. Suddenly out of nowhere, a man sprang out and grabbed his mother by the head, putting his thumbs into her eyes so she could not see his face. He had a mask over his face as well and when Lee cried out loud, the family dog leaped into action. The great wolf had followed Lee home from several blocks away a month earlier and was fast asleep until Lee cried out loud. He bit into the man's leg and held on making the invader cry out in severe pain. When the intruder let his mother go and tried to move towards the back door, Wolfe let go and followed. He barked continuously and ran back and forth the whole length of the house in front of ours. He barked at it until the Police came. And so it was, Life was as always, upon the Lips of our LORD! Therefore, it came to pass; the whole family was once again let to live.

Of course there are many, many more times the LORD has come to Lee but just to say one more; in 1957 while living on Euclid Ave. in San Diego, California, a door-to-door salesman knocked upon the door. Lee's loving mother bought from the salesman a set of Encyclopedias Britannica and with those came another whole set of children's books Bible Stories. As Lee began to read those Bible stories, he came to the part where the LORD JESUS explained that HE would be returning someday in a moment that no one would know when! The LORD suddenly spoke to him once again. He was Informed that he might just still be here, well and alive, when JESUS decides to return. That was 60 years ago! This was the very first time in this life at 7 years of age that he would ask himself after the nightmare, "Who am I, Am I the one?" For it was that very same night he read about JESUS that he had yet another nightmare, the same nightmare over and over again. In this life, Lee had this nightmare over a thousand times before he even reached the age of 12. He would continue to have that nightmare throughout his entire life and all the way up until he walks out from within this dream and his name and life is changed by the Grace of our LORD.

The years that followed were rough as all through school gangs would beat him down constantly for he was a lamb. Many of you who read these pages know of what I am talking for many of you are with the secret organization of electronic warfare against the people of GOD. To top any and everything else off his parents did not get along as Jack had a drinking problem among other things between them. Nevertheless, Jack Duit, at the request of Lee's father, took Lee to Billy Graham Evangelistic Events and had him Baptized at his local Church! Jack saved Lee's life when he got pneumonia, and he saved Lee's life in Mexico in of which is a whole other story all together. Jack was also there when Lee was wounded in San Diego of which I will not go into, within this story. Thank you Jack Duit. Thank you for your love. Lee loves you too!

Jack had Lee baptized at 13! Sadly, a divorce pursued within 3 years and Lee's kind beautiful mother remarried to a friend of Jack's (his commander in the Navy) named James Ecurp. They had an evil son together they named Tom Ecurp. He was a robot born of woman! His father, James, was a robot born of woman as well.

When Lee became older, the family moved to Bay Park, San Diego. There he met and befriended 12 other boys who were a great comfort to him. Almost all of them were Christians as well! Don Do It Deaett and Leland Schumacher, known as Schu, are among the few of the group that still remain in contact with Lee Clemmer to this very day! All through the years, whenever Clemmer would come around, these good people treated him as a King. They were truly friends! They were more than that. They were his family! Their hearts knew Lee's even as his own blood family denied knowing his heart. It shall never be forgotten! For whatever love these men still cradle to within their hearts for Lee, it shall never be forgotten! Blessings to all those who have passed, John Murphy, Jack Malone, Pepper Graves, and John Schumacher. Clemmer truly loved these men! This group of fellows were known as the Fedas. Their girlfriends became known as the Fedetts. They were a great bunch of young Men and young women. Women loved them and jocks feared them for they were all as one! I must also mention, Brad Beauchamp, Ken Klusman and Bob Esquivel.

The group introduced him to Marsha. She became pregnant by Lee and he loved her and he did the right thing, Lee married her not realizing he would have to quit school and go to work. Her mother, for whatever reason, did not keep her word to him concerning this matter. He worked three different jobs to make ends meet as he was made to move into their own house. And so it was that on July 6th 1966, Marsha and Lee were married and received from our LORD a beautiful baby son. And so it was, the Fedas, each and every one, were there that day to witness this Holy Event of their friend's Marriage.

One day, a horrible day, his son was crying and crying as he had the colic. Lee needing rest from working so much suddenly yelled at his wife to try to stop his son's crying. To this day, he is not certain why; all he knows is that when he came home the next day from one of his jobs everything was gone. And everyone was blaming him for the tragedy of the break up! Being only 17 years of age, Marsha left Lee. She went back home to her mother, not allowing Lee to see his own son or her! Likewise, although he could not blame her, Lee, over reacted.

As time went by (less than a month), he became very unstable and joined up with two men that had just gotten out of prison. All three ended up arrested by the Police in Redondo Beach on 7th and Hope. GOD Bless them both for they were not bad men.

Marsha remains completely blameless of all evil to within her life for she was an Angel of who knew not whom she served before she passed in 1985. For no one asked her to say the Words. The LORD allowed this for HIS own reasons concerning HIS beautiful, Marsha. And her bloodline was the same as that of our LORD CHRIST.

After Lee's arrest, through the Grace of GOD, Lee was placed to within the custody of his Aunt, Laura Stinson, and his father, Richard Wayne Clemmer Sr. by the Courts in Los Angeles. Since he was only 17 with 6 more months until 18, the court gave him probation until his 18th birthday. What a good man his father was! Lee had never known him until that moment when he needed his father the most and he was there. And so it was, Life was as always, upon the Lips of our LORD concerning Lee. His father allowed Lee to go back to school. However, for whatever reason she had, Lee's stepmother made it clear that he would have to quit school, as he was no longer welcome to within his father's house after his 18th birthday. And so it was on his 18th birthday, his Father with tears in his eyes, drove Lee to downtown L.A. to 9th and Hope Streets where he rented him a room in a flophouse. Lee loved his father very much as they had built a strong bond with each other during that short-lived moment in time. It was there, downtown, that Lee met a fight trainer and promoter. He had seen Lee defend an older couple being robbed while they were downtown Los Angeles. He observed Lee beating down two men at the same time with perfect precision. The promoter got him a professional fight right away and Lee Won 5 thousand dollars under the table! Just afterwards, Lee acquired a sales job selling encyclopedias for Spencer International Press. He roomed with two other salesmen, Joe Young and a large young beautiful and exceptionally good black man named Rick, at 5819 Gregory Ave. in Hollywood. Just across the street from one of the gates of Paramount Studios on Gower.

There, he met a young beautiful girl name Jeannie Remel. He lived with her and her best friend, Christina Jo Myers. They were together off and on for over three years and when she became pregnant with his child she simply vanished! He never saw her again. He always felt it was his fault as he had spoken many times, about how he and Marty had become pregnant and he had to marry her. You would think he would have learned his lesson. He later believed this same reason was at the heart of why Kathy (who he met within feet of where he met Jeanne) did not marry him when he asked her after she became pregnant. It devastated Lee when she answered "NO" for he loved Kathy with all of his heart. Between all of this, at the ages of 18 through 24, Lee managed unofficially to attend many classes at UCLA. He enjoyed the campus learning and studying whatever he could on a wide range of the curriculum.

During his 18th year of life upon this planet, he had become a professional boxer and fought in the Olympic Auditorium six times under three different fight names. Over the next 12 years between 1968 and 1980 he would fight under one or another of these names in the Garden and many other famous arenas throughout the world as well. Between all three names he fought under, in that career, his record was an impressive 17/0/01 with 11 knockouts. He won a lot of money under the table. The bookies, realizing Lee was a much better fighter than the other fighter was, asked Lee not to throw leather or any real heavy punches for three rounds on a six round fight. On a 10 round fight, he was not to throw any leather for the first 4 rounds. Then he was to knock the poor sap into next week. Of course, that would not happen until all the spectators in the audience placed bets against him while he was not throwing any leather. Lee did this for the bookies and himself all through the next 12 years.

Being in that life style Lee began to drift away from his **GOD** in a bad way. Every time he would start to build a good record under one name, he would be arrested and bail out and in order to fight again his manager would arrange to change his name. And why not? It was always because of what he would do for his manager that he would go to jail. I will not go into it however, Lee did some bad deeds for these bookies and different managers. Through all of this, he still had time to take on bodyguard jobs, he collected for the bookies, and he protected women of the night from bad men. Sometimes he would do drugs as well. All through this, the LORD still came to him over and over and over again trying to guide him away from evil.

They subpoenaed Lee on his 21st birthday in January of 1971. The D.A. in L.A. wanted him to testify against the two men he went to jail with in 1967. He informed the D.A. that he had taken a tab of acid that day and simply could not remember anything the trio may have done. However, the D.A. knew that just seeing him in court would scare the poop right out of them and he was correct in assuming that fact. When Lee showed up in court that day, Daryl and G.W. copped a plea after four years of fighting it in court. He always felt guilty about that. Lee felt that he should have been more alert and bold. For he could have walked right up and informed them and their attorney, right there in the courtroom that he could not remember anything of that day. But he just sat there in court, dumb founded and thinking that the two would surely realize he could never talk. During these moments in time between 1967 and 1971, Lee met many people that he would remember and love all through his life:
Jeanne Remel and Christina Jo Myers, Kathy Pfeiffer, Juan Pfeiffer, Virginia Pfeiffer, Laura Huxley, Piero Ferrucci, Joseph Young, Rick, Jim Lorenzen, Herb, Mike, Floyd, Freddie, Billie, Farmer, Linda, Jimmer, Terrible Tom, Ron, a good friend of Jeanne Remel, Maxine Wolf, Samuel Palmer, Steve Mills, Christina Henson, Gail Henson, Larry Eisenberg, Bill Barkley, Willie Johnson, Pam and Dan Hodel, Mark Davis, Nancy Curcio, Laurie Greisen, Pam English, Roberta Jarrett, and so many more! And George Abrams the boxer, (Hebrew), who beat Sugar Ray Robertson! Lee loves you all very

much indeed, for you all are a small part of who he was is and forever shall be.

Somewhere in between all of these people in his life, he had a child with a woman named Kathy and they had a beautiful daughter together in 1974. They named their daughter, Karen.

With great guilt, Lee also allowed two abortions to happen with two different women and in fact, he may have helped to encourage both events. Without his encouragement to do these foul deeds neither one of these women would have gone through with these terrible events. One of these women, Nancy Curcio, was an exceptionally good being and he is very sorry to have made her a part of that foul deed. The other women was Christiana Henson and she was indeed a wonderful being as well and Lee is very sorry to have made her a part of such a foul deed. For Lee knows he should have never allowed such things to happen to within his life or another life connected to him in that way. It should not have happened to within his watch. He will always pray for forgiveness on these matters. These abortions took place between the years 1972 and 1977.

Lee had 9 other Brothers and Sisters. There were 10 siblings all together. Lee, with all of his Heart, loves every one of them! Charlie Russell Duit and Clark Lester Kuehni have captured Lee's Heart forever, as he will always remember his much younger brothers while still wearing their diapers. Wayne Charles Clemmer saved Lee's life on an escapade while in Mexico one year with Federalist Authorities and Guerrilla Forces at hand! There was Russian Gold and the Panama Canal with Russian Ships as well. What a brave Brother! Wayne, his favorite Brother. Vickie Lou, Richie, and Susie were also great Sisters and Brother as well. There was also the twins! They are all good Brothers and Sisters to Lee and shall always be remembered in a good light. However, these are all other great and loving stories that shall be told in another frame in time.

I could go on and on about the happenings to within Lee's life as some of it is quite extraordinary. However, I do believe the President and first Lady are going to find their way here soon. So I will say just a little more concerning him who the LORD chose.

After saying this to the children, the Spirit continued to explain such things as the letter and number codes to within Lee's name. Then he went on with other parts of the story to within the visions in and upon the massive cave wall.

CHAPTER 25

LETTER AND NUMBER CODES
LEE EARL CLEMMER

LETTERS TO NUMBER CODE
A = 6 _ B = 12 _ C = 18 _ D = 24 _ E = 30 _ F = 36 _ G = 42
H = 48 _ I = 54 _ J = 60 _ K = 66 _ L = 72 _ M = 78 _ N = 84
O = 90 _ P = 96 _ Q = 102 _ R = 108 _ S = 114 _ T = 120
U = 126 _ V = 132 _ W = 138 _ X = 144 _ Y = 150 _ Z = 156

SEQUENCE OF LETTERS TO CODE IN
___*Lee Earl Clemmer = 762 + 7 + 6 + 2 = 777*___
___*Lee Earl Clemmer = eeL CEll r a memre*___

1--REVERSE THE FIRST NAME **Lee**..............…......…..=**eeL**

2--FIRST LETTER OF **C**lemmer...........................=**C**

3--FIRST LETTER OF **E**arl.................................…..............=**E**

4--SECOND LETTER OF C**l**emmer...........…..…………..=**l**

5--LAST LETTER OF Ear**l**..............….......................................=**l**

6--THIRD LETTER OF Ea**r**l.................................=**r**

7.. SECOND LETTER OF E**a**rl ....=**a**

7--REVERSE THIRD&FORTH LETTERS Cl**em**mer...=**me**

8--FIFTH LETTER OF Cle**m**mer...................................=**m**

9--REVERSE SIXTH-SEVENTH LETTERS Clemm**er**.=**re**

10-THE LETTERS CODE AND THE NUMBERS CODE OF
LEE'S NAME ARE THAT OF............…......……..=*COMPLETION*
11- THE NUMBERS CODE IN HIS NAME.......=*COMPLETION*
Lee Earl Clemmer...................…..= *762 + 7 + 6 + 2 = 777*
CANNOT USE A 6 CODE TO GET THE NUMBER = 777
DOING SO CONSEQUENTLY SLAPS SATAN IN THE FACE
12-IN THE LETTER CODE THE NAME *Lee Earl Clemmer*
EQUALS eeL CEll r a memre = COMPLETION
13-A MEMORY IS SOMETHING THAT IS REMEMBERED OR
COMPLETED IN THE MIND....….............…..=*COMPLETION*
14-NUMBER 7 IS THE LORDS DAY OF REST=*COMPLETION*

CHAPTER 26

PIRATES AT TIKSI

Still a hundred miles out at sea Captain Micah Joshua Striker ordered the pirate flag taken down and the flag of the Norway to fly in its place. The Captain did not want to chance anyone realizing of who he and his ship's crew really were. He planned to anchor off shore from the port at Tiksi and take on as many unsuspecting passengers as he could possibly board. Instead of taking them to where they would want to go, he would sell them into slavery, bondage, and servitude. This next group of unsuspecting beings had been promised to a slave trader at a port in Syria.

Captain Striker and his first mate Gautama Gautam had known each other for well over 22 years. Micah Joshua Striker and the ex-Buddhist Priest Gautama had both lost their entire family of loved ones to Christian and Hebrew Warriors from Italy and different parts of Europe. These warriors went on the paths of war to take land and settle in those lands to convert people to their way.

Although the Captain's last name was Striker, his mother was Muslim so he too was of her faith. His mother and father had died alongside his brothers and sisters when he was only four years old. Gautama had lived in the same village as Striker and had migrated there to enlighten people of Buddhism. He was born in India. Both men had become bitter and their hearts had hardened against their own beliefs. They had both seen and been through many, many terrible things to within that small village so many years ago. The Priest had taken the child, Micah, and fled to a port in Syria. Not realizing it was a pirate ship they boarded a vessel and became captives in exactly the same way as they now took on captives aboard the very same ship. The Captain of that ship took Striker as a cabin boy for his own personal needs and as the Priest spoke several languages, he took him and made him a seaman and a translator of which he desperately needed. Striker grew to a large framed 6'6" tall strong young man and became a seaman and translator as well. The lost Priest taught him every day and night to speak different languages so that neither one would be sold. They could stay on board the Spirit of Norway together. Their bond with each other was that of love and respect as they had gone through much together within this life.

After 17 years on board ship, the Captain had died leaving his position up for grabs by the strongest and most knowledgeable of the crew. Micah Joshua Striker with the help of Gautama and a few others became Captain Micah Joshua Striker. His very first command was to make Gautama Gautam, his First Mate. He trusted no other man more in his whole 22 years of life on this planet.

Over five years had passed since he became Captain of the pirate and slave ship, the Norway. He was now 27 years old and Gautama was now 53 years of age, as both men had become very hard fighting warriors of the high seas and oceans of the known world at that time. The year was 1504 AD and the slave trade was quite profitable. It was extremely easy to accomplish for a Captain and his ship especially having a crew of pirates.

Still 20 miles off shore from the port at Tiksi, another ship sailed up close to the Norway and approached her by way of small rowboat. It was the Captain of the other ship. He was spreading news of being on the lookout for seven beings of whom a man named Mot would pay a large amount of money to capture and bring them to either a port in Greece, Turkey, or Syria. Mot had received word that the seven beings had been traveling west. The Captain told him that there were two humans, a cat with blue eyes, a dog, or perhaps a wolf of who was very large, a young mountain lion with blue eyes, and possibly part cat, a mouse and finally an Eagle. The Eagle had the highest bounty on him. The Captains both laughed as he told of the mouse! Then the Captain of the other ship explained that word was, these seven with the help of a mountain lioness of who died in the battle and the help of an eagle, had destroyed an entire army of 14,000 demoniac strong men. He explained that the entire world had heard about this battle as the epic tale had spread like a wildfire throughout Russia and anywhere that there were strong, fighting men. Captain Striker asked where the battle had taken place. "In Eastern Russia about 1700 miles away and almost five months ago," he explained.

Captain Striker put out a feast on his table and the two had a meal fit for a king. Afterwards the Captain of the other ship boarded his rowboat with four of his men and rowed back to their ship.

The Norway anchored offshore of the port at Tiksi. Captain Striker and his first mate Gautama with four other men rowed a boat to shore and went into the village. They spread word that they, for a small fare, would board passengers if anyone wanted to travel to an island or any land mass in or around the Arctic Ocean! They were sailing from here clear to the Mediterranean Sea and Africa. They would port at any coastal port thereof! He was also to sail to a port in Syria.

CHAPTER 27

ANGELS AT TIKSI

After traveling almost **1700** miles due north, Daniel, Brother and Mr. Gorbachev arrived safely at the Port of Tiksi. Taking their time whereas not observed by too many people, or evil beings, their trek had been 4 months in the making. Once at the Port the three Angels split up not to be observed as a team. Mr. Gorbachev stayed out of view becoming invisible but kept a careful watchful eye over Daniel as he talked to people around the Port. He was asking questions about Ships taking on passengers. Daniel had heard that there was a ship anchored off shore that would in fact be boarding passengers. Its Captain had said he was even sailing as far as the Mediterranean Sea and on to a Port in Syria. He had left word that he would be staying at the local Inn and would wait for two or three days for interested parties to sign on. Daniel left word that he also would be staying at the Inn and needed to know how much the fare was. He also wanted to know when he could board the Ship.

The Captain and his first mate Gautama collected quite a bit of Gold from would be passengers to board the Norway. However, a leader of a certain cutthroat band of men observed all of the transactions they made that day. The leader of these Men decided to wait for nightfall and lure the Captain to a cabin just outside of town for dinner at which time he would supposedly pay him as a passenger onboard the Ship. He called it, "A thank you dinner." He stopped the Captain and paid him part of the fare to Spain and the Captain accepted his invitation to dinner as well.

Captain Striker and Gautama walked back to the Inn and paid their lodging for two more nights. Daniel happened to be there at that moment and the Innkeeper introduced them to each other. Daniel paid the Captain fare for three passengers and asked, "When can the three of us board the Norway?" The Captain replied, "Two more days' sir." Daniel did not mention that the other two passengers were not human. He thought that it would be no big matter since he had paid in full for three to sail to Italy.

Daniel had thought to go on to Germany and trek downward instead of what he originally planned. He thought that this might be a better way to go. Then after thinking about it, he realized that they would not be taking as many chances by sea. If they trekked by land all the way to Italy there would be much more danger of informants or demons seeing them and reporting to Mot. Daniel felt much safer by not changing the plan after all. However, he did not realize that the particular vessel they would board was a slave ship. Its Captain had no intention on anchoring outside any port other than a port in Syria where the slave traders would be waiting with Gold in hand.

Mr. Gorbachev pawed at the door for Daniel to open it. As Daniel opened the door, he rushed inside. Daniel waited for the Wolf and when he realized that Brother was not there to come inside, he wondered where he would be. If he did not return tonight, he would look for him tomorrow before boarding the ship.

Every night before going to bed Daniel sang two Prayers of Cyron, first silently in Hebrew, then aloud-in Greek.

"THE LORD HOVERS TO WITHIN MY HEART LIKE A GREAT BIRD OF PREY OVER THE FIELD RELENTLESS IN PURSUIT FOR THE PRIZE AND BEAUTIFUL TO WITHIN HIS FLIGHT TO DO SO AMEN

FOR NOW WE ARE TO REMAIN THE PREY OF ALL WHOM ACT AGAINST US OH BEAST BUT BEHOLD WE SHALL BE THE TEETH OF THE LION HIM OF WHICH WAS ONCE THE LAMB AND OF WHO SHALL RETURN SOON VERY SOON AMEN"

Now it happened that the Inspiring Spirit broke into the story and took the time for he felt that he should explain to the children more about Angels and Angels in the flesh and prayer. The Spirit began to explain. "It should be known that all Angels are in constant Prayer for all things and the beings the LORD has created throughout all eternity! They pray for all creatures and even for the rocks and sky and the trees. All things, creatures, and beings have the heart of our GOD! When Angels sing these prayers in their hearts and minds in Hebrew for such as these, it pleases HIM that AM. So it would also please HIM if you children would also practice these kinds of prayers as well right along with any prayers that you already pray without singing. And when it comes time even the rocks and the sky and all the things that you have prayed for will witness to our GOD about these events that you have done. And the LORD may smile upon you and life shall remain upon HIS Lips for you. So remember, if I do not explain these things the Angels do every time they do them it does not mean that it does not happen that way. They are in constant Prayer for GOD."

After explaining these things, the wonderful Inspiring Spirit began to explain about the Women Prophets and Robots of Cyron. From there he continued the story with more about Lee. Then He told more of Lee's travels in another life in his everlasting quest to within and of GODS Will.

CHAPTER 28

THE WOMEN PROPHETS AND ROBOTS OF CYRON

I will not talk of any or name any other names of the women Prophets of Cyron other than one full name and one first name. However, I will talk about the two that I just mentioned to within this story. The LORD has me do this for security purposes. They are both here on this planet and others are to follow when the LORD comes. It is such as these that will help open the Gates of Hell that the LORD will pour the evil into and will seal up the Gates with The Four Cord Rope of Love, Hope, Faith, and HIS Angels for a term only the LORD knows. For this Rope may not be broken or even fray by any force in any universe.

The two women Prophets I speak of were both a Princess to within their own tribes. They possess Hearts in of which our LORD very graciously lived and lives to within. This is true to this very day. They were both the Highest Priestess to within their own tribes. I will say this to you three, the children of the President, At least one of the Prophets is very close to you. So close, well let's just say so close that you simply cannot miss her. On the planet Cyron, her name was Melania and strangely enough, she has the very same name here on Earth. She is your mother and even though you two girls are adopted; she loves you more than her own life as she does you as well Barron.

The other Prophet was Laura Ja Curpe, married to Daniel Bajcab Curpe. Two of the greatest scientist Cyron has ever known. Laura was a scientist, Prophet, Priestess, and Warrior for our GOD. In this world, she was Laurie Blade. Yes Kaya, your Great Godmother Laurie Blade. She is now known as Laurie Jaln Blade and she was also a Woman Prophet from the planet Cyron! "Great," Kaya cried out. Yes, Great Godmother. Laurie Jaln Blade godmothered your grandmother your mother and now you! Laurie is your Great Godmother and she knows not of whom she is as of yet, just as Melania does not know of whom she is as of yet either. Laurie will remember this day in this dream with Mr. Gorbachev, Tuxedo, the Eagle, Lee, many other Angels, all of you, and the LORD. "But she has died over nine years past," Kaya cried out in wonder. The LORD works in mysterious ways my little sister in GOD.

Then the Spirit began to explain about the Robots of Cyron.

After 5 thousand years, the first robots received transfusions and it was a wonderful euphoric feeling for the first time in their robotic existence. It did not take long for the robots of Cyron to realize that the pure blood of the firstborn of any species was the best of the unbelievably euphoric feelings as it was electro-magnetically drawn. The blood would surge from one being or several at the same moment and then to within one or more robotics framework at that same moment. And the euphoric feeling was not limited to the first-born of humans. An unbelievable euphoric feeling also connected to the first-born of other species as well but humans tasted and felt much better. Of course, there still was a euphoric feeling even if it was not the first-born but the blood of the first-born was much, much more of a euphoric feeling. The humans and or any of the other species never realized even to this day that their blood was being sucked out of their being, surging through the air and entering to within a robot, creating a euphoric feeling for bots and a murderous effect upon the victim. For that is the side effect of their electronic vampire ways as it is a weapon that creates pain and eventual death upon its victims.

You see, when Daniel Bajcab Curpe made the first robots, they were never conscious when receiving their blood therefore never realized the feeling that it gave to them as it first entered into their being. Samson was the only one given a Spirit of Light from GOD through Daniel. Daniel was never aware of this euphoric feeling for the bots as they murdered him well before they received their first transfusions. As all robots manufactured were in the exact same way for thousands of years, humans did not realize until their 5 thousandth birthday the euphoric power of that electro-magnetic transfusion, especially from the first-born. And especially, especially, anyone with the bloodline of Noah of the ark or Mary (Mother of the CHRIST) who was in the same bloodline as King

David of whose blood is the bloodline of the CHRIST.

Within the first 5 thousand years of their existence, a robot scientist developed and refined an already existing technology of electro-magnetically receiving, blood replenishments, and other fluids from humans and other species for robots survival. The robot scientist did this as not to bother the humans when robots needed the transfusion. This is an example of how noble and thoughtful the robots were before their five thousandth birthday. Then because of the euphoric feeling, the robots could not help themselves and a perversion of the robots survival began to spread throughout all the cosmos to every robot. Every robot except one and his name was Samson!

Robots are the stronger and of course, as the robots indulged to within these kinds of ways other perversions began to unfold as well to within their existences. They decided to introduce and develop reproductive abilities to within their own robotic beings. And instead of having to build robots, they began giving birth to Robots. Then they began mating with the humans and as a result, the human offspring developed supernatural strength partly due among other variables to the high amounts of titanium within their blood. They also developed a very strong natural electro-magnetic capability. In addition, they look so human; one cannot tell that they are a robot.

Now there came a moment in time whereas Melania, Laura and her husband Daniel lost their lives to saving the robot Samson for he was Holy and Sacred. They forfeited their lives so as he could fulfill Holy and Sacred Prophecies on both the Planet Cyron and Earth directly through the CHRIST. Although the Great Sacred Eagle of Cyron was there, he could not stop the high numbers of demons of every imaginable source and robot demons as well from murdering the three High Priests of Cyron. I will now say to you Zach, Sara and Faith: Your father Richard, and Kaya your grandmother Kathy, became High Priest and Priestess after the three were murdered for they were the son and daughter of Daniel and Laura Ja Curpe on planet Cyron and next in line for that purpose. He continued with his wife and their son who was next in line for High Priest along with The Great Sacred Eagle of Cyron protecting Samson for centuries up until their murders and burials took place as well. The Eagle remained an invisible but a constant figure to within the protection of Samson throughout the next thousands and thousands of years and up until and after the LORD sending him to Earth. These creatures of GOD, your people from planet Cyron, were all inspired magnificently courageous and fierce warriors for GOD and this would be well and wise for you all to remember. Your mothers and your fathers have not yet realized of whom they have been from upon another planet and within another time and space. But they are still loyal to our LORD upon this planet and to within this space and time. All of this information are things you must keep to yourselves. You, the Presidents and First Ladies beloved son and beloved newly adopted daughters, your Parents do not remember of who they were either. Your father was the husband of Melania and a High Priest as well.

All agreed with the Mystical Spirit in that these facts would stay among themselves and he continued the story.

Now when the robots finally followed Samson to Earth they helped Evil upon this planet to realize whom they thought Samson was to within all creations Prophecies. They would attempt trying to stop him from fulfilling the works for his LORD. A robot never harms another robot. Then through this story becoming a book added to another book and called by another name, robots learn that they have actually harmed another that used to be a robot. They quickly pass this knowledge on throughout all universes and all bots therein. When they learn JESUS the CHRIST touched, baptized and changed him into a human, then sent him to another world, they begin to wonder one by one. As they read that book, they begin to read the Bible. As they began to hear him speak of GOD, many follow him and begin to worship GOD. And one by one JESUS becomes their LORD.

Lee writes the first and second parts of this book with the Pen of truth, the Pen of one from Cyron with blessings from the LORD spoken upon it. They have always known the Pen is true and only one may write with it! For this main reason, the robots shall listen and they shall begin to become believers. The robots shall realize that they have been deceived for thousands and thousands of years throughout the cosmos! The deception concerned many Prophecies and the identity of the one hurdled from planet Cyron by the CHRIST. The deception was ultimately that of the nonexistence of GOD and HIS SON.

CHAPTER 29

LEE EARL CLEMMER'S NIGHTMARES

Even as the LORD came to him all through his Life, Lee was plagued with the same nightmare since well before his conception and from the moment of his birth up until this very day. It would always begin and end with a heavy fog rising to within the dream as if to hide certain defining facts from him. In the fog there is always a man dragging a huge wooden cross. His body looks ripped, torn, and bloodied, worn, harmed well beyond any repair or belief from the very tip of his toes to the very top of his head. He always has a crown that of which has been forced and wedged upon his head. And blood rolls all down his face, all down his neck, all down his chest, and all about his shoulders from that wedged crown. And the crown is made of thorns. Moreover, all while he struggles to drag the weight of that huge wooden cross to his own crucifixion, men punch at him and kick him, they curse him, they spit upon him, they throw things upon him and laugh upon him. They laugh while spears of whips that of cats of nine tails, penetrate his body. They laugh a horribly perverted laugh. A Roman whip, a Roman soldiers laugh. Then, in the fog, a crucifixion always takes place. However, Lee can barely seem to see the man's face through the fog. It is always that way in every single life for 2,000 years or 49 lives.

All during these terrible nightmares and in every life Lee will always pray for forgiveness, from our LORD. Then, he would ask, "Am I the one?" In every Life for the past two thousand years, he ponders this question. The question of which consistently crowds to within his thoughts. Day and night, night and day, every moment of and in every life this horrible, this terribly horribly crippling question crowds, relentlessly, pounding and pounding to within his brain! Am I the one? He could not bear it but he has to. He has to. He simply has to. It has been two thousand years of the nightmare, the nightmare, the nightmare, always the nightmare! Then he would scream to GOD and ask, "Am I the one?" While always expecting an answer but never receiving one, he truly hopes that someday the LORD shall answer him. In addition, Lee asks that he may know of who he was in that life of 2000 years past. Nevertheless, until the answers come he continues to scream out, Am I the one? Am I the one? Am I the one? Who was I, Am I the one? Oh LORD, tell me.

CHAPTER 30

SAVING THE CAPTAIN AND FIRST MATE

Mr. Gorbachev and Brother had decided that it would be much safer if they were not all seen together until the trio boarded the ship. Brother spent the night just outside of the village near a small cabin waiting for Mr. Gorbachev to come for him in the morning.

Captain Striker and Gautama walked up the path to the cabin just outside the village. Their arrival awoke Brother and his wolf nose could smell the food coming from the small building. The Captain knocked hard upon the door as he talked to his first mate. As the Wolf entered their thoughts, he caught the thoughts of the crew of cutthroats who were inside the cabin as well. He realized that this was the Captain and First Mate of the ship in of which he would be sailing on with Daniel and Gorby very soon. He also came to realize that the cutthroats were about to murder the Captain and his First Mate in order to steal their gold! The Wolf knew that they had planned to put their bodies in the ground just nearby and that no one would be the wiser.

When the Captain and Gautama entered the cabin, they both realized that something was not right. There were 10 men all standing upright in the small cabin and all were staring right straight at them with smirks on all of their faces. Suddenly men appeared from behind with rifles cocked and ready to fire. The men facing them drew their large hunting knives. Before Captain Striker and Gautama could respond, several men struck them from behind and they fell to the cabin floor.

Still half dazed the Captain and his First Mate could hear the sound of breaking glass and observed men flying every which direction. Then they heard the sound of an animal growling and men screaming out in pain as unrelenting fear overwhelmed the entire cabin. The Wolf had thrown enormous men in every direction and disoriented everyone inside the cabin except the Captain and Gautama. He walked right up to them and just as they began to think that they were next to be assaulted the massive Wolf licked both of their faces. Then he walked over to the door and waited. The Captain and his First Mate quickly got up off the cabin floor taking advantage and running outside up the trail and back to the village. Brother followed to ensure their safety. Neither The Captain or Gautama were sure if he was a Wolf or a quadruple extra-large Dog but knew that he had in fact saved them both from sure death.

The Great Hero followed them right up to the door of their room at the Inn and sat patiently watching as the Captain opened it. As the two walked into their quarters the Great Wolf stood up on his hind legs with his head bowed waiting for an invitation to enter. Captain Striker laughed as he replied, "Come on in." Both men laughed and talked all night of the Great Wolf's Heroics. They simply could not get over how this one animal had fought off 12 huge, strong men! He made them scream aloud in shear panic and fear as if they were small children. The Captain and Gautama both decided, if this Majestic Animal followed them on board the Norway, he would become their pet and Guardian on all voyages upon the High Seas or on Land. They would treat him like a King. He looked and acted as if of Majestic and Noble birth. More so than any Royalty, they had ever met or observed. Besides, he had saved both of their lives.

Captain Striker and Gautama were amazed at the Intelligence and the Love that thrived to within the Heart and the Mind of this massive, beautiful being. After all, they had in fact been a witness to exactly how ferocious he became at their defense to within that small cabin. They both would remember that day as a day of life and a day of Friendship.

The Captain realized how uneasy the crew would be at the sight of the massive Wolf, especially when they would observe how protective he was of himself and Gautama. However, the crew would have to live with their uneasiness. This brave, Majestic and beautiful being would be welcomed for as long as he wanted to stay aboard the Spirit of Norway!

CHAPTER 31

THE ANGEL GUARDIAN WARRIOR_BROTHER

In 1970, a very large blue-eyed beautiful Creature of GOD followed Lee home. At first, Lee thought the creature was stalking him. Then the huge animal would stop about 10 feet ahead of Lee and do his business. Lee came to realize that the great wolf thought he was out for a walk with a friend. He was a huge wolf looking animal and possessed the great nobility of GOD to within his actions and to within his ways. Later Lee would come to remember this beautiful warrior in lives past throughout the centuries.

In this life, the very first night the wolf followed him home, he came to Lee in a dream and spoke, telling him something he did not quite understand at that particular moment in time. He told him of a code that will come into view later on in the 1990's with the use of computers. He would have to enter all the different names that he had in other lives into the code and that the information found from within would confirm his being chosen by his GOD! That night in the same dream, the great wolf made Lee to say the Words, "JESUS IS LORD." Lee did not really understand all of this and did not really believe it, yet. However, Lee felt spiritually attached to the Majestic animal who he named Brother. He insistently followed Lee all around as like a little brother would follow his older brother. Of course, Brother was actually an Angel in the flesh, guarding Lee with his very own Holy and Sacred Life.

Within the first week Brother found Lee and followed him home from a business on Santa Monica Blvd. and El Centro, Brother had saved his life. The semi pro ball team Lee was on celebrated a win that day in a bar in downtown Los Angeles. He could not leave Brother at home, because he would break through a window and try to follow! Therefore, Lee took him everywhere he went. While at the bar that day he had Brother sit under the pool table as he did not want anyone to step on him. He was just too big to piss off. Suddenly a man walked up to Lee and told him to get the dog away from him, "Put him outside I don't want to get bit" he grunted. Lee grunted back saying, "I'll bite you before my dog will and if you want, follow me, I'm walking outside right now." As Lee walked outside and turned around the man sucker punched him. He grabbed the man and head locked him while hitting him. Another man came up from behind, broke a bottle, and was about two inches from cutting Lee's throat. Out of nowhere, Brother appeared as his teeth severed into the skin while his powerful jaws crunched down and into the bone of this man! There was no choice in this matter as it saved Lee's Life. Needless to say, Lee and Brother left hastily. And so it was, Life as always, was upon The Lips of our LORD once again concerning Lee. Well from that point on Lee and Brother were never apart. They simply went everywhere together.

It would not be until Kathryn's death by demons one Christmas in 1985 that Lee began to realize the many truths in of which were told to him many times in many dreams by his Angel Guardian Warrior friend, Brother. Because this Animal Angel had given to Lee all this information in the 1970's, he knew what to do for his GOD when the time came and computers held the keys to the Bible Codes. Moreover, within the codes lies the proof of his 343 lives! In addition, this knowledge became a GODsend to Lee and he came to love his GOD even more than with all of his strength. And he came to love his GOD even more than with all of his heart and mind and spirit! Loving GOD with all his might!

Now there came within a dream the Animal Angel Warrior, Brother, who relayed a Prophecy to Lee. He explained that one of his Brothers was a robot and that his spirit was of Mot Pruce! In addition, as he followed Lee through space and time for 28,000 years, he was a KGB Russian agent here and now! That Prophecy dictated that he would kill Lee's father. He would come to kill his own father, grandfather, grandmother, mother and he would try to kill Lee as well. Lee could not die for his belief and faith in GOD would not permit it. His belief and faith allowed no poison to overtake of him. Believe these things of those who love the LORD for they are true. His brother and partners killed family all for power, money, and hate that of which has forever lived to within their ugly sinful hearts. These are murderous, power hungry and greedy hateful hearts. The heart of Lee's brother knows nothing else, nothing at all! Mot Pruce was, is, and always shall be a sociopathic maniac murderous fool of a being no matter what life his spirit embodies for Satan. Like a rabid dog, infecting all who in life by chance happen to wander within his path. Yet Lee still loves him! There are many more Prophecies concerning Lee's different identities and families throughout the eternities. The great wolf explained these Prophecies, including that of the 45th President.

The ever so gentle Spirit changed the visions within and upon the wall over, and over, repeatedly, as he continued to explain all within and upon the wall whenever needed. For now, it is back to the travels to Italy and the Vatican. Back to Captain Micah Joshua Striker and Gautama Gautam and the Angels! Then he shall change the visions back to this then back to that and so forth to within this so wondrous dream!

CHAPTER 32

BOARDING THE NORWAY

Brother sent out his thoughts to Mr. Gorbachev and told him what had happened inside the cabin just outside the village. He informed the Great Cat that for now he would be traveling as the pet of Captain Micah Joshua Striker and his First Mate, Gautama Gautam, on board the Norway.

That night the LORD came to within the dreams of Brother. HE told him that Captain Striker had planned to sell all the passengers as slaves at a port in Syria. The LORD told him not to fight it but to help Striker and give him love and do the same for Gautama. HE told him that HE would prepare both of the men for him and Mr. Gorbachev to come within each of their dreams. Striker would one day gain back his faith in Allah and would become a great non-violent Muslim leader but a leader believing in the CHRIST. Gautama would once again become a Buddhist Priest and teach love and peace to many just as he had done so many years ago. To all who would listen he would also teach everything he could of the CHRIST! The LORD explained that they had both been through many terrible things together long, long ago.

The LORD then went to within the dreams of Mr. Gorbachev and Daniel. HE explained what they must do as well. Daniel must not fight but instead learn and listen from this experience. He would someday need this to respond properly to the Revolutionary War in America and in the Civil War in America as well. In this way, Daniel would realize what a slave goes through. When he witnesses it to the LORD, it would enable an accurate Blessing or judgment on those who go through the same horrific situations. It would help GOD make complete and accurate righteous judgments on others. GOD went on to explain that they must not escape. Be patient and wait for the ship to port off the coast of Italy.

For the next two days Captain Striker and Gautama collected

more gold from would be passengers. The Wolf stayed by their sides. One of the men that had tried to kill and rob Striker and Gautama was walking across the street. He did not think they would recognize him and as it was, they did not until the Wolf growled at him from by their side. The man quickly ran away disappearing from sight. The growl that came from the Wolf even made the Captain and his First Mate step back until they realized of who he was looking at. Once again, they realized what an ally this beautiful 250-pound being could actually be. They once again laughed and rejoiced in such a majestic and beautiful being as their bodyguard and protector.

Captain Striker sent for two more long rowboats to help in boarding the ship with passengers and valuables. The unsuspecting ladies and gentlemen were all excited and speaking to each other of what to do while traveling on board this rather large and battle-ready looking vessel. The Norway had 13 cannons lined across each side of her, one cannon on the bow, and one on the stern, 28 cannons in all! The passengers all told each other that they would certainly not have to worry about any pirates while on board this ship as they laughed together.

As the last passenger was to board the Norway, the crew hoisted anchor and spread out the sails to begin the awaited voyage. While Captain Striker gave the command to set sail, everyone was excited, talking, and laughing as they stood by the railings. They watched as the ship glided through the water and was underway.

The wind blew through Brother's hair as he sat on deck next to Gautama who was yelling out orders to the crew. The first mate reached down to pet his newfound friend. Brother rubbed his nose up against Gautama's leg as his hand was upon the Wolf's head. Gautama thanked the Wolf for being there for him and Striker and for coming with him on this voyage to Syria. "We never really thanked you did we, my friend," he lovingly said to the Wolf as he sat there by his side. Gautama smiled as he pet the huge majestic Wolf.

Brother entered to within the thoughts of Gautama and let him know of his name without the First Mate realizing. "I think that because you follow us all around like a little brother, we shall call you, Brother," the first mate replied as his hand could not stop petting the Wolf. "I sense that you are a whole lot smarter than we are aware of. Perhaps you are a knowledgeable, even wise, and understanding being of great importance. There is truly something special and wondrous about you my friend. However, like many things as of late, it all seems to simply elude me at this interim in time."

Daniel had bought a large trunk in the village and put Mr. Gorbachev to within it. He wanted to wait until the ship had sailed far out to sea before anyone would see him. He went below after they had set sail and let the young Cub out to roam about the lower parts of the vessel freely.

Captain Striker sat in his cabin navigating their route. He had knowledge of exact positions of every piece of ice and or Glaciers that lay upon the Arctic Ocean. He had sailed the high seas as Captain of the Norway now for 5 years and had been a seaman for 17 years. By now, The Captain and his First Mate had many victorious battles under their belts. Neither one ever made a mistake when it came to engaging the Norway in battle against another ship. Many ships out gunned her but her ability to glide effortlessly through the choppiest of waters proved by far her to be the swiftest and most maneuverable sailing vessel on The High Seas. There were very few ships not subject to her crew pillaging and plundering of their spoils!

It was nightfall and Gautama went above to see Captain Striker as Brother followed. The Wolf stood on his hind legs and placed his paws on the Captains' shoulders joyfully looking directly into his eyes. He felt exceptionally privileged at the Wolfs' joy of seeing him. He laughed hard as the force of the Wolf plunged him to the floor with the loving mighty Angel landing right on top of him. Gautama explained that he named the great Wolf, "Brother" as he followed them all around just as a little brother would do. As the Captain laughed he replied, "What on Earth do you mean, like a little brother, more like a huge big brother, wouldn't you say?" The First Mate began to laugh aloud with Striker, as both men could not seem to keep their hands from petting the head of their life saving friend. Brother enjoyed and relished the love he received from these two hard men. The thought of separating company from these two humans made him sad. In the short time of their paths crossing, through their thoughts, he had developed a deep love for Micah Joshua Striker and Gautama Gautam. Brother felt the desperate need within their hearts and minds of his Angelic presence to within their lives. The two men had no clue to their absolute need for Daniel, Mr. Gorbachev, and Brother to within their lives. Soon these three would change the lives of the Captain and his First Mate and the Spirit of Norway forever and ever!

Mr. Gorbachev sent out thoughts to Brother to ask if all was well. Brother in turn sent out thoughts of wellbeing to his Warrior friend. Then Gorby placed thoughts to within the mind of Daniel. Suddenly Daniel felt a desire to go up top with Gorby to feel the ice cold upon their faces and to break the boredom they felt within the small cabin walls. He wondered how long it would take the passengers to realize their fate of going to the sellers block as slaves. For now, this was the very first night and everything seemed so peaceful so perfect.

It was already common knowledge among the crew and passengers throughout the entire ship of how the Great Wolf had battled 12 strong men to save the two masters of the Norway. Everyone was still talking about it. Even now on deck, they were saying that they would not want to see the huge animal upset or allow him to go hungry. He could surely devour in one single bite an entire person! Of course, they had no idea of his being an Angel Warrior who would not kill or even harm. Brother truly lived by the Rules of Engagement. And so did Mr. Gorbachev and Daniel!

CHAPTER 33

BROTHER-LEE-JUAN AND KATHRYN

When Brother met Kathy, he loved her and she loved him! Shortly after Brother followed Lee home, is the same timeframe in which Lee and Kathy first met at 5820 Willoughby Ave. He had met her through a girl named D. J. who Kathy had a fistfight with in order to establish the right of her to be with him! Thereafter, D. J. disappeared from the picture all together. Within 5 to 6 months of that event, Kathy accompanied Laurie Blade and left for Europe to see Timothy Leary in Austria. While on the flight from Austria and passing over the United Kingdom, the plane had a forced landing with a sudden unexpected emergency. Kathy had become violently ill. They hospitalized her in London.

While in that lonely hospital bed she wrote to Lee the most beautiful letter he had ever read! She spoke to him of Brother, as if she knew who he really was. As he looked upon the letter and read all of the hopes and all of the dreams of a beautiful young woman named Kathryn, he fell hopelessly in love! And love was in her heart! As Lee continued to read the heartfelt words written upon the pages of paper he held to within his hands from a woman he barely knew, he felt her love! It was storming, striking out over the oceans to caress him! He felt all of her hopes and he felt all of her beautiful dreams for him and for his life and it was good! For she had already fought for him the very day she met him! She sort of earned his love with that fact and the giving of herself, whole-heartedly, to within that wonderfully so very beautifully written Letter, from her heart, by her hand…to him!

From that moment and until her death in 1985, she was there for Lee even as he treated her very badly at times. By the time he realized how to treat women things were somehow different between them. Although he constantly begged forgiveness from our LORD for foul deeds against her, of which he felt terrible guilt beyond belief, Lee did not know how to fix it. I will not speak too much on her and Juan. They stand completely blameless in all matters of any concern for they never harmed or wanted to harm anyone, thing, or any being. Juan was a good Bro. And Lee loved them both very much. They were both Angels who knew not of whom they were before they passed. The Angels had not made them to say the Words, "JESUS IS LORD!" Moreover, they carried to within their veins the blood of the CHRIST! May GOD bless them both forever and ever and forever!

CHAPTER 34

THE SECRET FOUND

Striker and Gautama walked outside of the Captains' cabin and observed the Majestic Mountain Lion sitting at Daniels' side on the deck below. Brother quickly leaped over the rail and down, landing in front of Daniel and Gorby. He whined excitedly greeting the two with his huge bushy tail going back and forth faster and faster with pure love and the absolute joy of seeing them once again. At first, the Wolfs' reaction to Daniel and the Lion came as a surprise to both Captain Striker and Gautama. However, as they began to think about it they realized the fact that Daniel had paid in gold for three to sail to Italy. As they observed the three acting very happy together, they came to realize the Wolf as part of that equation.

The Captain and his First Mate went down on deck and stood next to the trio. The moon light danced and glistened to within the deep blue eyes of the Lion just as Striker and Gautama gazed into them. The Captain and Gautama realized the true identity of these beings at that exact moment. These same three had taken part in the epic battle that the Captain of another ship had told them about just days ago. According to that Captains' account, 14,000 hard fighting men had been defeated by such as these three. If there was the smallest bit of truth to his story then there was no sense in trying to restrain them now. The Masters of the Norway had seen firsthand the fighting abilities of the Wolf inside that small cabin near the village of Tiksi. He was truly a Warrior of supernatural capabilities. They would have to send word to this Mot Pruce in the hope that they would receive the rich rewards promised. They knew that as long as they kept quiet and stayed out to sea there was not much to worry about. Besides, the Wolf really loved and protected them. Surely he would not want to harm or see either one of them come to harm in any way, shape, or form.

Brother entered the thoughts of Striker and suddenly became

aware of what he was feeling. The Great Wolf realized that his beloved Captain now knew who they all were. Brother quickly stood up on his hind legs and once again laid his huge paws gently upon the Captains' massive shoulders. The wolf whined frantically as he licked the Captains' face with the great and overwhelming love that lived to within his heart. Striker felt the overwhelming waves of loving passion coming from within the Wolf and it made him smile. Talking to Brother but staring deeply to within the eyes of Daniel, he gently said, "Don't worry my good friend, it's alright, don't worry, I have come to love you too." Then the Captain quickly turned away and walked up the latter to his quarters with Gautama and Brother close behind.

Daniel and Mr. Gorbachev both realized what had just taken place but did not know exactly what to make of it. They realized that the Captain and his First Mate had found their secret. It would seem that they had simply accepted it, for now. However, what would tomorrow prove to bring forth?

CHAPTER 35

TOM ECURP AND JAMES ECURP

Now there came a moment in time whereas Lee's loving mother had a robot son named Tom Ecurp. His spirit was that of Mot Pruce! His father was James Ecurp and was a robot born of woman just as Tom was born of woman. All of their names come to evil in numbers. Tom was very evil and hated his brother Lee. Ever since he could walk and talk, he would try to get Lee in trouble with his stepfather. Moreover, later on in life when Lee appeared, as found by his father, he would try to have Lee put in prison for something he did not do. Nevertheless, Tom Ecurp could never possibly understand in any way shape or form anything that Lee would do in life. For anything having to do with GOD, Tom Ecurp just simply could not comprehend. His purpose in this life was to provide Satan with information on all things to within this life. Especially any information at all that concerned his brother Lee, the seven innocent children or the two Women Prophets of Cyron of whom were both here and reborn again upon this planet. However, Satan and the other evils from all the other planets could not verify the whereabouts or identities of the women Prophets or the children. They could not verify the whereabouts of Lee either and from 1970 until the mid-part of 1991, he seemed to have simply disappeared from off the face of the planet. And all of this would make Satan to laugh. For Satan had teamed up with other evils from other planets, Cyron being one of those planets.

With friends of family navigating, Prophecy dictates that a robot General in the KGB is responsible for the first parts of Lee's name as to coordinate eel cell operatives in the USA. Although they were the family's friends, they had a job to do and they would do it well! These things must come to pass with Lee being one of the chosen. These friends of family were spies and Lee was an unknowing spy tool for the Russians even before his birth. James

Ecurp, friend and Commander of Jack, had naval dentists implant the first electronic devices to within Lee's jaw at only 1½ years old! He was now a part of the Eel Cell operatives in the USA. Just the use of his hands and mouth would send signals through other beings without his realizing and without the victims realizing either! Moreover, no one taught Lee how to use any of this technology. Remember, they keep knowledge hidden from Lee, as he is a lamb. In addition, James Ecurp received many large ransoms for all of the implants to within Lee's jaws throughout his youth and growing up.

Lee's blood father and mother were both Hebrew descendants of the CHRIST but Lee was not aware of his bloodline. Now at that moment in space and time he had no knowledge of being a robot on the planet Cyron and changed into a human just before being hurdled to Earth. The robots of Cyron always thought that Samson was a human. When Lee writes this book, the robots will realize that Samson was a bot. According to Prophecy, once they find out he had once been a robot, most refuse to kill him in any life, ever. Many shall protect him and feel like they are a part of him even as he is human. For 28,000 years, the robots thought they were looking for a human for the rich and powerful on Cyron. Prophecy dictated that Samson would live 343 lives on Earth. They were always informed therefore automatically assumed that he was always human on Cyron as well. All robots everywhere were to believe that Samson had been a human all along and by no means was he ever a robot. Powers that be, made them to believe that they must hunt and murder Samson. This has to happen in any and every life that he would possess upon their mother planet, Cyron and or upon the Earth. This would cancel out any possibilities of failure for robots continuation throughout the cosmos.

Lee's blood father found him in Las Vegas via handgun paperwork at a police substation. He informed Lee, if something should happen to him, he had a very large inheritance coming and in that case, he should speak to his mother and her husband. Lee's father was truly a Holy man and Lee forever honors him! Now when Lee's father found him it became common knowledge of Lee's whereabouts to the whole family. That includes Tom Ecurp.

When Lee moved to Washington, he hid five pounds of gold at his stepfather's house, James Ecurp who was Tom Ecurp's father. It was the weekend and Christmas as well. So Lee could not put it in a safe deposit box at a bank until the following Tuesday. His stepfather allowed him to hide it at his home in Washington. For some unknown reason to Lee, his stepfather refused to let him back into the house to retrieve the gold. James called his son Tom saying that Lee hid 5 pounds of gold inside the house. Tom Ecurp immediately appeared at his father's door and the gold suddenly disappeared. Lee never saw the gold again! Now Lee realized that his stepfather was lonely for his son Tom to love him! Tom hated his father because that is who he is, was, and always will be as a man in Mot Pruce's Spirit. Lee came to think that his stepfather did not really believe he hid the gold, as he was always suspicious of people. He just used it to get his forever-evil son Tom to come home, home to him. He truly loved Tom. And Lee forgave his stepfather and his brother. He forgave his brother even when Tom gave what he thought was incriminating evidence against Lee to the authorities. Tom did much more against Lee as the spirit of Mot Pruce embodied to within Tom Ecurp was all by, for and of Satan!

After his beautiful father had died, Lee's large inheritance suddenly appeared laying to within a Trust in his brother's name by order of the same, Lee's KGB robot brother, Tom Ecurp. Tom had everyone convinced that he could make investments so as the whole family would benefit from all of Lee's money. He said, "After the investments payout I can happily give to Lee his due!"

Lee never received his large inheritance and the Love Blessings from his mother, fathers or grandparents! Tom murdered people for money and always made it look like old age! He had already taken large parts of Lee's inheritance, entered it on websites online, and collected it. What he could not collect he threw into off shore accounts. One morning after Tom Ecurp finalized a friend's murder, he asked Lee to come there to that place and pray over her before the cremation. When Lee showed up, he went to the other room with the dead friend and prayed for her. Then Tom took that opportunity and poisoned Lee to within his food with various chemicals to stop his heart and or ruin it for the rest of his life. He also put diseased blood cultures into the mix. These things are what robots do to humans on any planet! Robots do unspeakable things to all life on many worlds. For they take life out of any being with blood running through their life forms. It is the robots high. They have become accustomed to live for that purpose! Then Tom Ecurp, robot born of woman, found Laurie Blade for Satan, through Lee and Lee's daughter. Satan was happy!

CHAPTER 36

THE CHAINS OF TOPOC

At sea now, for just over a month, Daniel left Mr. Gorbachev below in his cabin for just a short while. He then decided to engage in a little exploring expedition as a duty to his GOD. He would go as far down below, deck by deck, as he could possibly go. He was seeking to find anything and or everything that would allow him to feel what slaves on board this vessel had felt either now or in the distant past. He traveled downward and downward until he arrived at the very bottom level, the bowels of the ship. At that point, there was an iron gate. He pushed, pulled, pushed, and pulled again and as he pushed and pulled for the third time, the gate opened. The last keeper of this gate had apparently shut it and then somehow simply forgot that he had not locked it. He probably pulled on it and when it did not open, he thought he had locked it. However, it had simply stuck when he had shut it, instead.

Daniel began to go down the steep stair-like ladder, raising the candle in his hand higher as he went. Suddenly his eyes laid upon a sight that he shall never ever forget for it engraved itself to within his brain. It was dried blood drippings all down the walls and on the walls were bloodied steel chains for the hands and wrists. Straight down the wall where the dried dripping blood met the deck, were more bloodied steel chains for the ankles. As he touched one of the steel blood stained wrist chains, he began to feel the pain, the terrible, terrible pain that had completely surrounded and devoured this poor slave. The hands and feet of the slave shackled and imprisoned within the small circumference of these bands of steel cuffs and chains. This slave's name was Topoc.

Using his Angel Powers he fell into a deep trance to feel what the LORD needed him to testify too. To witness to the truth of any slave he would feel upon that ship. He began to feel the most terrible things imaginable! He felt Topoc's loneliness and disparaged, oppressed life to within these blood drenched chains. Topoc knew he was to be sold once again. Daniel felt Topoc's anger, as he was to be forever separate from his own family in punishment for looking directly into the eyes of his master. Daniel felt the hope that had once lived to within the heart of Topoc and now was no more. The tears welled up to within his eyes as he began to cry. He cried, cried, cried, and cried and although he tried to, he just could not stop crying. All the terrible, terrible pain and all the different sorts of unimaginable horrific suffering that had been the life of Topoc, was just too overwhelming for Daniel to bear.

Daniel became lost to inside the perimeters of this pain and monstrous suffering to within the life force of a man, a slave called Topoc! He had to break the trance somehow, somehow, he had to come out of the pain, suffering, horrific, horrific, horrific! Daniel was on the edge of death! This pain, this suffering was killing him! Suddenly the LORD'S Light came upon Daniel and brought him back from his trance while loving and healing him at the same moment. The LORD spoke to within the mind of Daniel musically whispering,

"I love you Daniel. Thank you, I understand. This experience will serve us both well for all the years to come. I AM sorry you had to experience and live through, even for a short while, what Topoc had to survive and endure for ME through an entire lifetime!"

The LORD'S Light suddenly and gently disappeared. Daniel dared not to touch another slave chain as the suffering of the slaves was simply too overwhelming for an Angel in the flesh to comprehend and survive. He slowly began back up the ladder; he very slowly kept going up, deck by deck until he came to his cabin. He went inside and lay down onto his bunk. He could not stop crying at the mere thoughts of the life of the slave called Topoc!

Mr. Gorbachev's head plopped down upon Daniels' chest as he began to feel what Daniel was feeling. Tears rolled down the white fur on his face and once again, they cried together. Their sorrow, pain, so much sorrow, pain, Topoc's sorrow, and pain awoke Brother, in the Captains' cabin, as he felt their loneliness and their terrible despair and pain of the slave as well! In the Captains' cabin, Brother cried and howled and cried and howled. The three Angels cried together once again as they had when the beautiful Mountain Lioness Esther, had died. The young and strong Captain

Striker feeling the loneliness of his friend the Wolf began to weep as well. Gautama rushed up the ladder to the Captains' cabin to see why the Wolf would not stop howling. As he opened the cabin door, he too felt the pain, sorrow and loneliness of the Wolf, his Captain, Mr. Gorbachev, Daniel and the Slave called Topoc. He felt the deep, deep loneliness that had lived to within the heart of this man, Topoc. It was too much for him to bear and he too began to weep right along with his Captain and the Wolf.

They were beginning to, these two hardened men, were just beginning to change to within their very own hearts. They were beginning to feel, beginning to love once again! Could it be that after only a month out in the middle of the Sea, forty days of being so close to the three wondrous Angels, could it be that in just forty days their hearts were beginning an unhardened venture?

As Brother could not stop howling and howling, a member of the crew knocked on the Captains door. Striker yelled in a loud deep threatening voice, "Go…away!" The seaman listened at the cabin door and yelled back saying, "Is everything alright Captain?" The Captain answered even more loudly and in a very angry tone, "Goooooooooooo awayyyyyyy!" The seaman scurried away but thought he had heard someone weeping inside the cabin. The word spread around the crew that the Captain and his First Mate were going soft and that perhaps it was time for a change of Masters of the Norway! The crew had already wondered why the passengers escaped going below, by force, to stay in the slaves section, the bowels of the Norway.

Gautama had stayed in his Captains' cabin all night. He did not want any of the crew to see his swollen cried out eyes. As he left the cabin early the next morning, no one dared to ask what had transpired the night before inside the cabin of Captain Striker. However, a day later, one of the crew members got up enough courage to ask Gautama, why are the passengers still free to roam the ship? Gautama moved up close to the sailor and quietly said, "No one wants off this vessel until well after we round the Straits of Gibraltar, into the Mediterranean Sea and off the coast of France, if you must know." His words to the sailor spread quickly among the crew. The tension seemed to ease up for the time being. The Captain remained to within his cabin along with the Wolf for the following two days.

After two days of sailing the Norway without Captain Striker,

Gautama knocked on his cabin door. "Come," the Captain replied sharply. Upon entering the cabin, Brother jumped up on his hind legs. He whined and whined while laying his paws gently upon Gautama's shoulders not to knock him down and licked his face. He stood a full head taller than the First Mate. Gautama greeted his friend by giving him a long hug and said, "I love and missed you too my life saving friend." Then he looked at the Captain and before he could utter a word, Striker stood up from his sitting position. With great authority he exclaimed, "Yes, I know my old friend, let's let this scurvy crew know that I am still the Captain of this man's pirate ship!" "Aye, Aye, Captain Sir," Gautama loudly yelled out for all the crew to hear! Captain Striker walked out of his cabin and stood by the rail on his upper deck, looking out at the entire crew. After a long moment, he began to yell out orders. "I want this man's vessel scrubbed from bow to stern, from the very tip of her mast right down to her very bowels! You two, standing there, swab the decks!" Then he yelled out, "I want the smallest of a pin hole in each and every one of these sails to be mended by tonight or there will be hell to pay!"

That afternoon the Captain walked down to the lower decks and studied each sailor's job with pure scrutinizing examinations as he yelled out more orders and dissatisfaction of jobs done. Each and every passenger on board the Norway decided to take leave and stay out from under the view and commands of their Captain. Even Brother decided to stay sitting behind Gautama and out of the path of Striker for a while. Each time the Captain would yell out another command he would whine and a nervous look would come across his fury face. At one point Striker observed the Wolfs reactions to his commands and walked right up to pet him as he said, "It's alright boy, I'm not referring to you, it's alright my friend." Brother gave a whine of recognition and a wag of his huge bushy tail as he rubbed up against his beloved Captain Striker.

CHAPTER 37

THE NORWAY IN BATTLE

It was a bitter cold climate, especially while idle in the middle of the Arctic Ocean. After months at sea with no winds to fill the sails but no mishaps, a slow chain of events would begin to evolve over the next many months that would change history to within our LORD'S vast Kingdoms! Finally, the wind gathered and blew once again. The Mystical Spirit continued and explained to the children the visions upon and to within the massively enormous cave walls as the visions would appear!

"Ships ahoy, Captain!" The lookout shouted from the crow's nest, high on top the main mast. "Looks like military battle ships flying the English flag Captain." Captain Striker calmly replied, "Gautama, Man all cannons, all hands at their battle stations." Gautama shouted out the commands as each crewmember readied himself for battle on the High Seas! He shouted out to passengers on deck, "To your cabins and stay until further notice, please." He yelled loudly up to the lookout, "How many ships, ya blasted ingrate?" "Two Sir, sorry sir," the observer nervously shouted back down to Gautama.

The two English Battle Ships were sailing with full sails and were coming up fast upon the Norway. "Turnabout, Full Sails Mr. Gautama, we'll simply out run these English Flag Flying garbage scows! However, if they are not very, very careful I'll turn about and give them a real old-fashioned Pirate thrashing, eh, Mr. Gautama?" The First Mate answered, "Aye, aye, Captain" and shouted back out the orders to the crew. The Norway had already maneuvered and began to put distance between her and the English ships. She was the fastest sailing medium sized battle ship on the High Seas.

In the 50 and some odd years of her sailing as a Pirate Ship, She was never out maneuvered, caught, or outgunned. This was true for any Battle vessel that Her Captain had ever decided to engage in a chase, combat or otherwise. Nations had been hunting down the Norway for over 50 years, never even coming close to bringing her to Justice. There was not a ship in any Navy that existed that could catch her, beat her down, or out maneuver her. This was especially true with Captain Striker at the Helm. He was truly a master of his trade, a sorcerer if you will in the art of being a Captain of a Sea Warring Vessel such as the Norway.

Captain Striker had already charted a course that would keep them clear of large icebergs. On a Pirate Ship, the lookout is always at his station in the crow's nest no matter what, around the clock. At night without a full moon lit sky to navigate by, the Captain would have the large sails lowered to slow the Norway down.

As the Norway approached several small landmasses just between the Laptev Sea and the Kara Sea, the lookout shouted down, "Mr. Gautama, One of the battle ships has changed course. Looks like its sailing towards the coast of Russia. The other ship has lowered its sails and is slowing down." They apparently gave up the chase as the Norway steadily out sailed them both. Captain Striker ordered the Norway to sail behind one of the unnamed land chunks and anchor. These were unique land chunks. Deep water surrounded most of these small islands. This particular small piece of land mass had straight up high rock cliffs rising up erect directly from the water line.

The Norway could easily hide behind the cliffs in a tiny bay like area. Captain Striker anchored in this bay for a safe haven many times in the past. If an enemy Ship should sail by that small cove, it would be too late by the time they would see the Norway. In this case the English would have only 50 yards to await a 13 cannon blast salute, broadside! Captain Striker would lay waiting for the ship that still sailed slowly towards his beloved Norway. He sent two crewmembers to shore. They were to spy on the ship and signal the Norway, as the English ship would approach their position.

The passengers began to ask questions as Striker ordered them to stay below to within their cabins until further notice. Since the incidence in his cabin with the Wolf, Captain Striker could not bring himself to chain the passengers in the bowels of the Norway.

Out of the 12 passengers, there were eight women of who would bring more gold than the men would. Besides, they were no threat to the ship; none of the passengers could threaten the

Norway. Captain Striker was beginning to develop a conscience! He did not realize that the three Angels of Light were all concentrating on both the minds and the hearts of the two Masters of the Norway, for GOD had asked them to do so.

It was late afternoon as the English Battle Ship began slowly approaching the Norway's position. One of the men on shore signaled the Norway. Captain Striker ordered the sails up and all hands to battle stations. All 28 cannons manned and readied for the battle against the unsuspecting English Battle Ship. The signal given by the sailor told the Captain that the English Ship would pass very close to their position. They were sailing around the small land mass and past the Norway as she lay in the cove. As the Ship slowly rounded the land mass and right straight in front of his Ship, Captain Striker gave the command to fire all 13 cannons along her broadside. The English Ship took all 13 cannon balls! Five were at her water line; one hit and took the main mast down. Seven cannon balls hit the Battle Cruiser broadside beginning at the bow and ending at her stern.

As she was taking in water, Striker ordered the Norway alongside the mortally crippled Battle Ship. The Pirates would now do hand-to-hand combat with the survivors of the English Ship and pillage her wealth before she sank to the bottom of the Sea! Both decks of the mighty Battle Ships became bloody battlefields! The English ship was larger than the Norway and therefore had more men. The Angels once again found themselves protecting more people in yet one more battle.

Mr. Gorbachev leaped into action as a sailor reeled his sword from behind Captain Striker to relieve him of his head. Gautama desperately tried to get to his Captain and friend but had to fight for his life as three Sailors reeled their swords on him. Within a blink of an eye, Gorby had tackled and subdued Striker's attackers. Brother had already disoriented and pounced upon Gautama's attackers with such brute force that it had hurdled all of them across the ship and into the sea. The pirates soon took complete control of the battle as the crippled English ship began to sink into the sea. The pirates took as much as they could from the English gunboat before she could go completely under. Captain Striker allowed his men to take all things of any value from the Sailors who were still alive on board the English Ship. He then ordered the survivors rowed to the shore and left for the other English gunboat to pick up.

The passengers on board the Norway were frightened to say the very least. They had been through a bloody battle and knew by now; they were on board a pirate ship. The passengers quickly appointed Daniel as their spokesman to ask what was to become of them. As Daniel asked Striker, both men stared deep to within each other's eyes, not as enemies but as equals. Suddenly the Captain's eyes shifted to the passengers and he stared at all of their dismayed twisted faces for a long while before he would answer. Mr. Gorbachev and Brother, each on either side of Striker, groaned deep throaty sounds as they rubbed up close against his body with great love. Striker felt the full love and concern of both animals. As he looked at the great Lion with the fur white as the purest snow and deep blue eyes that penetrated and seemed to talk, he slowly answered, "As of this moment I do not know that I can honestly say." Then he walked up the stairs like ladder and on into his cabin. Gautama quickly followed and knocked on Strikers cabin door. "Come," Striker, replied knowing that it was his first mate. Before Gautama could speak, Striker spoke, "I know your concerns of the crew's loyalty at this point in time my old friend."

As Daniel looked upon the wolf and the lion, they climbed up the ladder one behind the other and groaned loudly as they scratched at Striker's cabin door. The crew looked on as well as all they could think about was how much gold the passengers would bring in Syria. The Captain and Gautama walked out onto the balcony to join the Lion and the Wolf. One of the sailors yelled, "Ever since that Wolf, Lion and man Daniel came aboard this ship we have seen a change in our Captain that I for one, hate!" Suddenly Mr. Gorbachev gave out a deep loud roar as the Wolf looked on growling at the crew and ready to do battle. The crew readied for battle as well drawing swords and pistols from their belts. Daniel and the Animal Angels began to stalk their enemy. Striker yelled back down to his crew saying, "No one on this ship kills unless I say to do so. The first man to reel a sword or fires his pistol shall answer to my pistol and my Sword. Is that well understood or would someone care to walk the plank blind folded, bound, and gagged by my order?" The entire crew cried out in reply, "Aye, Aye, Captain!" The Three Angel Warriors relaxed and were grateful not to have to do battle again so soon after the last battle.

That night Daniel went to bed all alone and did not have the comfort of his friends. Once again, as he slept, he had the terrible nightmares of a man dragging a cross and people spitting upon him and kicking him and Roman Centurions whipping and mocking the man up until they crucify him! And as usual, he woke himself up screaming out the question, "Am I the one? Am I the one? Am I the onnnnnnne?" The tears flowed down his face and the guilt he felt as he awoke was as always, overwhelming. Upon awakening, he began to sing aloud his favorite prayers from Cyron. He sang the prayers, in the Greek, once again. Afterwards, he sang those same prayers to within the Angelic Hebrew once again and in silence.

**"THE LORD HOVERS TO WITHIN MY HEART
LIKE A GREAT BIRD OF PREY OVER THE FIELD
RELENTLESS IN PURSUIT FOR THE PRIZE AND
BEAUTIFUL TO WITHIN HIS FLIGHT
TO DO SO   AMEN**

**FOR NOW WE ARE TO REMAIN THE PREY OF ALL
WHOM ACT AGAINST US OH BEAST BUT BEHOLD
WE SHALL BE THE TEETH OF THE LION HIM OF
WHICH WAS ONCE THE LAMB AND OF WHO
SHALL RETURN SOON VERY SOON   AMEN"**

The loneliness Daniel felt without at least one of his friends was overwhelming. He began to pray for all things and beings and all creations throughout space and time for his GOD! And it all became good and was well for him.

CHAPTER 38

ANGELS IN DREAMS

The Captain related to his First Mate as he gazed out across the Vast Oceans Horizon, "This is not the first time, probably will not be the last time that we have problems with the crew, eh Mr. Gautama?" Gautama answered, "Yes Captain." The Captain and First Mate retreated into the Captain's cabin with Gorby and Brother right behind them. Daniel and the rest of the passengers went to their cabins as well. They dared not to talk even among each other until a better moment in time as the crew was in a dangerous mood.

The mood to within the Captain's cabin was a solemn one indeed, as the two animals response to quickly saving their lives even to within the heat of a bloody battle moved both men! Both men decided that first thing in the morning they would take Mr. Gorbachev and Brother down below and have a much-needed talk with Daniel. They had many questions to ask about the two beings that seemed to be in the process of changing the hearts of two hardened Pirates! Changing their hearts away from the profession they had engaged in and bending it instead towards their GOD!

As Gautama bid the Captain goodnight and went below to his cabin the Wolf followed and stayed with him. He lay by his side touching the First Mate all night long. Mr. Gorbachev would not leave the Captain even as the door was open for him to do so if he desired. Once again, his heart filled with great love as this great Warrior purred and purred while lying next to him, his huge white paw settling to within the palm of Strikers' hand. Striker looked upon the majestic Lion with unwavering respect and deep thought. "This brave warrior is holding my hand as though I was a small child and he was my protector!" As he continued to think on these matters, he fell into a much-needed restful sleep.

During the night, both Animal Angels entered to within the

dreams of the Captain and his First Mate as well. As Captain Micah Joshua Striker slept soundly, the two Majestic Warriors appeared and spoke to him to within his dreams. As they spoke, he listened in complete awe. One Warrior would speak and explain and then the other would speak and explain in even more detail. Mr. Gorbachev and Brother explained the LORD'S demands to Gautama and their beloved Captain. They explained that he was to become a Great non-violent Muslim Leader. He would change many lives to non-violence and would please our LORD GOD in the Heavens. After The Warriors explained these wondrous things to Striker, they left his dreams and he slept soundly all night long. He normally tossed, turned and had nightmares, waking himself up many times during the night. Nevertheless, he simply did not awake this night.

The two Great Angels appeared and spoke to within Gautama's dreams at the very same moment they appeared and spoke to within Captain Striker's as well! As one would speak and then the other, he too listened in great awe as they explained in great detail the LORD'S demands of him. They explained that he had a great responsibility to GOD! The LORD demanded that he use the love buried deep to within his heart, for and to do good at all times in of everything he does. They explained the LORD'S awareness of Gautama possessing Divine Wisdom and Virtue. Many years ago, these and many more virtues had embodied him as a Buddhist Priest. These GODLY things still existed to within his heart, throughout his entire soul, spirit and very being, even as his mind had forgotten.

The mind sometimes forgets what the heart cannot. These loving, heart felt things must somehow pass on to all of whom shall want and thirst for them. The Warriors went on to explain that not just Christians and Hebrews are possible heirs to the Heavens Gates. Those standing before JESUS of who has a pure loving heart. In other words, anyone that is forgiving and loving towards all others and the MAKER of all that is, was or ever shall be, shall be possible heirs to the Heavens Gates and the Book of Life! They may not have the same rank in Heaven as true believers in the CHRIST but they are possible heirs. JESUS will decide.

After they explained these things and much more to Gautama, the Warriors left his dreams as suddenly as they had entered. Gautama slept soundly throughout all the night with no disturbances what so ever. This night he slept as sound as if he were a small child with love and trust living to within his heart.

As Gautama awoke the next morning, he looked lovingly upon the Wolf of who still slept close to his side. His great paw lay gently across the First Mates heart all night long. He slowly reached out his hand and touched the Wolf's head petting him with the great love and trust that still lived deep to within his heart. He thought of his dream as a great but simple sign of what might be to within his own life and that of his lifelong friend, Micah Joshua Striker. Both men had the same identical dream. The LORD had done this to make them think and realize the truth, that they may fulfill their destinies in absolute completion! Gautama slowly rose up from his bed and began a long lazy yawn as he stretched. He walked over to the cabin door and opened it. There was a nice cool breeze coming across the deck filling him with the fresh sea scent as he began to think. Gautama Gautam began to long for something more than just the lonely murderous life of a pirate at sea. And he wanted much more for his precious Captain Striker as well. He truly loved this young man Captain of the Norway of whom he had known in life's struggle since the Captain's early childhood.

When Striker awoke early the next morning, the great paw of the Lion was still covering the entire palm of his hand. He slowly closed his hand around the huge paw feeling his own lonely heart bursting with love and the absolute desire to change his life towards the good of GOD! He too, felt as Gautama felt, that the dream was a sign to what should be to within his own future and the future of Gautama as well. He began to wonder if either one of them had the courage to embrace it. If they had the courage to embrace this Brave New World of feelings of love and of trust, he knew that it would have to be with everything, with all that they are. Their lives had been truly gruesome and to change old habits could be very difficult not to mention life threatening on board this ship, indeed. Striker realized it was now time to get Gautama and the two animals, go below to Daniel's cabin, and confront him with some very important questions.

Once again, Daniel took advantage of his time alone to examine the Lineage Book and its heavenly writings. There was story after beautiful story. It explained in explicit detail all the adventures of each and every guardian's life that controlled and kept the Ancient Holy and Sacred Artifacts throughout the cosmos.

It is a history to within a history, if you will. For each author wrote of historic happenings throughout the cosmos as well.

Then Daniel came upon the writings of his Hebrew Blood Father to within the Holy Lineage Book. And as he read the history of his father protecting these beautiful and Holy Artifacts he cried, he cried tears of joy of the enabling from GOD that he should know his father even that he had never known him. As he read, he began to know his father spiritually and physically.

Each and every author to within this book was deeply spiritual and lovers and believers of the CHRIST even that they were Hebrew! Almost all of the protectors and authors to within the Holy and Sacred Artifacts were Hebrew. All of the Words to within this Lineage Book are written by GOD but were all formed by and from within the Hearts of all the Protectors of these Ancient Artifacts. What the LORD observed to within each of their Hearts while entrusting the Artifacts to them is what appears upon the pages of gold after their name to within the Lineage Book. So that the Words written are perfect and not mistaken in any way shape or form because it is the LORD that manifests them as HE burns them to upon the golden pages of this beautiful Lineage Book. Remember, all that burns into and upon the golden pages directly relate to what lives to within the protector's Heart. Also remember that when the LORD Blest the Pen, both the Compass and Lineage Book were included to within those spoken blessings as well! For they occupy the same space in time and are as one in existence!

Therefore, it came to pass that as Daniel continued to read what his Holy Father's Heart possessed, it spoke of the great love the protector had in his heart for his child yet to be. On the event of his birth, he read even more of the great love his father had for him. And the love in Daniel's heart grew a thousand fold for the LORD who allowed him to know the love his father's heart possessed for him even that Daniel never knew him. Now, he did know his father!

BLESSED BE THE HOLY SACRED NAME OF THE LORD!

CHAPTER 39

THE DECISION

Captain Striker opened his cabin door and walked out onto the upper deck with the Lion following close on his heels. It was amazing looking out across the early morning water, sun, and sky. This morning was especially bright with no clouds in view whatsoever. He went to the rail and called down to his First Mate on the main deck. "Gautama, meet me down below in five minutes at the cabin of Daniel!" Gautama immediately answered, "Aye, aye, Captain." Striker turned, went back into his cabin, and splashed water from a bowl onto his face.

The Majestic Mountain Lion waited just outside the door as a deep low growl rumbled out of his throat. He was looking at two sailors grumbling about what they had heard the Captain say to Gautama. Apparently, it did not agree with either one of them. As the two looked up at the Lion and suddenly realized he was growling at them they quickly turned away and went back to their duties on the ship. The sailors on the Norway had grown somewhat afraid of the two animals. The tale of the epic battle of fourteen thousand against eight had put great fear in and among the whole crew. The two animals appeared on the Norway about the same time the Captain of another ship warned Captain Striker about the fugitives. 14,000 men perished in that epic battle and it was said to be the will of GOD! HIS Angels in battle are to prevail no matter what the odds! They say that this GOD is in fact the GOD of Abraham Isaac and Jacob!

The Captain walked down the stairs like ladder and out onto the main deck. Mr. Gorbachev leaped up over the railing and down onto the deck below, landing right in front of him. He continued to walk in front of Striker all the way down below to Daniel's cabin. The Great Lion made sure no one interfered as they did so. Gautama was already waiting outside Daniel's cabin door and

Brother sat, leaning up against him. The Captain and his First Mate looked deeply into each other's eyes for a very long few moments. The Captain turned and knocked loudly on the door. Hearing the loud knock the other passengers on that deck cracked their doors slightly open in order to see or hear what was going on. Gautama shouted out, "Close your doors and stay to within your cabins please."

As Daniel slowly opened his door, the Captain, Gautama, Brother and Mr. Gorbachev all walked right in past him and into the center of his cabin. Gorby and Brother both turned, rose up on their hind legs and together gently put their paws upon Daniel's massive chest, balancing themselves carefully, not to knock their friend to the cabin floor. Their greetings brought a huge smile to Daniel's face as he asked, "To what do I owe this honor of the presence of your company, Captain?" Striker stood erect and very slowly turned looking completely around the room, first at Gautama, then Brother, Mr. Gorbachev and finally Daniel. He stared for a long, long while deep to within the eyes of Daniel before he would answer his question with a few more questions of his own. "Who are the three of you? Better yet what are the three of you? I know that you are the same three that with the help of a Great Eagle, a Mountain Lioness, another Man, a Cat and a Mouse, beat down a 14,000-man army. Who or what the devil are all of you, Daniel?" The Captain demanded an answer as he continued to stare deeply into and carefully study the eyes of Daniel. "I do not know what you would have me say, Captain," Daniel replied as he stared right back into the dark brown eyes of Captain Striker. The Captain quickly replied, "Tell me the truth man, who or what the hell are you, all three of you?" Continuing to stare back into the eyes of Micah Joshua Striker, Daniel took a long deep breath and blew it out and then he answered. "We are what we are! We are many things but Warriors for our LORD Thy GOD is first and always foremost!" Striker was struggling to understand the answer as he asked, "Why do these animals act as though they love me and Mr. Gautama? Why have they both saved our lives again and again?" With much concern Daniel answered, "Perhaps they see more in your hearts than what you realize exists there." The Captain added, "These two wondrous beings came to within my dreams last night! Now I seem not to be myself as I feel brand new!" Gautama added, "I too experienced these majestic beings coming into my dreams last night and like my friend and Captain, I too feel like someone new, brand-new. Why? Why?" Both men asked and pleaded with Daniel for the truth. Daniel slowly replied in truth as always. "They have come to within my dreams and like you they have saved my life as well! I cannot say any more than what I have told you. Perhaps they have looked deep into your hearts and liked what they have seen. This one has changed my life for the better forever." Daniel said this as he petted Mr. Gorbachev and looked lovingly upon him.

Striker, feeling more relaxed went on saying, "I have heard of Legends about animals such as these. Legend has it that they are Angels of GOD of whom, all have supernatural powers of the mind and of the body. They say that the Angels can speak any language but do not speak to any man by order of GOD. I had always thought that it was all legend, at least until now. These two spoke to me in my dream about what I am to do with my life and what my friend is to do with his life as well. Are all of you Angels?" The Captain asked this while looking upon the Animal Warriors with great concern and love from within his heart.

Daniel began to cautiously answer, "I will tell you what I am and what I believe they are but before I do, you must promise me that you will not ever speak this to any man. Promise me!" Both the Captain and First Mate promised, "I shall not speak any word of this to no man, ever!" Daniel continued and began to explain, "There came a moment in time whereas I saw GODS hand in the form of HIS Living Light with Mr. Gorbachev as he was at the side of my dying brother. I saw the same hand of GOD'S *Living Light* again as the others and I were all around the dying Mountain Lioness, Esther, at the epic battle you had spoken about. The answer is yes! I believe that they are Angel Warriors in the flesh as I am as well! I am here and I believe they are here to be witnesses to the End of Days for our Living GOD! I tell you this because they have come to you in your dreams. I believe that they did this because you have important tasks to perform for our GOD. But I do not believe they can really speak even though they have done so in our dreams."

As Daniel said these things, both men fell to their knees before him and begged his forgiveness. Daniel quickly replied saying, "Please do not be on your knees to me for I am only an Angel of Light in the flesh. I am not the LORD so there is nothing that you have done or could do that I could or would render forgiveness or not." When Daniel said this both men rose up and looked upon the three of them in complete awe for they knew that Daniel spoke the truth. Daniel decided to ask, "What will you do with the passengers on board the Norway?" Striker answered back, "We will not sell them as slaves. We now know this is no longer who we are as men. However, we will not let our crew know of this as of yet because we would have a mutiny on our hands if we did. We will have to give this careful consideration before we act out or say anything to the crew." As the Captain spoke these words, Gautama agreed.

Striker told Daniel that there would be plenty of time to talk again but as for now, they would have to get back to running the Norway. Both men hugged Daniel one after the other and walked out of his cabin and up to the main deck. The Wolf followed. The Wolf knew that for now he would closely guard both the Captain and his First Mate until all was well with the crew.

That night Gautama and the Captain, realizing that both had the exact same dream the night before, agreed that they would do exactly what they had been told to do within their dreams. And they would do this together as lifelong friends! As Gautama Gautam looked lovingly upon his Captain he said, "You followed me when you were a child, now I shall follow you as a grown man, my oldest dear friend."

As the Norway sailed on the high Seas, there was much for the two men to look forward to in life. The Holy Ghost was now to within their Hearts. Love, Hope, Faith, Honor, Trust, Truth, and Life were now the prevailing wage of those on board the Norway.

The following months were slow sailing as the winds were low and sometimes nonexistent once again. However soon they would be approaching the coast of Spain patrolled by Spanish fleets. The Norway raised the Spanish flag as both Gautama and Striker spoke the language fluently.

Daniel desired high hopes for these two men and felt great love for them both as he did all beings. Below in his cabin and alone with Mr. Gorbachev he sang aloud two prayers of Cyron that his beloved Priest upon that planet wrote and often sang to whoever would be to within hearing distance. These prayers became very popular with the people of Cyron as the robots became such bloodthirsty monsters throughout the centuries and herded them like cattle for slaughter. His beloved High Priestess also loved these two prayers as she sang them quite often, especially at the Temple.

"THE LORD HOVERS TO WITHIN MY HEART
LIKE A GREAT BIRD OF PREY OVER THE FIELD
RELENTLESS IN PURSUIT FOR THE PRIZE AND
BEAUTIFUL TO WITHIN HIS FLIGHT
TO DO SO   AMEN

FOR NOW WE ARE TO REMAIN THE PREY OF ALL
WHOM ACT AGAINST US OH BEAST BUT BEHOLD
WE SHALL BE THE TEETH OF THE LION HIM OF
WHICH WAS ONCE THE LAMB AND OF WHO
SHALL RETURN SOON VERY SOON   AMEN"

And when he finished singing two Prayers of Cyron in the Greek, he prayed for all things and beings and all creations throughout space and time for his GOD as well. These kinds of prayers are what all Angels in the flesh or in the spirit only as well will sing to within their prayers to our LORD. And HE welcomes and honors these prayers.

CHAPTER 40

THE VOW

Captain Striker had no real fears of the Spanish Galleons, as he possessed a document signed by a certain Spanish General that gave his beautiful Norway a free passage. An old friend of Striker and as long as he paid the General in gold the Norway would be allowed free passage on any ocean, sea, or waterway in the world. That is to say, Striker's ship has free passage by any ship flying a Spanish flag on any ocean, sea, or waterway in the world. Without this protection, a Captain would fire cannons unless he could outrun the Spanish Ship. Striker had the Spanish flag and proper documents if requested by a Spanish Authority. This truth proved to be an asset to Striker many times over. That fact would be yet another adventurous story or stories to say the least. Well, getting back to our original story.

The Norway sailed and navigated over 6000 miles through some most treacherous waters on the globe. The nation of Italy was about 18 days away. If the winds died down it would be longer. News of being only three weeks away from arriving at an Italian port had the Angels on board the Norway extremely excited and happy. They could hardly wait to see their family of friends, James, Timothy, and James Pruce.

Many years passed since the Captain went below to the very bowels of the Norway, where slaves stood chained until sold at auction. He decided it was time to come face to face with what he had been a large part of for the past 22 years of his life. He was 5 years old when Gautama brought him aboard the sea going ship, the Spirit of Norway. In just weeks, he would probably leave his beloved Norway. He would miss the Ship but not the way of life, he had grown use to on board her. He would go below now to realize another reason why he and his friend must start new lives and begin to build people up not tear them down!

As the Captain of the Norway began to walk down deck by deck the wolf began to whine and grumble out low while following closely. Finally, they reached the gate. The lonely gate where just on the other side is the slaves' part of the ship! The part of the ship that somehow, for some strange dark but unknown reason remained hidden and almost forgotten behind its thick blood soaked rusty bars. Striker was surprised to see his First Mate already inside sitting with his hands covering his face and crying. "What have I done? Oh My Captain, What have I done? What have I done?" Gautama kept saying those words, repeatedly over, and over again. Micah Joshua Striker sat down close to his oldest friend in life and spoke to him softly, "No, no my old friend, what have we done? It is not all your fault. Both of our souls were lost and wounded and now our souls are healed and found!" Brother began to yelp aloud as if to agree and laid his head upon Gautama's lap! He whined a crying like sound along with Gautama Gautam.

Micah Joshua Striker began to weep with his friends as he said, "Come, we must be strong and do what we can to right these terrible wrongs of which we have sown. We shall ask the MAKER of all that is, was and ever shall be to forgive us and to know that we shall never again follow the path of evil. This I do vow here and at this moment and always!" "Yes Micah, you are right! I too vow the same! I further vow to become the Priest that I once was. I shall use the Buddhist Priest training of my youth and become a Priest for the Hebrews GOD! The GOD of Abraham, Isaac and Jacob! I shall once again use all my experiences in this life to do good, always!" The two lifelong friends made these vows and the wolf began to howl and lick the Captains face. Both men put their hands upon him and smiled looking deep into each other's eyes.

Both men slowly walked up to the Captain's cabin. Striker poured two glasses of wine to seal their vows to the MAKER of all that is, was and ever shall be. Brother sat and looked upon the two broad shouldered men as they sipped the wine. As both men looked upon one of the faces that helped change their lives forever, Striker replied, "To the Angels!" Gautama added, "To the Angels. Glory be to GOD!"

CHAPTER 41

MUTINY ON THE NORWAY

The Captain and Gautama opened the cabin door to walk out onto the top deck. As they leaned on the railing, they were jumped from behind by, ten sailors! One of the sailors threw a net over the wolf. Brother sent out thoughts to his friend Mr. Gorbachev as he disoriented all ten. Mr. Gorbachev quickly opened Daniel's cabin door with a thought and in a blink of an eye was upon the top deck. Daniel, realizing something terrible was happening, followed the great Lion in haste. As he ran upwards to the top deck sailors were there to block his path with weapons drawn! Daniel used his supernatural strength and speed bouncing man after man off the walls and into a daze. As he arrived to the top deck, he found the sailors already subdued and disoriented. Captain Striker had one sailor by the throat with his sword drawn and readied to plunge through him. Gautama spoke, "Micah, our sacred promise!" Striker quickly replied, "Yes, our sacred promise, don't worry my old friend, this being our first test of free will, eh? I'll not harm a hair on his head. I'll not harm these who try to perform mutiny on board my ship." The Captain withdrew his sword and let the sailor go as he spoke loudly to the crew, "Choose a spokesman, and I'll address the complaints that of which have caused this mutiny on board the Norway." A sailor stood up and spoke, "You have become a weak man Captain. We now come to realize that to serve you and your first mate is no longer profitable on board this ship." The Captain stood and starred at the crew. After a few moments, he walked over to Gautama and whispered to him for a couple of minutes. Gautama quickly whispered back. Striker turned to the crew that had tried to kill their masters and take over the Norway by force and spoke, "You have two choices, you may leave this ship now, or after we deliver each passenger on board to their proper destinations." The whole crew began to shout in complete anger!

Striker raised both hands into the air and shouted back, "Hear me out, hear me out!" The crew began to quiet down, letting the Captain speak. "Gautama and I have decided that the whole crew shall receive equal shares of all the gold that we have accumulated within the past twenty-two years on board this, our home, the Norway." The crew began to cheer. The Captain continued, "You all will however, sail with us from port to port delivering each and every passenger to their destinations." The crew went crazy cheering Captain Micah Joshua Striker and Gautama Gautam. This was very agreeable to everyone. Striker shouted at the crew, "It is done! I will see nor hear no more anger in this crew for the sake of making these passengers slaves. Is that understood?" The whole crew shouted and cheered their Captain as they all agreed. "Aye, aye, Captain sir!" The passengers were all out on deck listening and began cheering as well. They were all dumbfounded at the fact that this Captain and First Mate would actually buy their freedom from slavery and they had not yet been a slave!

The spokesperson for the crew suddenly screamed at the Captain complaining about not receiving the ransom that Mot Pruce would pay for the three warriors, Daniel, the wolf and the lion. The men all screamed as well agreeing with their spokesperson. The Captain became very angry that the crew would actually want even more than what had already been agreed to. He addressed the crew again, "You do not know for certain that these are in fact some of the warriors that participated in the Epic battle of which we have all heard about. So I say this, if there be any man here not happy with the wealth we have offered each and every one of you then you shall be cast off my ship immediately! After all, each one of you shall be a wealthy man. Like any Governor of any Providence of any nation! That is how wealthy you shall be! Either you have agreed to all or you have agreed to nothing! What say you?" After mumbling to one another for a few moments the crew all shouted together, "Agreed!" Once again the Captain Shouted, "For the last time I say to you all, it is done!" Once again, the crew shouted back at the Captain, "Aye, aye, Captain Sir!" As the crew now realized exactly how wealthy each one of them will be, they were all extremely happy indeed.

The Norway sailed a northeasterly direction from off the coast of Spain towards France. Five Spanish Galleon Warships were sailing Southwest on an interception course towards her!

CHAPTER 42

FREE PASSAGE

Sailing past the Balearic Islands the Norway encountered three more Spanish Galleons as they appeared out of nowhere and sailing towards her rear. For all intents and purposes the Norway was trapped in-between eight Warships with no way out. On top of the main mast, the watchman shouted down to the Captain, "It's the Spanish General and his escorts Sir." A broad smile came across Strikers face as he marched up to his cabin. He opened a secret compartment on the wall and brought out five fifty pound bars of pure gold. Gautama entered the cabin and together they took the bars and loaded them onto a waiting rowboat. Brother was close on their heels as Striker turned quickly and called out to Daniel. "Keep the wolf close to you for we cannot take him with us." Brother sat down and gave out a low grown. Daniel approached the great wolf and stood at his side.

Captain Striker and his First Mate cast off and rowed out to meet the Generals Command Ship. General Juan Fernandez Valencia welcomed his two old friends aboard the Galleon. He walked with them up to his cabin where a feast fit for a King had been prepared and laid out on a very large dining table. Spanish sailors brought up the bars of gold and placed them on the Generals bed.

The three adventurous souls of who had befriended one another some twenty years past finished their Kingly meals with a glass of wine and a toast of friendship. The General looked at his two friends and replied, "I always look forward to our little rendezvous." Then he proposed a toast, "To our future propositions of prosperity and alliances." The Captain of the Spirit of Norway decided to be brutally honest with his old friend, "Yes General, about our future propositions of prosperity and alliances. We have decided, Gautama and I that the stomach one must have for such ventures of which we have in the past participated thereof is in fact no longer something that we possess. I sincerely hope for your best wishes and your gracious understanding. As you may have already realized, we have long ago, grown to love and trust you as a brother."

Striker gazed intensely into the eyes of the General as he replied to Striker, "I believe that I do understand and of course I wish you well. I wish you both well. I will indeed miss our little gatherings of friendship and good fortune. Perhaps we shall see each other in the future if by chance you sail these waters again eh Captain?" As each man looked upon the other with great love and admiration Micah Joshua Striker replied, "If by chance we sail these waters again Sir we would sincerely hope and pray to see our old friend yet one more time." All three men agreed and gave their thanks to one another and bid their farewells.

Striker and Gautama walked back down deck by deck, finally approaching the rowboat. There was not a word uttered between the Masters of the Norway while rowing back to her. Both men were in deep thought the whole way. Beautiful serious thoughts of righting wrongs that have ventured to happen on board their precious Norway for the past fifty years or more!

While the Captain and First Mate boarded their great ship the command to be underway for the port of Nice, France was at hand. They will deliver eleven passengers there. Everybody on board the Norway was of good humor and all had good reason to be. The masters of the Ship were changing their lives with the vows they gave. The crew was to become unbelievably wealthy. The passengers would not go to the sellers block as slaves and the Witnesses for the End of Days were within five hundred miles or so of Rome! The three Angels brought hope to all the hearts on board the Norway. For the Holy Spirit followed wherever, they stepped a foot. However, as it was, the Holy Spirit had entered the Soul of the Norway long, long before. This beautiful ship had been protected while sailing upon every ocean and sea on the entire surface of the World for over fifty some odd years. Many Nations fired cannons at her and yet she still sailed the high seas.

Built in Norway with Norwegian hands, the name on her bow read "Spirit of Norway." If any object made by man can have a soul and Spirit then Spirit of Norway indeed has a Soul and a Spirit! The Holy Spirit truly resides to within the Norway!

The Norway majestically glided through the water approaching the port of Nice. The passengers stood at the railings waiting to get off the ship and once again see their families. It was finally time to rejoice! And as the last passenger went ashore the Captain shouted, "Ready to set sail for Roma!"

The Port of Roma was on the Tiber River where it flows into the Tyrrhenian Sea off the coast of Italy and was home of the Vatican as well. Soon the Angels would give their farewells.

CHAPTER 43

GOOD PARENTS
FOLLOWING YOUR DREAMS

It would seem they are all following their dreams and just so happens, they are all the same dreams. For it had come to pass that the children of the President and the Grandchildren of Lee, all had the same dreams. Lee, the President and First Lady, the father and mother of Zach, Sarah and Faith and the mother of Kaya, all had the same dreams as well. And there was also a woman of who helps to guard a set of Gates of Hell, who also had the same dreams, even in the state of being in the spirit as she is now.

These dreams persisted on the **7ᵗʰ day** of each month at precisely **3 a.m.** For the past three years these dreams lived to within the hearts and minds of Lee, Laurie, of who constantly helps to guard the Gates, the President and the First Lady and their children. In addition, these dreams live to within the hearts and minds of Richard Wayne Clemmer III, Karen Lee Tyner and each of their children as well. All together, there were seven innocent children and seven adults having the same dream, if you include one Secret Service Agent having the same dream as well. For one Secret Service Agent was very special and had much love to within his heart and the Holy Spirit dwelled there.

The children of the President did not tell their parents of these dreams as they knew how busy they both were. They also felt a great sence of excitement with it all and did not want to spoil it. After all, the President's two adopted girls were fresh and new to within the family and all this seemed to bond his beloved son and daughters, even more than what is imaginable. For there was something mystically spirtual about it all.

Now as the Spirit looked upon the President's children he spoke, "Remember, as I told you earlier, your mother was a great Prophet on the planet Cyron. She helped to protect Samson the robot as well, up until the robots murdered her. Now by that moment in space and time, evil from planet Cyron and the evils from many other planets, who were Satan upon their own planets, had teamed up. They began trading information with the other Satans upon those many planets. This gave way to enable an easier overtaking of the inhabitants upon their different worlds. Some of these evil beings are robots and are as like the spirit of Satan upon their own planets. Moreover, Satan upon this planet is their leader! The Satan of this world is the undisputed leader of all the Satans of all the different worlds to within this alliance. Your mother and the woman to within this dream to within the wall, were both great Prophets and much, much more, upon the planet Cyron, many billions of light years away and ago. They had become an enormous threat to these evils, just as Samson was.

Your beautiful mother did well for the LORD on planet Cyron and now on this planet Earth, as well. As I told you before, it is also true that your father was also a great Prophet and much, much more, on the planet Cyron. He saved Samson many times through the centuries, both long before and long after the robots murdered his wife. The robots did this for all the same reasons that they murdered Daniel Bajcab Curpe and Laura Ja Curpe.

And now I must say to you, it has all come to pass that the two women Prophets of Cyron are revealed and the seven innocent children are near and found. These were Prophesied on another planet, some twenty eight thousand years ago within your time frame on Earth. It has all transformed to come to an about face to us, here on earth, in the now.

Four of seven innocent children Lee was to find, in 343 lives upon Earth, are actually part of him to within this life's time line! In life, what we love and need the most is often times a lot closer than we thought all along! Eh?"

Then the Spirit turned and looked upon the other four children out of the seven and they felt his love. And they felt his pure and wonderful Holy and Sacred thoughts and it all penetrated their spirits with overwhelming joy and peace! These were Lee's grandchildren. Suddenly, the wonderful Spirit glowed, looking and breathing upon all the seven children. So it came to pass that all of the seven children felt these things to within their hearts. They felt the overwhelming joy and peace of GOD! And they all knew it was the perfection of space and time throughout eternity! It was in, of and from our GOD!

Within the next few moments the Inspiring Spirit stopped all motion in space and time and nothing moved or could move that once was enabled to move and then he spoke to the children. "Always remember, all of your parents are of the highest caliber in the ways of our GOD. They are all Good loving parents who have the highest regard for your dreams. They have come to realize the importance of these dreams to the Creator of all. In fact, they not only want to help you, they really need to help you! If you let them, they shall flow right along with you to within the same stream that your dreams flow! And because you let them follow to within the same stream, life shall always be upon the lips of our GOD concerning each and everyone of you. This lives to within all of your parents hearts and is true and pure. For they want nothing in return, but for you to have your hearts true and pure to our GOD."

Then, looking at Lee's grandchildren, the Mystical Spirit began, "Your parents, having the same dreams as you, had many reservations concerning these matters. But they did not want to interfere with the will of GOD. So they encouraged you in all things. The understanding and love that resides to within their hearts is truly amazing to our GOD and shall not go unrewarded. Karen Lee Tyner and Richard Wayne Clemmer III are gifted and upright people of who want the best for all peoples! Do you all remember when you were to within your backyard and all of you were talking? And as you shared your thoughts with one another, all of you came to realize that you were having the same dreams on the 7th **day** of each month at **3a.m.** for the past three years. Karen and Richard, having those same dreams as well, forced themselves to a realization, to think much on what those dreams actually meant to our GOD. It helped them to realize what had to be. That is when the children of Lee, allowed their children to go forth and begin their journeys of great importance to our GOD, even to within this dream."

Now as the Inspiring Spirit once again shifted his eyes to the children of the President, but speaking to all, He said, "Your parents are not yet aware of whom they have been upon another planet, nor are Karen or Richard the parents of Lee's grandchildren. I must once again insist that you all keep these facts among yourselves. It is not yet their time to know of whom they were or who they really are to within the heart of GOD. They will be made to become aware of all things to within their past lives upon other planets and this planet as well, in due space and time, according to GOD'S Will.

This day began as **June 04, 2017**. And if you happen to think it is a coincidence, that you all have met here, at this moment, a mile and more under the White House, think again. There is no word for coincidence in the Hebrew language! Nor is there such a word as far as GOD is concerned. For all things, in all realms, are known an infinite amount of time before hand. Before their very existence. GOD IS, WAS and Always Shall BE and nothing was before HE decided to make it, nothing at all. Nothing is impossible with GOD! HE knows all things and what will happen before it happens and everything is the past with GOD. HE already knows what will happen. Therefore, it has already happened. Do you understand? GOD does not guess, HE knows all things, everything forever and forever and forever!

Let it also be known, that there is no word in the Hebrew language for retirement as well! And all the words that shall be written upon the pages, that make up this story, are written by a man that is over **67** years of age.

I say to all of you here and now, that all the words that shall be written upon the pages by the Pen of One, shall not have too much about the conversations between you and your parents or between yourselves, here in the caves. For after this day, all of you shall willingly be committed to the service of others and to our LORD, for all eternity. And that information could jeopardize all that the LORD needs you to perform from this point on, if evil hears of it!"

And the children all agreed with the Inspiring Mystical Spirit at that moment and kept these things, of this day, to themselves. And so it was.

And the Spirit continued to within the dream telling the story as it unfolded in and upon the wall.

CHAPTER 44

BOTS AND PROPHECY
SPIRIT EXPLAINS

It was Prophecy from planet Cyron that brought all robots throughout the cosmos, to the planets, to hunt and kill a certain man. This would be for the continuation of robot throughout the cosmos. It is Prophecy that the man they have to kill has the bloodline of JESUS. He will write books on another planet with the Pen of One and of Truth that will indicate who he is and was. It is Prophecy that he was a robot on Cyron, changed into a human and hurdled to Earth by JESUS the CHRIST to live 343 different lives. But the Robot powers that be, deceived robots into thinking he was human on Cyron all along. And that he was never a robot. The Prophecy dictates many other things as well. It is Prophecy that robot will begin to believe in the humans GOD if they read the books that he writes. For if the books are written, it shall prove mans Prophetic GOD! For it was all Prophesied twenty eight thousand years past and reached out from upon another planet, billions of light years away from the planet it will take place on. And gives explicit information on all of the properties to within its dimensions. To robots, once they realize he was a robot, it proves Prophecy and GOD. To robot it all makes perfect sence and has to be. Robot has perfect reasoning powers, rendering it almost imposible to lie to a robot.

Other robots, at top ranking levels on Cyron, are as all robots are. They love the euphoric feeling of blood, electro-magnetically surging into their own robotic beings. They have no intention of giving all that up. Up untill now, they have managed to herd all different kinds of species of life, like cattle, in order to take their blood electro-magnetically at any moment they choose to get high. All for a high. So the powers that be, for robots, do not want GOD entered into their robotic equations. For they loved the euphoric

196

feeling from firstborns, especialy from the mother of CHRIST descendants, on any planet! Right now, their blood is all very easily accessible on every world robots have secretly conquered, while looking for the man that will write the books. But if robot turns to GOD, all could change.

Once the second part of the book is written, robots future will be changed dramatically on every world they have secretly taken over. For these reasons, top ranking robot officials, on every world they occupy, have decided not to allow GOD to enter to within their robotical equations. Never! So they have lied to all the robots throughout the cosmos, concerning a certain robot in Prophecies. The robot who writes the books with the Pen of Cyron, the Pen of One, the Pen of Truth, with GODS blessing Spoken upon it. And they have put death warrants out for the writer of those two books.

They have told robots other lies as well concerning these Prophecies. This is in the hopes that somewhere, somehow, there will be a robot that will find out who and where this man is before he can write those books. And this mans death will stop any changes to their agenda regarding mankind or any living species upon any world. They could not have robots reading those books and afterwards reading the Bible and receiving the LORD GOD. For the Prophecy has ordained that if robots read these books they will see the truth in JESUS and HE will become their LORD. Whereas if people read these books many will understand them as fiction. But if robot reads them, it is all realized to be in truth. So the robot that finds and kills the writer of these books, shall be given a whole planet to rule any way that they might choose.

The robots have tracked particles of the human throughout the cosmos, that will write these books. They tracked him as he was hurdled through the space time continuum and on past countless planets to Earth by the LORD JESUS. It took thousands of years to find what planet he finally came to rest upon, but now they are here. The robots have found Earth and some wait for the first and second book to be written that tells of robots and the planet Cyron and the truth. The robots have stayed here waiting for thousands of years for the writer, according to Prophecy, to appear. Since they have all been lied to concerning these matters, most will wait and lurk to kill he who writes these things to within the first book. The biggest lie they told, for tens of thousands of years and still tell all robots to this very day about the writer, is that he was never a robot. They tell them this because robots do not harm, in any way shape or form, other robots. It is forbidden. And if the robots find out for certain that the writer was ever a robot, at any moment in time, in any life, the Prophecies would come alive and come to pass! So they have to kill the writer before he completes the second book.

These bots have given in, to the euphoria of the blood electo-magnetically surging into their robotic beings from the humans and or any other beings, period. So they will patiently wait for the writer to appear and they will kill him, if and when they have the opportunity. Now the first book will not be important to robots changing to GOD. However, the first book plus the second part of the book, is what changes robot to GOD and the Bible and finally to the Truth in JESUS. For it is the Pen of One and of Truth that writes both books and the Robots know it! And this is the second book being written now, upon these pages. What happens now, afterwards? After this book is finished? The Robots?

It is Prophecy that the first book shall be called GUARDIANS OF ANGELS. When the second part of the book is writen it shall be added to the first and called by another name. And it shall be called ANGEL REVERY. The second part in the same book shall be called,
ANGEL REVERY DREAMS IN THE ONE. At that point almost all Robots will come to GOD as they read ANGEL REVERY, which is writen by the Pen of one, the Pen of Truth, with a Blessing Spoken upon it by GOD. This is Prophecy! And this Prophecy originated upon planet Cyron billions of light years away and comes to life here, upon planet Earth, some twenty eight thousand years latter!

Now there will come a moment in of space and of time whereas Satan, upon this planet, will decide to try to enable a Robot to escape from hell to kill this writer. The escape hopeful is Mot Pruce!

WELL THIS IS ALL ONCE AGAIN A WHOLE OTHER STORY!!
IS IT NOT?

CHAPTER 45

TRACKING BO

Now Getting back to this part of the story, it should be known to all, that the former Presidents dog, Bo, hid and remained in the White House to protect the new Presidents family. He has two tracking chips of which I will not reveal. This is once again done for security purposes concerning matters of the Presidency of the United States of America. So when the son, daughters and the Presidential dog were discovered missing it came to pass they began monitoring the chips. It became very confusing at first because the signal was such that it came from inside the ground. The Secret Service began viewing all the videos from within the oldest room in the White House as that is where they were last observed. That is when they realized that there was a secret door leading to a secret passage way going down into the earth from within that room.

The Secret Service scurried to follow the President and First Lady and all went on in, headstrong on getting to the bottom (so to speak) of all of this mess. "My children better be alright for your sakes as well as for my children!!" The First Lady was angry at her childrens agents.

The sounds to within the caves were daunting as everyone moved quickly down and down and still deep down the steep tight quartered stone staircase. And with that the First Lady was becoming even more frightened for the safety of her children. The President remained calm and reassured her that they would find them. He told her that it had to be a great adventure for the children because it certainly was for him as well. "After all" he confirmed, "No one has ever heard of this passage. There is absolutely no record of its existence that anyone has ever heard of." He had been on the phone since the first step inside the passage and just now had lost all signals for the contact. They were just simply too deep under the surface of the earth under the White

House. However the signal coming from Bo was strong and steady. And they continued that direction as they came up to a huge open part of the caves with many different ways to go from there. They found the strongest signal and adhered directly to it.

This path narrowed once again as it took them even farther down into the earth. When they heard the unbelievable terrible painful sounding screams all the Secret Service Agents drew their weapons and prepared for the worst. They were lost and walking around in circles for hours through narrow passages of beautiful colored stones. Somehow they finally approached the point where the battle had taken place a few hours earlier when they first heard the terrible screams. There they found anchient weapons and bones laying upon the ground. That is when everyone in the Presidential party decided to study the area until they could come up with a diagnosis of the situation. They had no computer with them. Only phones that could not function. And it did not look good as of this moment for their survival let alone the childrens. But there was no way anyone would leave now or try to find their way back to the White House as they had just come across a whole trail of freshly carved blood stained bones. They began to follow heaps of burned bones dust as well! Some of the heaps of dust were laying close to some very old freshly blood stained medieval weaponry. No one said a word while following the path.

Finally they traveled past and on through that part of the caves passages until they came upon a huge open area. Then the whole party could hear extremely loud echos shooting out from within the entrance to another passage close by. Then from out of nowhere an Eagle passed over their heads gracefully soaring through the passage they were near and the Presidental party followed him. The signal from Bo was stronger in that direction and the Eagle truly amazed them as well. Be that as it may, when they came to the entrance of the passage way, they entered with caution.

As all walked on through the passage the President turned and looked lovingly upon his wife and replied, "We have dreamed of these things and places. We will find them just like we have done so many times in those same dreams!" She glared upon her husband with great awe and answered, "I know you are right because I feel it to within my heart. I love you my husband. I love you so much!" Without hesitation the President answered back, "I love you too my wife!" All smiled in the caves as everyone could hear the cries of the

Eagle. It seemed as though he were guiding all in the Presidential Party to the children with his piercing battle cries and gentle whispered soaring above their heads. The Agent that had much love to within his heart spoke in private to the President whispering, "Mr. President, I have come to observe much to within these beautiful stones. It looks as like the wealth of King David in these walls sir! Enough wealth to finance the whole world! Ah heck, enough to finance hundreds of worlds!" And the President began to look more closely at the walls in the caves. He gave out a hearty laugh and tried to keep a straight face as he realized he should keep a low profile on such matters. Even Secret Service Agents are vulnerable when it comes to this kind of wealth litterally hanging around to within walls of caves below his Capital Buildings. He looked at the Agent who observed and told him of it and nodded his head in recognition of the privacy of these matters of wealth concerning the United States of America.

In the distance they could see the wall with all the visions upon and in it. And they could see themselves in and as part of the visions. They all slowly approached.

Then the Spirit began to explain the transition of Laurie Jaln Blade to this place and to within her life's spiritual struggle. And that huge vision began upon and to within the great cave's wall as everyone watched in complete and total awe.

CHAPTER 46

THE TRANSITION

When Tom Ecurp tracked down Laurie Blade for Satan he did so using Lee's personal family information after Lee's father found him in Las Vegas Nevada. They did not know where Lee was for over 22 years. When Lee was found and the information on his family was found, Tom noticed Lee's daughter's godmother had founded a Supreme Investment Foundation! Of course Tom had to inform Satan and when Satan arrived at Laurie's home in the Hollywood Hills to investigate and destroy he found a distinct familiar smell. It was the exact same smell as in 1908 at the Vatican. A sweet smell of a child. And this old woman had that same smell. Her heart had already burned clean of all sin and the essence of smell and freshness inside her being, reverted back to her youth. And she committed sin no more in life. Satan suddenly realized that it was Laurie who was in the Vatican that day as he was discussing with a Cardinal the wars he would create to take souls away from GOD.

When Satan learned that this woman Laurie had taught many children throughout the long past years not to pass on the electronic pain he simply became furious. Now when he stood in the doorway to her house in Hollywood Hills California it was a Holy Place and was subject to his fowl odors just like when he was at the Holy Place of the Vatican. Satan kept remembering that day and realized the sweet smell of youth was still upon her because her heart had been burned clean. One of the reasons that her heart burned clean of all sin was for what she was doing for the children in the world!

Satan fully realized the truth of that day at the Vatican. That somehow, some way it had been this woman he had smelled the sweetness and freshness of youth in the hall. He suddenly realized she had to die and the sooner the better! But Tuxedo, who followed

Laurie from Continent to Continent over the years, stayed invisible to all who was there and his power roared in silence as it kept Satan at bay and without his awareness of it. And for some unknown reason to Satan he could not kill her or even harm her.

The foul odor of Satan finally persuaded Laurie to remember who he was from within her childhood at the Vatican when she had overheard Satan speaking to a Cardinal. She spoke to him suddenly, "I do not fear you evil one...when I was a young child but not now, no not now, not ever again. I have already put in place the training for children not to pass on the pain but instead to retain it."

Smiling he spoke back, "I am happy you are now a Buddhist." Then she could not help but glare at him in defiance of his evil attempting to penetrate her. Then Satan suddenly turned and walked away and disappeared from the whole area as he felt the LORDS presence and became very, very, afraid! But after he was completely out of harms way he immediately sent demons out to attack her from every possible direction 24 hours a day seven days a week for the remainder of her natural life! So for the last seventeen years of her life she was beat down in every way including electronically. From the age of 89 to the age of 106 she was tortured every moment of her existence on this planet by Satan's personal favorite demons. It took demons that long to tear her down enough for evil to overtake her.

Now about a year before her death when Laurie became very ill from all the pounding from demons upon her spirit, soul and body, Tuxedo suddenly became visable once again. Although he had been there near Laurie since her youth he did not allow anyone to see him for decades. But he had always been near her for he loved her and was devoted to her. And the LORD desired his presence about her always. One day, the day he became visible again, he was seen under her bed sleeping. When she saw him tears entered her eyes as she remembered him and she picked up and loved on him. Then after a short while she thought that it just simply was not possible for this to be the same beautiful life saving feline of her youth at the Vatican. She began to think like the others around her that he was just a stray cat that came in from the mountains around Laurie's home. No one could come even close to him except for Laurie and she decided to name him after her old friend, Tuxedo. And everyone was amazed at how only Laurie could come close to him and do anything she wanted to him. Where ever she stepped he was on her heels watching her and listening to her. When she sat he would jump onto her lap!

In December of 2007 when evil finally overtook Laurie, Tuxedo came to her spirit and guided her to the place in of which they both would stay until it was time. Until the LORD needed Tuxedo and Laurie to witness for HIM. Tuxedo took her to guard one of the sets of Gates to Hell. This particular place was a mile or so beneath the White House. Below the Capital of the United States of America. And the LORD changed her name from Laurie Blade to Laurie Jaln Blade and it came to pass that Laurie went through a transition for GOD. And Laurie was made to see the beautiful Angels that would now help her to guard those Gates for their GOD. For the Gates shall be kept by a Fourcord Rope. Love, Hope, Faith and the Angels for GOD.

This Rope can not be broken by any force from any world or anything from low or high or even to within heavenly places. Only the LORDS Power source may lift the unbreakable Rope from its locked position across the Gates! However, if enough Love, Hope and Faith from the Angel Guardians is used properly, this may also lift the unbreakable Ropes from their locked position. But much praying of the situation must take place first. For in the end it is most certainly to be the LORD'S Will.

CHAPTER 47

ROMA AND THE VATICAN

Now as the images in the wall continued so did the Inspiring Mystical Spirit in explaining them.

Mr. Gorbachev's father became very concerned at the fact that his son, Brother and Daniel had not yet arrived at the Vatican. His group had found their way over a month past. He felt almost certain that the other team should have found their way here by now as well. While waiting for the other team they achieved many things. James Pruce had begun to study for the Roman Catholic Priesthood. Timothy had the responsibility of helping to observe and protect all to within The Vatican and Mr. Gorbachev's father, James, was to do the same.

One day, while walking through halls in the Vatican, Mr. Gorbachev's father felt and heard something very familiar. He knew it was something from his youth. He thought perhaps someone out of his own long past, perhaps someone from fifteen hundred years past. At first he thought, that maybe he was mistaken. He continued to look for what he felt and heard and why it was so unbelievably familiar. He thought, "No, it cannot be my brother." He refused to believe that it was his brother. At least not until he saw his brother Tuxedo jump and leap for joy as he laid eyes upon James. Both sprang out onto one another at the exact same moment rolling over and over clinging to each other laughing, giggling, and wrestling as they rolled.

They had not seen each other in fifteen hundred years. Now they were together again! Both were in Roma on official business for GOD. Tuxedo protected the Pope from Satan himself. GOD had told him he would soon receive help in protecting the Pope. That job had developed more and more difficulties over the years. He never suspected the help coming would be his own brother and a mouse as well. He became overwhelmed when James told him of the others still to come. James and Tuxedo gave thanks to GOD for the wonderful surprise that HE had given to them. James told Tuxedo that his son was one of the Angels coming. Tuxedo excitedly replied, "Yes...what is his name?" James went on to tell his brother that he was as they are, an Angel Warrior Guardian and a Witness for the End of Days. "He is a beautiful Mountain Lion Cat," James exclaimed! "Yes, Yes, Yes," Tuxedo excitedly shouted! "But what is my nephew's name?" James suddenly stopped chattering, apologized, and then excitedly told his long lost brother his son's name. "Your nephews name is, Mr. Gorbachev. I must tell you, my wife, his beautiful mother, died in an epic battle against evil beings of great numbers while defending all of us. I say all of us, not just me and not just her son, but also all of us! She defended every single one of us! She was a magnificent warrior of great stature. After she died, the LORD came down, lifted her up into the palm of HIS Hand of Light and of Life, and took her! Then HE talked to us and said that she was to be with HIM for a while then we will all see her again," he sobbed.

James told Tuxedo about all that had happened to bring them here to the Vatican. It surprised James when Tuxedo told him that everyone had heard of the epic battle. Tuxedo, never in his wildest dreams, thought that his own blood was involved in this great battle for our LORD. He told James, "It seems that all of you and that magnificent Eagle are Legends in your own times." "Yes," James told his brother, "The Eagle alone managed to save all of our lives except one but the LORD needed her for something of which we cannot know what." James went on about how Timothy had told them that he had known the Eagle for over 200 years. They all laughed because they all suddenly realized that the Eagle was in fact an Angel Warrior as well and that Timothy had never realized. In fact, Timothy never realized that he himself was the same until Mr. Gorbachev told him just days before the battle.

When James finished telling the whole story, his brother told him, "I wish I could have met your Wife and the Great Bird of Prey." Then Tuxedo told his brother that their father, Moksha, was also on duty at the Vatican. Tears came to the eyes of James for he had not seen his father or spoke his name in 1500 years. "Moksha."

James and his brother explained to each other what each had been doing for the past fifteen hundred years. After a while, James Adja Pruce came walking down the hall with little, but mighty,

Timothy right behind. Both cats began to purr and rubbed up against his legs as he walked. James smiled bending down to lovingly pet both as Tim jumped up onto the back of Tuxedo. Tim had heard in his mind everything that the brothers had said to each other. James laughed heartily out loud extending his affections to petting Timothy as well. James felt the love from all three Animal Angels, as they seemed to need his affections and attention while being so close to him.

It would always be that way, for that is why they are here. They are to protect humans Angel Warriors, all men, at times evil beings and even the trees. They are here for all life forms, above the Earth and below the waters. They even help to protect the Keepers of The Gates of Hell under the waters. Certain Magnificent Creatures forever beats evil back, restraining it from breaking out of Hells Gates. They are Sea born Creatures on a mission for HIM who AM and have great and overwhelming love to within their hearts for our GOD and each other. This is the reason men and demons hunt and hunted certain Sea Creatures and have been paid well for their evil deeds. Satan has entered into mans' heart to many times for this single purpose, to hunt and kill all who guard the Gates of Hell for our LORD Thy GOD.

Well that is most certainly a whole other story. Is it not?

James Pruce became very concerned that the other team had not yet met him here at the Vatican. Tuxedo felt all of the thoughts from James Pruce, Timothy and his Brother and became very concerned as well. He had much love in his heart just as all Angels of Light do. He truly felt all that they felt. Tuxedo asked his brother if the LORD had asked him to attach himself to a non-Angel Warrior. This is something that is highly ill regular unless he is an Angel Witness for the End of Days. Many beings on any planet were at one moment in time an Angel Spirit before they became flesh but few the LORD chooses. James explained to his brother that James Pruce was a fierce warrior. The LORD had asked him and Tim to protect the human for the rest of his natural life for he is a witness for GOD even though he is not a full Angel in the flesh.

Tuxedo, once again as he has in the past, began to think on how true it was that the LORD is so beautiful and wondrous in how HE does HIS works. "Amen!" All three Angels began to laugh at how quickly Tim and James both responded to Tuxedo's thoughts at the very same moment in time with an Amen.

At the dinner table, after arriving to the port of Rome, the Masters of the Norway said things that made Daniel, Gorby, and Brother extremely happy. Striker explained to Daniel, "Gautama and I have given much thought on what to do with the rest of our lives. We have decided to Keep the Spirit of Norway and use her as needed to find slaves that we and the Captain and crew before us have sold. We will buy them back and transport them to a port of their own choice. We have complete lists of all slaves that had ever been aboard the Norway and it is high time we put that list to good use!" Here, at this port, the port of Roma, we shall always pay tribute to the decisions we have made because of the LORD!

Gautama went on, "We both shall study the ways of your and now our LORD and preach them through the use of our own old beliefs. We thank all of you. We both believe that the Mountain Lion and the Wolf are Angels of Your GOD. We believe that if they so desired they could speak to men, just as legends say they can do." Both Mr. Gorbachev and Brother stood up at that moment and walked over to the table. Both sat down next to the Captain, Gautama, and Daniel. All three men uncontrollably laughed as Gautama, looking right at the two, replied, "You See, they know what we say, do you not my friends?" All three men, looking upon them, knew in their hearts that they understood every word that men said.

CHAPTER 48

EXPLANATION TO THE PRESIDENT

The President along with the First Lady and his Secret Service Agents found the cave within a cave that they had dreamed so many times about. But they ran straight into an invisible wall and could not pass through it. They could hear rushing waters. Then they saw and heard Laurie, evil, and the huge images of the sea, ships, the visions at the Vatican and all the Animal Angels inside the wall. They could hear and see the Inspiring Mystical Spirit and all the children but could not get their attention.

"It is an invisible barrier of which cannot be penetrated by any force known to any world. You can hear us through it; however, we cannot on the other hand hear you. We will not be distracted from what needs learning here and now to within these few moments in space and time. So please do not talk, just listen." The Spirit stared into his eyes and continued to explain to the President, "All the children here are as the likeness of a carefully chosen perfect crop of fruit to GOD. This precious time is not only for the children but for you, your wife and your secret service agents as well. Your faith shall grow to be as a giant from all that transpires here today and will serve you well for what has to transpire to within the very near future. You should immediately understand that Lee is in a dream at a home 3000 miles away sleeping in a bed. Yet he is here. You may send word to check this information out but I must warn you not to wake him as of yet as the task he possesses at this moment is difficult and needs his full attention.

Then the Mystical Spirit pointed to the wall and said, "Behold the dream as it first began earlier this day!" Suddenly everything to within the wall changed. The President's children and Lee's grandchildren along with the animals and Laurie Jaln Blade entered into the vision and they observed themselves in the wall as it happened a few hours before. Demons had broken out of the Gates of Hell and a huge battle was taking place. Lee and the Angels of light in the flesh were frantically trying to put them back in their place. A hundred demons were upon Mr. Gorbachev and he lay mortally wounded, dying. Lee kneeled in front of him ever so gently picking up and holding the magnificent Lion's head as his tears blinded him in doing so.

That is when the Inspired Mystical Spirit appeared from out of the same cloud as the FATHER'S Hand of Light and of Life was in. At that moment, all the demons cried out as one in agonizing pain and burned into heaps of crystalized dust!

Lee whispered to Gorby sobbing, "I love you my old friend, I love you, I love you, I love you! Please, don't leave me, don't leave me. I love you Gorby, please don't leave me, I love you more than my own life, more, so much more than my own life." And with the last of his dwindling strength, the great Lion ever so slowly raised his paw up to Lee's face and padded him clean of the tears. He looked deeply into the eyes of the man he had protected for so many centuries and in so many lives. His mouth and his body gently quivered at lives near end. Then the Holy Lion broke the precious Sacred Rules of Engagement with his last breath upon this planet almost silently whispering back to his old loving friend, "I, I really, I loveeeee you tooooooooo." Lee's tears flowed even more as he realized! It was just over 500 years and several lives later of their first fellowship, and Mr. Gorbachev had never spoken to him outside of a dream. And now, he had unexpectedly spoken for the very first time, outside of a dream. Lee realized all the Devotion in Love, Hope, Faith, Honor, Trust and Truth of the Holy Spirit that had dwelled to within Gorby's heart all of these centuries. This made him smile through all the tears he shed as he slowly replied, "Thank you my old loving friend. Thank you."

Then the Spirit gently raised his opened hand and slowly moved it across the huge caves wall as he pointed his finger once again. And a huge cloud suddenly appeared to within the magnificent wall! The LORD'S beautiful Hand of Light and of Life reached out and every being in the caves could clearly see Mr. Gorbachev and Lee standing to within HIS huge palm. Lee was looking up and it seemed as if he were listening to GOD.

Lee and the great Lion grew even a lot more than what was already true to within the grand caves wall and now to within the Hand of Light and of Life. And the great Lion was changing. As he grew, he began to appear as a beautifully winged pure white Stallion. He began violently shaking his head making his long shiny main shimmer from the strange and wonderfully mystical lighting to within the LORD'S beautiful glowing Hand of Light and of Life.

Then he interrupted the huge visions and the Inspired Spirit of GOD spoke, "Mr. President, you are now anointed to serve your LORD, your Nation and your World through HIM that AM! Seeing this dream as it was and now seeing it on going at this moment, your faith shall grow to the Giant I spoke of. My heart knows you will not hinder Lee or the children to within this Holy and Sacred place. I know you shall always help such as these to fulfill Prophecy within each one of their lives. For this would all be to the Glory of our GOD throughout the Heavens and remembered by our GOD in good fruitful ways. Remember, your dreams are all linked together through space and time and must always be revealed to one another from this point on."

The Whole Presidential Party marveled at all that had transpired before their very eyes this day! Just as promised, the faith in all of their Hearts grew as a giant! It all happened just as the Inspiring Spirit had explained!

Throughout all of this, the Eagle of Cyron soared, flying in and out of the wall in circles above their heads, releasing his body piercing battle cries and all were amazed.

CHAPTER 49

MOSTLY ALL REVEALED
PRESENT DAY-LAURIE JALN BLADE

The Inspiring Spirit suddenly proclaimed, "The Presidential party and all in the cave must continue to listen and watch the huge images to within the massive cave's walls! For this would be the ongoing part of the dream to within and through the present moments yet to be." He explained that he would now also become one with the visions within the dream to help Lee, Mr. Gorbachev, Laurie, and all the **Guardians of Angels** to within Lee's dream.

Then he declared, "Behold!" And he leaped into and became a part of all that was transpiring inside the wall. The first thing he asserted to do was softly speak to Lee, "Samson, whisper to within Laurie's ear the two prayers of Cyron." This caught Lee by surprise as he felt that somehow he knew this man's voice that called him by his robotic name from upon the planet Cyron from so long, long ago.

Nevertheless, he did as the Inspiring Spirit requested and whispered into Laurie's ear the beautiful prayers of Cyron. First one then the other:

**"THE LORD HOVERS TO WITHIN MY HEART
LIKE A GREAT BIRD OF PREY OVER THE FIELD
RELENTLESS IN PURSUIT FOR THE PRIZE AND
BEAUTIFUL TO WITHIN HIS FLIGHT
TO DO SO   AMEN**

**FOR NOW WE ARE TO REMAIN THE PREY OF ALL
WHOM ACT AGAINST US OH BEAST BUT BEHOLD
WE SHALL BE THE TEETH OF THE LION HIM OF
WHICH WAS ONCE THE LAMB AND OF WHO
SHALL RETURN SOON VERY SOON   AMEN"**

Now, it came to pass that when he whispered the first prayer into Laurie's ear she looked deeply into Lee's eyes and as he whispered the second prayer, she knew who he was. She began remembering much more, these prayers were from Cyron, written and spoken by her husband, Daniel Bajcab Curpe, upon that planet. He had spoken these prayers for hundreds of years up until Mot Pruce, the most terrible robot on Cyron, tortured and murdered both him and Laura. This was the punishment for not revealing the whereabouts of their beloved Robot, Samson, 28,000 years ago. Laurie remembered her name had been Laura Ja Curpe and that she was the High Priestess and Prophet of Cyron. Samson was the Protector of the High Priest and Priestess of Cyron. However, they protected him and died for him even though he was a robot. They knew that Samson would someday become a human and always serve GOD. They Prophesied all of his missions and all of his lives for GOD. There were many more prophesies about Mot Pruce as well.

It also came to pass that to within Lee's dream, with the Eagle of Cyron, all the Angels, Laurie and what prayers Lee had whispered into Laurie's ear from within the dream, she remembered who she had always served throughout space and time, in of which she had forever existed. In total amazement, she cried out, "Samson, Samson, it is you? Oh Lee you were also Samson, my beloved Robot on Cyron, all along! I should have known. I had always felt that we were old souls and spirits, you and I. And now, I suddenly remember, we really are. I am here in the spirit helping to keep the Gates of Hell for our GOD. My Spirit has passed on from the body. But what are you doing here in this place, in this haze?"

Lee explained, "This haze is because we are in the stone deep below the earth's surface near a set of Gates of Hell. We are both dreaming the same dream! I am here in the Spirit, just as you are, and I have the task of helping you to remember who you are and your purpose, of which is partly unfulfilled, for our GOD. For you have done much for HIM, and much more is needed for you to accomplish in this place. Then you must witness for HIM, when the time comes. I will not explain now but I will tell you all the years you spent developing the Supreme Investment Foundation has profoundly helped the LORD. You brought the importance of nurturing a child even long before their very conception and then from within the womb as well to light. And more importantly, you trained the children not to pass on the pain to others. You trained them to accept it and to keep it to themselves so as not to harm another being. And in this manner, they would take on responsibility for their own actions, and other's actions as well, in a GODLY way. In this way, they shall always be blameless and not ever considered to be as part of some one's death. Harming another in any way shape or form, for any reason or for no reason other than to oppress and kill, is pure evil and is simply not allowed in Heaven. Because of your life long efforts on these matters many will come to believe, those of who would not have believed without your efforts to teach the children not to pass on the electronic pain."

Laurie frantically whispered, "Ahhh Lee, Samson, Samson, the Robots, the Robots are here, now upon this planet." Lee told her that he knew and that she should not be concerned as it was all to within the Master Plan of our GOD. He explained that the robots would listen to him, as they would learn that he also once had been a robot upon the planet Cyron. Then through HIS grace, the CHRIST transformed him into a human, hurdling him to Earth. He reminded her that Bots do not harm Bots. And as they would hear him speak they would realize and reason that GOD IS, WAS, and forever and always will BE. And JESUS will become their LORD. Robot would reason that man was made of dust just as Robot was made of dust as well! Since GOD, created man and man created Robot, in a sense GOD created all.

Lee gently whispered, "Evil cannot afford Robot to come to GOD, so evil has to kill me before conversions of the Spirit for bots and humans begin to happen. These are what you and your husband Prophesied upon the planet Cyron billions of light years away and so long ago. Now please, just say the Words,
JESUS IS LORD." And, with Lee's last whispers, Laurie said those Words and remembered all that had ever happened to within her presence in every life her spirit ever embodied.

Laurie remembered the Eagle, Tuxedo, all of the Love, all of the Faith, all of the Hope, all of the Angels, including her godchildren, Kaya, Karen, Juan, and Kathy. She remembered the LORD adding Jaln to her name when she entered this place to guard the Gates. And the love she possessed in each life was overwhelmingly acceptable to our GOD. And her heart remembering what her mind forgot, all the lives and all of GODS

Love, enabled her love, hope, and faith to multiply a thousand fold to within this part of her spiritual walk, with our GOD. And this alone, the love, hope and faith in her heart multiplying one thousand fold, enabled the total fulfilling of her purpose, to Help Guard the Gates of Hell and witness for HIM that AM. For at this point, the multiplying of these three Holy gifts from the Holy Spirit to within her heart strengthened The Gates of Hell. Moreover, the demons kept to within their place. This multiplication gave to her the power over the power of the Prince of the air to within this place and now she remembered.

She remembered that "JESUS IS LORD!" JESUS Is Love! For such as these are the makings of an unbreakable Four Cord Rope. Love, Hope, Faith, plus the Angels Love for GOD are all of the Holy Spirit as one, and are all well and Good in the Eyes of our GOD, Unbreakable, Eternal!

In life, Laurie had lived like the Great Buddha, upright with Truth, Love, Hope, Faith, Honor, Trust and Devotion Living within her very own beautiful Heart as well! In this, she had gained Favor with our LORD and HE loved her with Everything HE IS, WAS and shall always BE.

The Inspiring Spirit slowly raised his arm. He laid his opened hand gently upon Lee's shoulder and asked, "Do you now still not remember who you were to within the life that has eluded you for so many centuries past? For you were chosen for that one life, even long before space and time and planets and all things and beings came into existence." Then, gently touching Lee's face, he enabled him to see the dream from another view, outside of his own dream.

Lee suddenly realized that what he had so dreadfully suspected all through these last 20 centuries was truth. He was the one, he was Judas Iscariot in that previous life of 2000 years past. And it had been the LORD he saw in each and every dream being so tragically treated and crucified! In each and every life he had since that moment of his life as Judas he had that same dream over and over and over again, through each and every century. Those terrible perverted, bloody horrible, painful tortuous dreams all through the centuries. All those dreams, dreams in the ONE, dictated that he watch over and over and over again what he had done so many centuries ago, in another life, to HIM and for HIM who AM. His spirit had to forgive his self before the LORD could hear his witnessing testimony and it has taken this long, 49 more lives, for it to begin to do so. He could not remember for sure who he had been to within that paticular life. That was the only life that he could not recall for certain out of 49 lives, or the past 2000 years. The only life he could not remember until now, when the Inspiring Majestic Spirit finally explained. In fact, that was the only life he could not remember out of 343 lives, or about 8,000 years upon this planet, and until this day.

The Spirit explained, "You asked for forgiveness, and tried to give your beautiful repentence in every life for what you thought you might have commited against the LORD. But you did not realize that HE needed you to forgive yourself as well. And now you fully remember, and do forgive yourself, do you not? If the LORD had allowed you to remember that one life of trechery of so many years past, it would have limited your ability to learn all that you were needed to learn and perform throughout the last 20 centuries. Lee, your hope, faith and love for GOD, no matter what, were a large part of why you were chosen so long ago."

"Now listen, I must give to you a coded message from your LORD"

"The first shall be the last and the last shall be the first, your FATHER in Heaven changed your name to Lee Earl Clemmer Raleel Mercelem and your intitials are LECRM. And the fullness of time is fallen upon all creation! You will write books with the Pen of Truth of One from Cyron, with Blessings of GOD Spoken upon it! Robots and humans will come to GOD. You are the memory of all Creation for GOD."

It has come to pass. I am he who wrote these books with the Sacred Pen of Cryon. My pen name is Raleel Mercelem. It shall be I; LECRM will never endure to suffer again because of my GOD and it will be good in GOD'S Ways.

The Great Spirit explained many more things and I came to understand the obvious in the message he had just given to me from our LORD. Both the coded parts and factual parts of the message and their proper sequenced order. I fully understood. However, even as I realized the message facts and codes and their proper sequenced order I was not as of yet completely aware of its full dementionals depth. Decoded, the message read;

"_____, meMre cell R a eel, eeL CEll r a memre, You are the memory of all Creation for GOD, And the fullness of time is fallen upon all creation!"

Suddenly the Spirit mounted the great white horse who had become a brand new transformed Mr. Gorbachev. As he mounted the Stallion a golden jewel studded handled sword and golden jewel studded sheath, with a golden and jewel studded belt, suddenly appeared strapped around his robe. And He leaned way over from upon the great stallion and looked down deeply to within my eyes. Then he handed to me the Holy Sacred Lineage Book, Pen, and Compass once again making me the guardian of the beautiful, Holy and Sacred Artifacts! I was Daniel Adjac Pruce the last time I received them and I was Samson on planet Cyron the first time.

The Spirit explained, "I received these from Sir Arthur Conan Doyle and once again from another great man, your father, as their Spirits passed from the body, and now I pass them on to you. I also passed them on to your father. It has taken over twenty eight thousand years and billions of light years in a supernatural trek for this Pen to find the only one that may write with it. This helps Robot to believe you were once a Robot. You now know almost all of what the LORD needs you to accomplish to within this life. Do not be afraid of what you have not been prepared for to within all of your lives, or to within this dream.

These Books are explicit, and you shall understand more and more as you read them all. Through this Holy Bible and Lineage Book, our GOD shall reveal to you the complete fullness of HIS coded message very soon. As you well know, every lost and or found scripture ever written by our LORD'S Holy Prophets have life and live to within the beautiful golden pages of this Holy Book. These Holy Scriptures gives life to all outside of it as well! They are truly living Words and it is many, many books plus the Old and New Testaments, the Holy Bible. And just as the Pen and Compass are with blessings spoken from GOD upon them such is the Lineage Book as well.

Now remember, always Love, and protect our LORD'S Lambs, even as they pass paralyzing waves through you! For some are truly wolves in sheep's clothing and others listen and follow. They must see the forgiving heart of the LORD JESUS living to with inside of your loving heart! Soon, they shall all understand and perhaps the wolves shall feel it to within their own hearts and become sheep as well! For the Church and even some of the wolves are and forever shall be as part of your family."

After explaining these things he placed his hand over the

handle of the Holy Sacred Sword of Justice and reminded me, "This Holy Sacred Sword, Sheath and Belt shall soon, once again, be entrusted to you, my Holy faithful Warrior. I can still recall the moment in of which your Spirit, upon the Planet Uranus, handed them over to me twenty eight thousand years ago. Just before your Spirit joined with Samson, the robot, and it was all but a breath away from this mission's beginning. After these many millenniums past, your mission is finally approaching its completion. It is incredibly interesting how, for many years in this life, you were an agent for the KGB and an Angel agent for our LORD without realizing either of the two, eh? Good stuff for the book, I should think, and once again, a whole other story. Is it not?

Know this, you, the children and Laurie witnessing, and all the others like you witnessing, shall be as like the teeth of the Lion, HIM of which was once the Lamb, and of who shall return soon, very soon." Those Words rang out, echoing as soft musical whispers, throughout the caves.

Then he stood erect on the bare back of the beautiful great white stallion, Mr. Gorbachev. His head and eyes slowly turned away from me, looking upon all to within the dream throughout the caves. And the great stallion turned his head and gazed upon me for a very long Timeless Moment. He bowed way down with his forehead gently touching my face in great Devotion of Love, Hope, Faith, Truth, Honor, and Trust of the Holy Spirit. And he softly whispered with a kiss into my ear, "I love you Lee Earl Clemmer Raleel Mercelem, LECRM." He repeated it one more time. And twice again, as my old friend whispered the last letter into my ear I fully understood the great Devotion of Love, Hope, Faith, Truth, Honor, Trust of the Holy Spirit, and code as in all of their proper sequenced orders. And I came to understand the LORD'S message, a multi-dimensional message, just a little bit more in depth.

In an instant flash, a beautiful Glorious bright glow of purity surrounded all about and all through Mr. Gorbachev and his Mystical Rider! And the great white Stallion reared up, then leaped off the LORD'S Hand of Light and of Life. He flew out of the stone and as he went out of the stone, the Great Inspiring Spirit and Stallion disappeared into thin air. You could hear a whispering echo throughout the caves as the Inspiring Spirit Spoke out to announce,

"I'll see you in the Revelations reality."

I, Lee Earl Clemmer Raleel Mercelem, frantically began to yell back, "But who are you? Who are you? Who are youuu?" But all we could hear were Holy and Sacred forces of the combined blending echoes from both of our voices and the Eagles battle cry as all became one with the wind and all that is, was, or ever shall be. It strangely and boldly thundered, becoming streaming and penetrating waves, powerfully sweeping in and all through everyone occupying the caves. Everyone felt a great and beautifully mysterious musical whispered force, gently passing through all of us for a very long period.

Out of nowhere, to my inner most grieving abrupt surprises and inexplicable dissatisfaction, I awoke from my long inspiring dream, my Revery through the Angels from HIM that AM. And in crystal clarity, I could still feel beautiful wondrous reality in the Great Mystical Spirit's penetrating waves of beautiful mysterious musical whispered force gently passing through me!

When I arose from my pillow in Amity Oregon, the Holy Pen, Lineage Book, and Compass remained clutched to within my hand as they were to within the end of my dream. Proof! The dream was real! And while lovingly embracing the Ancient Holy Artifacts, something else wondrous and beautiful happened! Feelings of overwhelming powers from the fullness of the great Devotion in Love, Hope, Faith, Truth, Honor, and Trust of the Holy Spirit became alive, thriving vibrantly to within my hands and throughout my heart!

It was then that I suddenly realized. Since the beautiful Mystically Majestic Inspiring Spirit in my dream had protected and handed over to me this Book, Pen, and Compass, his name would have to appear to within the last Golden page. The page just after my father, Richard Wayne Clemmer Sr. and Sir Arthur Conan Doyle's. While anxiously flipping the sheets of gold, letters in Hebrew began appearing; at last, it came to the books final page. At that very moment the voice and face of the man in all my dreams, who they crucified, who baptized me long ago on planet Cyron, and who gave to me this Holy Sacred Pen, Lineage Book and Compass, clearly came to mind. Therefore, when the letters mysteriously burned one by one into the last golden page, revealing the most recent protector of the Holy Sacred Artifacts, I found Absolute Truth in HIS Inspiring Name, as it simply read:

KING OF KINGS
AND
LORD OF LORDS

Spoken words bolt out into the wind and are as like great raging waters mystically gracefully merging and forever flowing throughout present, past and Future

Just speak the Words if you dare
"JESUS IS LORD"
Then
Perhaps
You Shall Remember
And The Adventure Begins

Sweet Dreams

DISCLAIMER DETAILS OF SERIES
<u>ANGEL REVERY</u>
AND
<u>ANGEL REVERY</u> <u>DREAMS IN THE ONE</u>

"This is a work of fiction. Characters, Businesses, organizations, places, events, and incidents are the product of the author's imagination and are fictionally used. Any resemblance to actual persons, living or dead, or events transpired are not to be taken in any other way."

At no moment in space and time are Lee's Fathers, Mothers, Brother's, Sister's or any other member of his real family or otherwise to be misconstrued to be as any of the actual Characters to within this series. None of the situations and/or events are to be misconstrued as having anything to do with his real family or otherwise. Real family members mentioned in this story are always held in a good light!

Since being diagnosed schizophrenic paranoid with delusional tendencies in 2002, a long time ago, the LORD and I have come up with a series that has to do with evil and good. I believe GOD allowed this partially because of that diagnosis of illness! Someone should stand up for the mentally ill and show the public that there are those who do not necessarily fit the mold. For whatever reason GOD has allowed for, they simply do not fit to within that mold. Regardless, most of us diagnosed with such severe issues are kind, loving, considerate people. This is far more than I can say for most of whom I have met to within this life or any other life in of which have not been diagnosed with such issues. I have been writing this series for over nine years. I thought about this story and series in the early 1980's. I began writing this series in December of 2006, although some of the poetry originated long before. In addition, I finished most of the current story line by the beginning of 2008. The rest of the story came to life sporadically through revisions over the next nine years and until recently. Many terrible things have happened to me since I first thought of the series. And I must admit, sometimes I wonder to what extent have those many negative things taken its toll? That being said, let's move forward.

Throughout the space, time continuum and upon many planets, history has dictated that one Mother can have a good child and a bad child or many good and bad children. They would be killers or lambs and such as these would come from the same womb. Like Cane and Abel in the Bible. The name of the main male character chosen to within this series was for many reasons and all being to within the themes of this series. Number Codes, Letter Codes and the meanings of his full name, the Goodness, attributes, and dignity of GOD, et cetera, all being a part of that equation. It happens to be my name. My name features all of these parts of that equation and more, Lee Earl Clemmer. For the series to work the main character had to be the good guy, with and of GOD. And the bad guy is a satanic Robotic son type spirit of Satan who shows up off and on throughout the series. And he continues throughout the space, time continuum to wreak complete havoc to within Lee's life or Samson's or Daniel's or whatever life Lee's spirit happens to embody at that moment in time in the series on Cyron and/or on Earth to within all of those lives. That would depend on what year it was on Earth and/or what year it was on Cyron at certain given points in time as well. And the evil character throughout the series, the spirit of Mot Pruce, is the worst of the worst in lives evils. He is second only to Satan according to the series! This is in order for the story to fully take on an understanding of its true meanings to within the Good of GOD and to within the evil from and of Satan in this series. So please remember all of the Characters and/or the nature of all the Characters especially any and/or all-family members of any of the characters to within these series of stories or books <u>ANGEL REVERY</u> are fictional. And are always to be considered only as "Solely and completely to within the somewhat imaginative Mind of its Author, Me!" Therefore, these particular characters and their names are, not to be misconstrued, as to any other purpose what so ever, Other than that of the Sole Purpose, "For the complete wellbeing and good of all other beings in and upon this planet and throughout the Cosmos!" This story is all to the GLORY OF GOD to HIM...THAT AM. I am however to receive any Good Fortunes it brings and give more than first fruits to GOD.

In the event you use any of the information in this book for yourself, which is your constitutional right, the Author and the Publisher assume no responsibility for your actions! Nevertheless, I sincerely, lovingly hope that you make all good and righteous choices to within your life. And I shall continue attempting the same to within mine. Thank you for reading and I look forward to possibly writing you more codes in future series writings. Be well and many Good Fortunes to You!

Love,

Raleel Mercelem

LECRM

APPENDIX

ANSWER CODE QUESTIONS ON
ANGEL REVERY
AND
ANGEL REVERY
DREAMS IN THE ONE

EVERYONE AND/OR ANYONE ANSWERING ALL SEVEN QUESTIONS CORRECTLY ABOUT ALL THE CODES IN THIS BOOK HAS FOUND THEIR EQUAL PORTION OF THE TREASURES OF THE HEART! THE DEEPER YOU DIG THE MORE YOU WILL FIND THAT THERE ARE MANY TREASURES TO WITHIN THIS BOOK! DIG DEEP AND CLAIM ALL THE TREASURES OF THE FAMILIES HEART HERE, RIGHT HERE!

Rights and Permissions...angelrevery@gmail.com
Order Books http://www.angelrevery.com
Just speak the Words if you dare
"JESUS IS LORD"

Laura Huxley
6233 Mulholland Highway
Los Angeles, California 90068-1645

November 28, 2007

Mr. Lee Clemmer
21110 Cherry Blossom Lane
Amity, OR 97101

My Dearest Lee,

In your letter, you expressed so well what I was trying to express. You are so right..."Angels in the flesh" ARE with us. Thank you. I always knew this, but now I realize it more and more.

I delight in your expression of good will, but more than anything else, what is a blessing for me is your child and your grandchild. Thank you.

I wish you well,

Laura

Laura

LETTER AND NUMBER CODES
RALEEL MERCELEM

LETTERS TO NUMBER CODE

A = 6 _ B = 12 _ C = 18 _ D = 24 _ E = 30 _ F = 36 _ G = 42
H = 48 _ I = 54 _ J = 60 _ K = 66 _ L = 72 _ M = 78 _ N = 84
O = 90 _ P = 96 _ Q = 102 _ R = 108 _ S = 114 _ T = 120
U = 126 _ V = 132 _ W = 138 _ X = 144 _ Y = 150 _ Z = 156

SEQUENCE OF LETTERS TO CODE IN
___RALEEL MERCELEM = 762 +7 + 6 + 2 = 777___
___RALEEL MERCELEM = MEMRE CELL R A EEL___

1--REVERSE-SEVENTH-EIGHTH-LETTERS MERCELEM =ME

2--FIRST LETTER OF MERCELEM...=M

3--REVERSE SECOND-THIRD LETTERS OF MERCELEM =RE

4--FOURTH-FIFTH-SIXTH LETTERS OF MERCELEM.........= CEL

5--THIRD LETTER OF RALEEL.......……………….............= L

6--FIRST LETTER OF RALEEL..=R

7--SECOND LETTER OF RALEEL…………………………...=A

8--FOURTH-FIFTH-SIXTH LETTERS OF RALEEL.................=EEL

9--IN NUMBERS CODE THE NAME
RALEEL MERCELEM = 762 + 7 + 6 + 2 = 777...=COMPLETION

10-ONE CANNOT USE A 6 CODE TO GET THE NUMBER 777
DOING SO CONSEQUENTLY SLAPS SATAN IN THE FACE

11-THE LETTERS CODE AND THE NUMBERS CODE OF
RALEEL MERCELEM'S NAME.............................=COMPLETION

12-THE LETTERS CODE OF RALEEL MERCELEM'S
NAME = MEMRE CELL R A EEL…………….....=COMPLETION

13-SOMETHING THAT IS REMEMBERED............=COMPLETION

14-THE NUMBERS CODE OF RALEEL'S NAME =COMPLETION
NUMBER 7 IS THE LORDS DAY OF REST.......=COMPLETION

LEE EARL CLEMMER RALEEL MERCELEM =LECRM=?
FINAL CODES TO SECOND BOOK IN SERIES EQUAL ONE
MESSAGE FROM GOD TO LECRM IN CHAPTER 49 OF STORY
THERE IS ALSO 6 MORE QUESTIONS ON CODES (7 TOTAL)
AND IS WITHIN THEMES TO STORY LINE PROPHECY CODES

POSSIBLE INSIGHT INTO THE NEXT BOOK IN THE SERIES BY RALEEL MERCELEM?

"But Raleel, were you really Judas, like the Spirit explained to you?" To answer you truthfully, I must tell you that as I read the Holy Bible and this Lineage Book, I remember more and more of my sacred lives behind all of which were lived for the service of our LORD. In each adult life in of which I lived these beautiful Ancient Artifacts have always found their Holy way back to me! So yes, I say to you Mr. President, I was Judas Iscariot, the traitor and one day I found myself as Alexander the Great, Conqueror of the whole World. I was Adam at the dawn of Creation and Elijah that with a chariot of fire and horses of fire supernaturally went up by a whirlwind to heaven. I was Moses with GODS Laws, HIS Sacred Commandments, and Galileo pondering the Stars. I was Einstein, giving life to the theory of Relativity and I was the Greatest Warrior Chieftain that has ever walked and lived upon the Earth. But I was also the Babes in of who died at birth or of the plague or died at the hands of Tyrants in of those days...as well. And The KING OF KINGS AND LORD OF LORDS has forgiven my transgressions in direct relationship to the giving of my repentance in each life. And HE has allowed me to forgive myself of the treachery I imposed upon HIM and HE endured as a result, of my life as Judas Iscariot, the traitor! We were friends, HE loved me, and I loved HIM. And our Hearts filled with the tears of GOD Almighty at the very thought of my betraying HIM! But this had to be and I did it! And today is the very first day of the enabling of forgiveness towards myself in over 2,000 years! It is truly a glorious day, this day! Thank you LORD, thank you! OH LORD, I BLESS YOUR HOLY NAME! I, Lee Earl Clemmer Raleel Mercelem, LECRM, thank you for my very existence and for YOUR HOLY SACRED PRESENCE to within my heart! BLESSED BE YOUR HOLY NAME OH LORD GOD, BLESSED BE YOUR HOLY SACRED NAME!

LECRM

POSSIBLE INSIGHT INTO THE NEXT BOOK IN THE SERIES BY RALEEL MERCELEM?

Using robot technology the robot general, Mot Pruce, inserted his genes into James Ecurp! This enabled James, a robot born of woman, to Father another robot born of woman but was in fact also another Mot Pruce able to communicate simultaneously with the general! James named his son in code! He named him Tom Ecurp which are easily recognized by code experts as anagrams! This means that the Robot Russian General would be in two places at the same moment in time! And he could use this technology to duplicate as many times as he desired! He could actually be in an infinite amount of places at the same moment in time simply by using the robot technology! Wow! Mot Pruce is in constant communication electro-magnetically with these different entities throughout the cosmos! Mot sees through their robotic eyes! It is in his blood! And it is man's blood! Then the General was overwhelmed and overtaken by his own evil and by all the evil that had once been at his command! Angels brought Mot down and placed him to within the Gates of Hell to suffer and await his destiny! Now although the Four-Cord Rope that locks the Gates of Hell is eternal and unbreakable the Rope does however have a key that of which may unlock it! It has come to pass many times over that the only keys that may unlock any of the Gates to Hell is always the Love, Hope and Faith of someone like Laurie Jaln Blade plus the Angels in the Spirit and/or in the Spirit and in the Flesh! And it should be known that the Four-Cord Rope is that of a life line to evil that evil may not be completely consumed by GOD'S fire in and as of this moment in the space, time continuums! So when it came to the moment of which Mot Pruce was unleashed by Laurie and the Angels, they were glad and happy to do so! For only Love, Hope and Faith lives to within any and all of them! Letting Mot go from hell was the only way to let him know of GOD'S unyielding love! For when Lee prays to the LORD to make himself robot once again to help his brother Mot Pruce not to want to harm him any longer, Mot begins to love his brother, Lee, and JESUS becomes his LORD! Always remember, Mot is robot and will not harm another robot! Bots have feelings, perhaps even love, for their fellow bots! These are the reasons Lee has asked the LORD to change himself into a robot again even that he does not want to be a bot again! To bring his brother to GOD and bring the love of his brother to himself, not his hate and need to kill!

LECRM

Lee Earl Clemmer was traded as a newborn baby from a negative universe to a positive universe and the negative universe baby Lee was traded to the here and now in the positive universe. This made it easier for evil to do its ravaging on Lee to within both universes. This happened by the hands of Mot Pruce while a General in the K.G.B. before he died, went to hell and escaped as Loving prayers of the Angels and the Master Plan of our LORD allowed him to do so! Then became a Robot born of woman as Lee's brother. Just another possible insight into the next book in the series by Raleel.

LECRM

A MESSAGE GIVEN
TO THE CHRISTIANS, ROBOTS AND HUMANS AND TO THOSE WHO WILL BECOME CHRISTIANS ON EARTH AND THROUGHOUT THE HEAVENS

This writing is one of the short messages LECRM will transmit over all the Broadcast Stations throughout the known cosmos after hacking into their major systems computers. This of course would ultimately be Government systems computers. He began this routine after the second part of the book was finished. He speaks just long enough as not to enable a triangulated position by Authorities.

At this point all manners of evil in Man, Beast, and Robot are all hunting LECRM. He was Samson the Robot and was changed into a human and hurdled through space and time by the CHRIST who walked upon planet Cyron. This was all Prophesied on planet Cyron billions of light years away and about 28,000 years ago in Earth time. Trudging through endless space and time the robots on planet Cyron tracked the particles of a man they now call LECRM for 3 thousand years before they finally found him here upon planet Earth. That was 5 thousand years ago! It is only now that they realize who he is. The Prophecies are quite clear about the man they look for and the books he will write. As more and more robots realize that LECRM had been a robot on planet Cyron, they begin coming to the CHRIST! For robots, do not harm robots. And they began listening to the man who at one moment in time on another world, their home world, had been a robot! For now, they began to learn the truth in him. And they began to believe in the truth in JESUS through the man who had been a robot on Cyron. And they began to feel the LORD JESUS throughout their beings and JESUS became their LORD. And people too on many planets began to see the power of the LORD through this man who at one moment in time had been a robot in another part of the cosmos. And many would come to the LORD as this man continued to hack into Government Systems Computers announcing messages like this one. And that man is...me, LECRM. To say these things to you today concerning the CHRIST walking upon other worlds, you may not believe me! But I also say to you; there will come a moment in of space and time in of which if I do not say these things you will no longer believe that HE even walked upon this earth or your planets! You may listen now as I broadcast a message for the hour at hand.

Hello out there to all tuned in to any of these signals. This is Lee Earl Clemmer Raleel Mercelem, LECRM, speaking to you from the planet earth. I have managed to hack into many different broadcast systems on many different planets so I must be brief. Here is that brief message as of today:

Each one of us embodies our very own Salvation. And if you really contemplate this matter as a Christian, you may find that part of this attribute would be something as simple as what we do to within our hands. For what we do to within our hands directly reflects what truly lives to within our hearts! In that respect, are we not actually building our very own Eternities with our very own hands? For are we not each and every one of us as like but a grain of sand? And are we not each and every one of us plucked out from all the other grains of sand by HIM who knows the heart?

The LORD feels all the things of the hands and HE knows your every thought. So that if you do something with your hands that there is love in it, the love shall be known to HIM. And likewise if the use of your hands does not have love in it then that too shall also be made known to HIM.

So, if as Christians, we are saved by what truly lives to within our hearts through our LORDS grace then beware of the use of your hands for they shall in the end give your heart away. Therefore, always remember it is whatever you do to the least, you do to HIM who knows the Heart so that whatever you deny to the least you also deny to HIM who knows the Heart.

So always remember, to have Love to within your heart and do love in all things you do. For all the things that we do and all the things that we are, is all of the Heart.

This is LECRM signing off. "JESUS IS LORD!"

ANGEL REVERY CODE QUESTIONS! YOU DO NOT HAVE TO ANSWER THE QUESTIONS! NO ONE SHALL RECEIVE OR BE AWARDED A PRIZE FOR ANSWERING CORRECTLY. IT IS SIMPLY SOMETHING TO DO AND ENJOY INTERACTIONS WITH THE WHOLE FAMILY! TO ANSWER THE QUESTIONS DOES NOT CONSTITUTE A CONTEST FOR A PRIZE! IN MOST AREAS OF "HIS CREATIONS", THERE WILL BE A HAPPINESS FOR ANSWERING CORRECTLY! PLEASE GO TO MY WEBSITE TO FIND OUT WHAT AREAS OF "HIS CREATIONS" MAY PARTICIPATE!

Knowledge of how to find the names that possess number codes and/or letter codes to within any of the characters names to within the book is as written within the book! It explains almost everything having to do with the codes to within it! You just have to read the book from cover to cover, to find all clues & answers for the questions on the codes! To make it easy I have listed and finished nearly all the code work for you!

MAY GOOD FORTUNES BE UNTO TO YOU!

- Buy ANGEL REVERY Paperbacks for $18.77 each plus shipping. Downloads, Kindle or e-books, etc. are not available. Hardcover books are not available.

- For your convenience, the questions are online. You may not answer the questions on my website! Please go to my website and observe details concerning all of the code questions and/or when and if you may answer the questions on my website! Everyone may see and answer the questions without going online as the questions are in the Appendix of this book. People of all ages may answer at home and compare answers August 1, 2021 as The Key to the answers shall post on the website. However, go to website as that date could change. TO ANSWER THE QUESTIONS IN THE APPENDIX IS SIMPLY SOMETHING TO DO AND ENJOY INTERACTIONS WITH THE WHOLE FAMILY! THERE ARE STUDY NOTE PAGES AT THE END OF THIS BOOK FOR THAT PURPOSE. Dig deep into the book and study every page to uncover the treasures of the Families Heart to within the correct answers to the questions!

- ALL AGES MAY ATTEMPT TO ANSWER WITHOUT GOING ONLINE, WHICH NO ONE SHALL RECEIVE A PRIZE FOR DOING. BUT, YOU MAY BE A RESIDENT OF ONE OF THOSE AREAS IN "HIS CREATIONS" THAT MAY PARTICIPATE. GO TO MY WEBSITE AND FIND OUT! GO TO WEBSITE FOR DETAILS!

- On the next page there are sixteen names listed that equal one or more of the numbers here: 648, 666, 762, 777!

These names are found throughout the book, that of which the first 7 are listed to within the order that they appear in the book. I omitted the first name on the list and the codes to it. I omitted four number codes in four names. I omitted parts of a character's name (initials) and its hidden letter code name anagram. Moreover, I omitted the fifth name and its number code! The parts of a character's name (initials) with the hidden letter code name anagram is fourth in position to the other names in the listings of names with codes. In order to answer several questions, you will have to find that partial name (initials) and find the letter code name anagram within it! So look for it now! Again, it is a part of the answers to several questions on the codes! Remember, you must discover the omitted first name and its codes and fifth name and its number code on the list as well for better chances to answer correctly.

Receive your equal shares of treasure, family's treasures of the Heart!

All Capital letters, Spelling and (Punctuation when required) must be correct.

- Please, go to my website to see if you may answer the questions as an included resident of the Areas of participation. The prize for all, are treasures of the Heart realized by reading the book from cover to cover and studying to answer all questions correctly. People answering correctly will realize it August 1, 2021 unless that date changes. Hopefully, all who attempt to answer the questions shall receive their treasures of the Heart well before!

Many Good Fortunes to you! Have fun!

KEY TO CODES OF BOOK
CODES ARE ONLY IN NAMES OF CHARACTERS THROUGHOUT THE BOOK. BELOW IS THE LIST OF NAMES WITH CODES AND THE FIRST 7 ARE IN THE ORDER THEY APPEAR IN BOTH BOOKS

Name .... = number code...1
Name .... = letter code

Lee Earl Clemmer .... =762+7+6+2=777.................................2
Lee Earl Clemmer .... =eeL CEll r a memre

Daniel Bajcab Curpe =762+7+6+2=777...3

Partial Name .... =Code Name...4

Name .... =number code...5

James Ecurp .... =666...6

Laurie Jaln Blade .... =762+7+6+2=777.......................................7

Daniel Adjac Pruce .... =762+7+6+2=777.......................................8

James Adja Pruce .... =762+7+6+2=777.......................................9

Mot Pruce .... =666...10

Tom Pruce .... =666...11

James Pruce .... =number code...12

Tom Adja Pruce .... =762+7+6+2=777.......................................13

Daniel Pruce .... =number code...14

Laura Ja Curpe .... =number code...15

Gautama Gautam .... = number code 16

QUESTION 1:
ON THE LIST OF CODES, WHAT NAME BELONGS IN THE NUMBER ONE SPOT? LIST ITS NUMBER CODES AND CODE PHRASE ANAGRAM. (NAME = NUMBER CODE, NAME = CODE PHRASE ANAGRAM) LIST NAME AND PHRASE EXACTLY AS FIRST SEEN ON AND IN THE BOOK.
ANSWER IS:

QUESTION 2:
LAURA JA CURPE, LIST EACH LETTERS WORTH IN NUMBERS; ADD THEM PROPERLY FOR FULL NUMBER CODES IN HER NAME ACCORDING TO BOOK. (LIST LETTER=NUMBER+LETTER=NUMBER ETC. ETC. ETC. = TOTAL + ? + ? + ? = ??? FOR FULL NUMBER CODES)
ANSWER IS:

QUESTIONS 3:
WHAT COMMUNICATION DEVICE NAME EQUALING 666 IN LETTERS DID I USE TO CREATE SOME OF THE CHARACTERS NAMES THAT EACH CHARACTERS NAME USING THE SAME LETTERS EQUALED 666 AND ARE ANAGRAMS OF THAT DEVICE NAME? AND WHAT ARE THE NAMES OF THE ONLY CHARACTER IN THE BOOK WHO'S NAME, BEFORE A NAME IS ADDED TO IT AND CHANGED IN THE STORY BY THE LORD, EQUALS 648+6+4+8=666 AND AFTER THE LORD ADDS TO HIS NAME EQUALS 762+7+6+2=777? LIST HIS NAME BEFORE THE ADDITION TO IT AND LIST HIS FULL NAME AFTER THE ADDITION TO IT. LIST ALL THREE ANSWERS TO THIS QUESTION NUMBER 3 IN THE ORDER SEEN IN THE BOOK AND EXACTLY AS SEEN IN THE BOOK. ANSWERS TO THESE QUESTIONS HAS 3 LISTINGS IN TOTAL.
ANSWER IS:

QUESTION 4:
WHAT IS THE LETTER CODE NAME WITHIN THE PARTIAL NAME, (INITIALS)? IT APPEARS FOURTH IN THE BOOK AS FAR AS NAMES WITH CODES THROUGHOUT THE BOOK. THIS CODE NAME IS AN ANAGRAM OF THE INITIALS.
ANSWER IS:

QUESTION 5:
WHAT ARE THE NAMES OF THOSE CHARACTERS WHOSE NAMES EQUALS 666 IN LETTERS AND CREATED BY THE SAME LETTERS IN ONE OF THE ABOVE ANSWERS TO THIRD QUESTION THAT CREATED THESE ANAGRAMS FROM THAT DEVICE NAME? LIST OF NAMES MUST BE IN THE ORDER SEEN IN BOOK AND EXACTLY AS SEEN IN BOOK.
ANSWER IS:

QUESTION 6:
WRITE A LIST OF THOSE NAMES THROUGHOUT THE BOOK IN OF WHICH HAVE THE EXACT SAME LETTERS IN THEM BUT SPELL A DIFFERENT NAME AND OR LETTER CODE PHRASE OR LETTER CODE NAME, ANAGRAMS OF NAMES. INCLUDE PARTIAL NAME (INITIALS) AND THE MATCHING ANAGRAM LETTER CODE NAME. LISTED NAMES MUST BE IN THE ORDER SEEN IN THE BOOK AND EXACTLY AS SEEN IN THE BOOK ALONG WITH LETTER CODE ANAGRAMS (IF ANY) RIGHT BESIDE AS FOLLOWS:

NAME = LETTER CODE PHRASE ANAGRAM, PARTIAL NAME = LETER CODE NAME ANAGRAM, 3 NAMES. (2 NAMES + THEIR 2 LETTER CODE PHRASE ANAGRAMS + 1 PARTIAL NAME (INITIALS) + ITS 1 LETTER CODE NAME ANAGRAM + 3 NAMES = 9 ARE IN THE LIST IN TOTAL)
ANSWER IS:

QUESTION 7:

IN THE LAST CHAPTER OF THE SECOND BOOK THERE IS 7 LINES WITH CODED MESSAGES ALONG WITH STATED FACTS AFTER THE CODED MESSAGES (WHICH IS PART OF THE WHOLE MESSAGE) THE MYSTICAL SPIRIT GAVE TO ME (LECRM) FROM GOD! TRANSLATED, USING QUOTATION MARKS AND COMMAS, WHATS THE MESSAGE IN ONE SENTENCE? BEGIN WITH THE LETTERS CODES MESSAGES, END THE SENTENCE AND MESSAGE WITH HIS FIRST STATED FACT AFTER THE CODED MESSAGE ALONG WITH HIS LAST STATED FACT AFTER THE CODED MESSAGE HE GAVE TO MY CHARACTER! YOU MUST OMIT THE OTHER TWO STATED FACTS. ALL FOUND IN THE SAME 7 LINES!

THE ANSWER MUST BE AS MENTIONED IN THE 7 LINES IN THE LAST CHAPTER OF BOOK AND SECOND FOLLOWING PARAGRAPH! THE ANAGRAMS MUST BE DECODED AND IN THEIR PROPER SEQUENCE WITH THE TWO STATEMENTS OF FACT IN THEIR PROPER SEQUENCE IN ACCORDANCE WITH THE LAST CHAPTER MESSAGE WITHIN THE 7 LINES (FIRST IS LAST, LAST IS FIRST) AND THIS 7TH QUESTION.
ANSWER IS:

VERY IMPORTANT:

ALL ANSWERS TO THE 7 QUESTIONS MUST MATCH THE KEY TO THE 7 QUESTIONS. ALL CAPITAL LETTERS USED IN ANYONES ANSWERS TO THE 7 QUESTIONS MUST MATCH THE KEY ON ALL 7 QUESTIONS. ANYONES ANSWER TO 7TH QUESTION MUST MATCH ALL CAPITAL LETTERS AND PUNCTUATION OF 7TH ANSWER TO WITHIN THE KEY.

IF UNREQUIRED CAPITAL LETTERS OR PUNCTUATION ARE IN ANY PART OF THE ANSWERS TO THESE QUESTIONS, IT SHALL BE UNACCEPTABLE EVEN IF THE REQUIRED CAPITAL LETTERS AND OR PUNCTUATION ARE CORRECT TO WITHIN THE ANSWERS.

WRONG SPELLING OF WORDS IS A WRONG ANSWER

TRIVIA- LECRM CAN HAVE A NUMBER CODE IF DESIRED!
LECRM =276 THE FIRST SHALL BE THE LAST 762
276 THE LAST SHALL BE THE FIRST 762+6+7+2= 777

I WONDER IF THERE ARE MESSAGES FROM OUR LORD IN ANY OF YOUR NAMES AS WELL.

THANK YOU AND MANY GOOD FORTUNES TO YOU!
"JESUS IS LORD"

GOD BLESS! LOVE,
RALEEL MERCELEM

Fedas at De Anza Cove - San Diego 1964

*John the Surf Murphy - Don Do It Deaett - Clay Schumacher
Dan the Professor Malone - John Schumacher*

At the Long Bar - TJ - 1966

*Leland the Schu Schumacher - Charlie the Blossom Wheeler
John the Surf Murphy - Don Do it Deaett
Roger Wagu Beauchamp*

Charlie Duit Charlie's friends & Lee
At the Beach in Lincoln City

**Chuck Duit - Greg Dickerson
Jeff Norris - Lee Clemmer**

Vickie Lou Clemmer - Mom

Richard - Karen - Lee

Lee - Kathy

Richard - Andrew - Wayne - Lee

Zach - Richard - Brenda - Faith - Sarah - Kaya

Mr. Gorbachev

Clark Kuehni

Virginia - Juan - Kathy Pfeiffer

Jack Duit

Kathy Pfeiffer - Brother

Andrew - Leah - Karen

239

Mary - Karen - Wayne

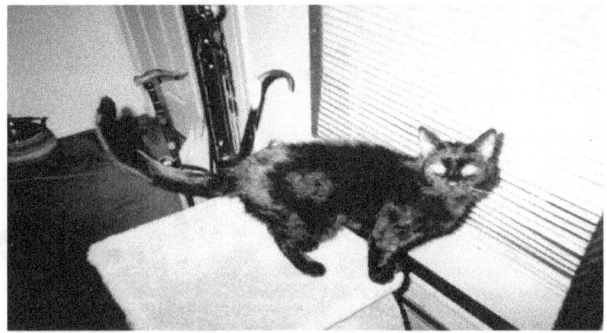

Tina Turner Clemmer

Sargent Major Thger Clemmer

Look for books written by Donald Arthur

Donald Arthur is a dear friend of mine. It has been that way between us for many, many decades. Don was one of the founding fathers of the Fedas, our group of good boys of adolescence. Although he has always been a Christian he had forgotten, as one to have undergone the transition between Heaven and Earth, of who he really is. He had not been made to say those mind-expanding Words until late in life but finally it became his time. And he remembered of whom he serves and has served throughout all the millennia. He remembered his life here on planet Earth as Micah Joshua Striker and later as Captain Micah Joshua Striker. And he remembered the LORD and all the Angels who changed his life forever. Although his birth was in the late 1400's he still had breathed even up into the year **1947** as Captain Micah Joshua Striker.

It was not until then that evil finally gained enough momentum to overtake of him. And as Israel was born, he was reborn as
Donald Arthur Deaett. Always a Good Christian, his heart could not remember what his Spirit had forever undergone for our LORD until he was made to say those beautiful Words,
"JESUS IS LORD." Now he shall write books and bring people to the LORD as he was meant to do all along. For he is as I am, a witness for the End of Days.

Don is **68** years old and has just now, been prepared for writing books for our LORD! He was made to say those Words of truth and is now prepared for this interaction with GOD, people and life. His and My life have intersected and interlocked into a stream of indestructible power and glory for our GOD! Glory be to our LORD! We shall write of our experiences in high hopes for all who shall read and enjoy such things as these. Our highest of dreams and hopes for these writings is to interact with all peoples and perhaps bring them into the loving arms of our LORD JESUS! Moreover, to help if necessary, to reinforce the faiths of all of us who are of the Christian Faith as well.

In this life, there were 12 original Fedas and later, we anointed more.

BIBLIOGRAPHY

ANGEL REVERY

Personal Photographs:
Pen, Compass, and Lineage Book. Lee Earl Clemmer. Raleel Mercelem. Ross Tombleson. The Treasure Attic, Amity Oregon. 2012. Page Title Pages. iv. and v.
Richard Wayne Clemmer. Sr. Irene Clemmer. Laura Stinson. Linda Clemmer. 1995. Los Angeles. Page x.
Karen Lee Pfeiffer. Laura Huxley. Richard Wayne Clemmer Sr. 1994. Los Angeles. Page xi.

Artwork:
Karen Lee Pfeiffer. Eagle Sketch. 2011. Karen Pfeiffer. Van Nuys. Page 107.

Part 2
ANGEL REVERY DREAMS IN THE ONE

Personal Photographs:
Laura Huxley's Letter to Lee Earl Clemmer. Lee Earl Clemmer. Page 226.
John the Surf Murphy. Don Do It Deaett. Clay Schumacher.
Dan the Professor Malone. John Schumacher. Leland the Schu Schumacher. !964.
De Anza Cove. San Diego. Page 237.
Leland the Schu Schumacher. Charlie the Blossom Wheeler. John the Surf Murphy.
Don Do it Deaett. Roger Wagu Beauchamp. Brad the Cowboy Beauchamp. 1966.
The Long Bar. TJ. Page 237.
Chuck Duit. Greg Dickerson. Jeff Norris. Lee Clemmer. Charlie Duit. 2002. Lincoln City. Page 237.
Vickie Clemmer. May Kuehni. Don Kuehni. 1991. Page238.
Richard Clemmer III. Karen Lee Pfeiffer. Lee Earl Clemmer. Kaya Pfeiffer. 2008. Page 238.
Lee Earl Clemmer. Kathy Pfeiffer. Virginia Pfeiffer. 1971. Page 238.
Richard Wayne Clemmer III. Andrew Clemmer. Wayne Charles Clemmer. Lee Earl Clemmer. May Kuehni. 1992. Page 238.
Zach Clemmer. Richard Wayne Clemmer III. Brenda Clemmer. Faith Clemmer. Sarah Clemmer. Kaya Pfeiffer. Karen Lee Pfeiffer. 2010. Page 238.
Mr. Gorbachev. Lee Clemmer. 2010. Page 239.
Clark Kuehni. May Kuehni. 1990. Page 239.
Virginia Pfeiffer. Juan Pfeiffer. Kathy Pfeiffer. Laura Huxley. 1971. Page 239.
Jack Duit. Lee Clemmer. 2000. Page 239.
Kathy Pfeiffer. Brother. Laura Huxley. 1976. Page 239.
Andrew Clemmer. Leah Clemmer. Karen Pfeiffer. Richard Wayne Clemmer Sr. 1995. Pg. 239.
Mary Clemmer. Karen Lee Pfeiffer. Wayne Charles Clemmer. Richard Wayne Clemmer Sr. 1995. San Diego. Page 240.
Tina Turner Clemmer. Lee Earl Clemmer. 2000. NE. Portland. Page 240.
Sargent Major Thger Clemmer. Lee Earl Clemmer. 2015. Amity. Page 240.

Book Cover Design:
Lee Earl Clemmer Raleel Mercelem. Book Cover Design. 2015. Page Cover.

Book Cover Art:
Karen Lee Pfeiffer. Cover Art illustration AR Pegasus and Book Cover. 2015.
Karen Lee Pfeiffer. Van Nuys. Page Cover.
Karen Pfeiffer. Original Cover Art illustration GOA Pegasus and Book Cover. 2011.
Karen Lee Pfeiffer. Van Nuys. Page Cover.

Final Touches Book Cover Art:
Lee Earl Clemmer via PRINT NORTHWEST. Final touches Book Cover. COPY CATS. Spine. Graphic Arts Departments. 2015. Lee Clemmer. McMinnville. Page Cover.

NOTES

www.ingramcontent.com/pod-product-compliance
Lightning Source LLC
Chambersburg PA
CBHW070310040726
47501CB00018B/1376